THE MIDDLE AGES
OF SISTER MARY BARUCH

The
Middle Ages
of
Sister Mary Baruch

FR. JACOB RESTRICK, O.P.

© 2016 by Jacob Restrick
All rights reserved. Published 2016.
Printed in the United States of America

ISBN-13: 978-1530915491
ISBN-10: 153091549X

Cover image by Lawrence Lew, O.P.:
Cloister Walk at Mary, Queen of Hope Monastery . . . Maybe

Cover design by Ignatius Weiss, O.P.

*To the Dominican friars,
on the eight hundredth anniversary
of our founding by St. Dominic in 1216,*

*and to the Dominican nuns,
who have prayed for us from the beginning.*

More and more impelled by the love of Christ, that all-embracing divine friendship, they should become all things to all. In the common life of the religious family to which they are united in a closer bond through chastity, they should cultivate sisterly affection and serene friendship.

—*Constitutions of the Nuns of the Order of Preachers* 26.II

foreword

The Middle Ages of Sister Mary Baruch is just as dramatic a story—if not more so—as its predecessor, *Sister Mary Baruch: The Early Years*. How could this be? After all, in *The Early Years*, our heroine, a young Jewish woman coming of age in 1960s New York City, finds herself drawn inexorably into closer friendship with God, in ways at once wholly strange and entirely familiar. This deepening friendship leads Becky Feinstein first to become a Roman Catholic, and then—as if that weren't enough to shock her mother—to enter a monastery of Dominican nuns. Shouldn't *that* be the end of the excitement? How much adventure could await in the life of a cloistered nun?

In truth, the most transformative part of Sr. Mary Baruch's story only begins *after* she enters the monastery. Her life as a Dominican nun may seem routine and limited from the outside, but inside it is filled with spiritual drama. Entering religious life does not magically change a person; rather, it tends to reveal that the qualities of the "old girl" are much more enduring—and deeply rooted—than previously thought. Overcoming attachments, and growing in virtue, involves a long process of being stretched by God. Nor are one's confreres plaster-cast saints, either. Living the religious life honestly and authentically means living sisterhood intensely—and there's nowhere to hide. Deep spiritual friendships, along with painful personal struggles and misunderstandings, mark this community. And of course, the lives of those Sr. Mary Baruch knows and loves beyond the monastic enclosure continue to shape her, often in unexpected ways.

God has chosen Sr. Mary Baruch to be consecrated to himself from the very beginning. Her conversion, entry into the monastery, and profession as a Dominican nun are all Sr. Mary Baruch's responses to God's gift of a vocation. She makes a complete sacrifice of herself, and gives everything back gratefully to God, who gave her everything in the first place. The real story begins in the monastery, because it is there that Christ is transforming her after his own image and leading her to the perfection of charity that is only possible through his grace. It's a story of real suffering—where God speaks in the obscurity of faith—and of powerful consolation. In all this, *The Middle Ages* offers lessons in profound spiritual wisdom for every Christian in realizing a closer friendship with God amidst joys and sorrows alike.

—Henry Stephan, O.P.

preface

A popular song recorded by Dinah Washington in 1959 opens with the lyrics: "What a difference a day makes, twenty-four little hours." Well, what a difference twenty-five years make. *The Middle Ages of Sister Mary Baruch* begins when she turns forty, and covers her twenty-fifth jubilee and a few years beyond.

Rebecca Abigail Feinstein, a nice Jewish girl from Manhattan's Upper West Side, became a Catholic in 1965 at the age of twenty. Five years later she entered a Dominican cloistered monastery called Mary, Queen of Hope, in Brooklyn Heights, New York, where she became Sister Mary Baruch of the Advent Heart. The "early years" were full of challenges, heartaches, family turmoil, and lots of faith, hope, and charity.

Having lived the life of a cloistered nun now for over twenty-five years, Sr. Mary Baruch still finds her life full of challenges, heartaches, family turmoil, and lots of faith, hope, and charity. The same, perhaps in many ways, but "what a difference a day makes." The spiritual journey is a continual conversion of heart, day after day and year after year. The monastic life of a cloistered nun faced many changes and "differences" in the post-Vatican II years. A community, like an individual, is on a journey of faith.

Meet Sr. Mary Baruch and her sisters, her friends, and her family in her middle age. She and all the sisters, as well as the monastery and her family and friends, are all fictitious. But hopefully you will identify with her "middle ages" in your own journey.

Many thanks to all who have shared with me their reflections on Sr. Mary Baruch in her early years. Special thanks to Sr. Mary Dominic, O.P., from the Monastery of Our Lady of the Rosary in Buffalo, New York, and to my Dominican brothers Peter Gautsch and Barnabas McHenry, O.P., for their editorial skills and expertise. Many thanks to Fr. Lawrence Lew, O.P., Sr. Mary Baruch's favorite photographer, and Br. Ignatius Weiss, O.P., who designed the covers. Thank you to Br. Henry Stephan, O.P., who has written the foreword, and to all my Dominican brethren who have been a great support in my poor efforts to make Sr. Mary Baruch "such a blessing" in our lives.

Fr. Jacob Restrick, O.P.
Easter 2016
Dominican House of Studies

one

Welcome to the Middle Ages, read the front of the card I received from Gwendolyn for my fortieth birthday. It was the best card I received, and it helped me laugh at the traumatic reality taking place—the end of the fourth decade of my life and my leap into the fifth! I realized that I didn't feel forty years old, judging on what I thought being forty felt like when I was sixteen. But still, turning forty was more traumatic than when I turned fifty!

Gwendolyn Putterforth was a youthful thirty-four when I first met her. She was the owner, manager, and chief bottle washer at a quaint British tea shop on the Upper West Side of Manhattan, near Barnard College and Columbia University. The shop was named Tea on Thames, and became my haunt during my early years at Barnard and my eventual conversion to Catholicism.

It was at Tea on Thames that I met Ezra Goldman, a student at Columbia, who informed me on our first meeting that he was a Jew who had converted to Christianity; he was a Catholic. He didn't know how much he was an answer to my simple prayers during those autumn days of 1965. I was feeling so alone and caught in a terrible Jewish dilemma. I had come to know *Jesus as the Lord*, to quote St. Paul, another Jewish convert. I was reading the New Testament and the autobiography of St. Thérèse of Lisieux, *The Story of a Soul*, and I didn't have anyone to talk to about all this. And Ezra walked into my life—well, he walked into Tea on Thames—and that was the beginning of a wonderful and God-sent friendship.

It was hard to believe when I entered into my "middle ages" that that was all twenty years ago. In some ways, those days seemed to be lived in slow motion, but they also sped by so quickly. Little did Ezra, Gwendolyn, or I know on that crisp October day in New York that Ezra would become Fr. Matthew Goldman and I, Rebecca Abigail Feinstein, would become Sister Mary Baruch of the Advent Heart.

Sometimes it just takes time to look back on things and realize how much God has been doing it all, while He lets us think that we're doing it—*we're* discovering who He is, *we're* in control of the whole situation. One of the graces of late middle age is to realize that God has been in control and has loved us through everything.

Gwendolyn was a God-send too. She's also my god-mother, and a wonderful godmother she has been all these years. She was a young widow and went through the terrible experience of losing her only child. He was thirteen years old when he was hit by a drunken driver while they were on vacation at the shore. Born and raised in York and Leeds, England, they came to New York on a visitor's visa, and Gwendolyn was eventually able to get a work permit. For the first five years of her New York life, she was a legal secretary in Midtown and loved the pulse of New York at rush hour, except for the subway, which she said was not as quiet or elegant as the London Underground. In nice weather she would walk home from Fifth Avenue and 57th Street, stopping in the Plaza Hotel for a "smart cocktail" in the Oak Room, then continuing around Central Park to West 75th Street between Broadway and Riverside Drive. She lived in a fifth-floor walk-up apartment. (Gwendolyn called it her penthouse flat, since the building only had five floors.)

Tea on Thames was famous among tea toddlers, as it specialized in English teas one couldn't get anywhere else. Gwendolyn also served traditional and some non-traditional English foods that made it a British "high tea" or an American coffee-break-gone-British. Tea was making a comeback among the young set who "grooved" on coffee and cheap wine. But it was the atmosphere of the place which kept us tea toddlers coming back. It was small, with little tables, each covered in real linen, the necessary condiments for tea, and a small vase of fresh flowers. The back wall, which separated the front dining room from the kitchen, was lined with five shelves of fancy teapots, added to by customers who would bring Gwendolyn a teapot or mug or fancy cup and saucer.

Tea on Thames was also famous for its collection of penguins—not real, of course, but every sort of artificial figure imaginable, from porcelain to stuffed velvet. At Christmas Gwendolyn would have a Nativity set in the front window, and, instead of sheep, a rather large flock of penguins waddling to the crib. Inside, as you entered, there was a freestanding round table, which usually held a large bouquet of flowers, but during the winter held instead a lifelike penguin. The penguin's name was Ruben, after my father. Gwendolyn had become close to him in the year that he passed away, which was also the year I had entered the monastery, Mary, Queen of Hope. My father was my biggest supporter among all the members of my immediate family. Such a blessing he was in my life exactly when I needed it. And how many times since have I called on him, who I'm sure lives in Heaven with all the saints. He's a regular at the Celestial Communion of Saints Café, a heavenly version of Tea on Thames. It of course includes saints both canonized and non-canonized.

My little sister, Ruthie Feinstein, was also a support in her own non-judgmental way. I was always grateful she had become friends with Gwendolyn, whom we used to call Lady Gwendolyn, and Ruthie would put on her own British accent and request the daintiest of teacups.

Letting go of the need to control and of my stubborn self-will has been a big part of my journey. Mother John Dominic, my first prioress, used to call it the "old girl," meaning the self-centered Rebecca who entered the monastery and thought she left "Rebecca" outside. It didn't take long to realize she had schlepped the "old girl" right in with her. I prefer to call her the "little girl" because the "old girl" can act like one when she doesn't get her way. I'm over fifty years old, and I still pout!

My first spiritual director, Fr. Aquinas Meriwether, may he rest in peace, was the Dominican priest from St. Vincent Ferrer's in Manhattan who gave me my *instructions*, we called them, when I became a Catholic. He baptized me and gave me my First Holy Communion. He became and remained for many years my spiritual father. He introduced me to the "old girl" well before Mother John Dominic met her.

Surrendering, Fr. Meriwether assured me, comes in many disguises but is present in all the twists and turns of our lives. And so does our resisting it! (Fr. Meriwether pointed that out to me too . . . more than once.) I knew that a surrender was being called for and made when I became a Christian. The "cost of discipleship" was evident in my scandalizing my poor family. My older brother, David, accused me of betraying the Jewish heritage which our parents had imparted to us, which was rooted in a long tradition of Feinstein Jewry from Austria. David was a self-proclaimed agnostic for most of his teenage to adult life. His only religion was medical science. Mama was so proud of her firstborn: "My son, the doctor." And Papa was as proud as a father could be too, when it came to David's healing and helping people—but he also saw his ambitions for material possessions and acclaim. Papa was so wise. Growing up, I knew he was the smartest man in the whole world.

When I wanted to become a Christian, David suddenly became an expert in Jewish law, Feinstein heritage, and the Talmud—all to refute my asinine idea of becoming a Christian, let alone a Catholic cloistered nun! *Mamma Mia* (as Sr. Rosaria would exclaim whenever something unusual happened, which was about fourteen times a day)! David thought the whole idea was stupid. How could anyone in her right mind, in our day and age, give in to the oppressive mind-control of organized religion? I guess Judaism didn't fall under that—although, again, David didn't practice his faith, but I think for different reasons. With David, it was more the God Question. I guess it's always the God Question; that's the bottom line if one is clear enough in one's head and heart to go there!

6

When I discovered the Gospels, I entered into a whole new world and found the meaning of life, because I found the love of my life—Yeshua of Nazareth! (I love to say *Yeshua*; I love the sound of it, and I cherish it because it's the name Mary and Joseph would have used.) Perhaps it was in my hours of chatting with Ezra over Earl Grey tea or walking in the park and talking about the spiritual life that I realized that the crazy world we lived in also had its own "gospel." Still does. It can be very seductive and attractive, but, in the end, very vacuous and the great delusion. Money, fame, good looks, "thinness," sexuality, and the accumulation of stuff do not make one happy. Granted, there are those things which make us content and satisfied and happy for a time, especially the good things that kind of point the way to a higher, more ultimate happiness. And I think that's because this pull or drive towards happiness is innate in us human beings. It's all mixed up with our disordered egos, of course, and we search high and low for happiness, for meaning in our lives, because we know we cannot be happy if everything depends on our own power, our thinking, our being in control. It's one thing to know that or talk about that when you're twenty years old and strolling through the park with a friend like Ezra, and another to realize you're still working it out when you're forty and have been a nun for fifteen years.

My only older sister, Sally (short for Sarah), was always proclaiming the adage of the sixties: "If it feels good, do it." She got caught up in all the social movements, looking to feel good and be happy. But she always seemed more angry than happy.

I guess you could say I became a nun because I wanted to be happy, and the Lord made me happy. My solemn profession was a happy high point of my life. Solemn profession is our making final vows until death. Thinking back ...

I had packed my bag to leave some months before my profession because my agenda was not Mother Jane Mary's agenda. She was my second prioress after Mother John Dominic, and she didn't want to do it my way, the "old girl's" way! My dear friend, Ezra Goldman, was then Brother Matthew, a Passionist brother since he was twenty-one. He was being ordained a priest in Springfield, Massachusetts, and I wanted to attend. This was three months or so before my solemn vows. There was a precedent for attending ordinations: Sr. Trinity's brother had been ordained at St. Patrick's in Manhattan that same year, and Sister and a companion were permitted to attend. How marvelous! I logically concluded to myself that I would be able to go to Ezra's ordination too. To save Mother the trouble, I had worked it all out: I could stay with our nuns in West Springfield, and—best of all—Fr. Meriwether was going, was staying at the nuns' monastery, and would be able to drive me to and from the cathedral. I wasn't planning on going to any kind of reception—that was pushing the envelope too much—but if I stayed overnight I could go to Fr. Matthew's first Mass the next day.

I was also hoping (and planning) that Sr. Anna Maria could go as my companion, as we always traveled with another sister, and she would be able to meet the sister at West Springfield in charge of their laundry and they could compare notes, or detergents and stain removers. (Sr. Anna Maria was our laundry sister, but she aspired to be the altar bread supervisor—ABS for short!) It was all worked out in my head.

She was also my closest friend in the community. We had met in the guest quarters before either of us entered, when we were discerning our vocations, as she put it.

When I went to Mother Jane Mary to tell her my plans, or, rather, to "ask her permission," I was flatly refused. It was like someone punched me square in the stomach. I had the wind knocked out of me, emotionally. I don't remember anything that Mother said after that. I kind of walked comatose-like to the chapel. That was all the work of grace, of course, that I would head for the chapel, and not for my cell and the wardrobe room to collect my four pieces of wardrobe that I had arrived in five years before.

In the chapel, there was the grace—yes, truly it was all grace—of surrender. I surrendered it all to Our Lord, including myself and my manipulating self-centered will. And I offered it up for Ezra and all that he might be surrendering to as he prepared to be ordained. If the "old girl" didn't die then, she was knocked unconscious . . . for a while.

I only learned much later that that was the final test Mother was looking for in my regard. Before then she had regarded me as rather self-willed and needing to control everything, including my own life. I was asking to make a solemn vow of obedience, and I hadn't really surrendered yet. It all worked out in a way I would never have planned. But why did it have to be so painful?

The whole incident opened my eyes and my heart in a way that I hadn't opened them before . . . and five years is a long time to try to get your eyes open! I realized that these sisters were also surrendered, each in her own way, and that our life together would be one of deeper and more profound (solemn) surrenders until death. I saw that this is all the work of God. I have also realized over the years that none of us nuns does that perfectly, and we sometimes forget that it's all God's work within us and within our community. I'm sure the battle with the self-centered will goes on right into Purgatory!

When I recovered from having the wind knocked out of me, I was free and discovered a joy I hadn't really experienced in the five years that had brought me to this point. I looked ahead with joy at giving my life totally and freely to Yeshua.

Three weeks before my solemn profession I was able to go on retreat. You don't really go anywhere, geographically, but you are excused from the common recreation and work, if possible. (Your charge is modified or someone else substitutes for you.) This gives you ample time for prayer and lots of time to reflect on what you are about to do—or, as I realize now, what the Lord is about to do in you and for you.

Such a private and individual retreat is never preached like our yearly community retreat, but you may listen to tapes from former retreats, and we had an abundance of these. I had spent several months organizing the tape collection in a room off the library. I called it the Mediatatio Room (a play on words for the four levels of prayer: *lectio, meditatio, oratio, contemplatio*; or, in English: reading, meditating, praying, and contemplating). It was a separate room at the back of the library formerly used for bookbinding and repairs.

Sr. Mary Hildegard had been our bookbinder. She was born in Germany and came to America in 1923 when she was just nine years old. She grew up with books and learned to do bookbinding from her uncle, with whom she and her mother and brothers lived when they waved hello to Lady Liberty and passed through Ellis Island. Uncle Max lived in a brownstone apartment on West 98th Street in Manhattan. He was a typesetter for a small German newspaper. He was also a part-time shoemaker and a part-time bookbinder.

Sr. Hildegard (I never heard what her name was in the world) learned to make shoes, or at least how to replace old soles. She also learned how to re-bind old books. Sr. John Dominic told us when she was prioress that Sr. Hildegard would humbly boast of "restoring your sole and mending your back."

Sr. Hildegard died a couple years before I entered, so I never knew her, but her stories and wise sayings were remembered often at recreations. Her mother and her uncle Max opened their own shoe repair shop, and Uncle Max let go of the typesetting and bookbinding jobs. Bookbinding became more a hobby than a profession, and Sr. Hildegard liked hobbies.

When I was appointed librarian by Mother Jane Mary, I cleaned out Sr. Hildegard's bookbinding room, with all the presses, tools, and supplies Sr. Hildegard had neatly organized in cardboard cupboards. There was a drawer for everything, and everything was labeled and arranged in alphabetical order.

Cleaning out the room was only accomplished, of course, with permission, as a faction of the elderly sisters almost revolted at the thought of moving Sr. Hildegard's bookbinding paraphernalia out of the room. I realized that change is not always welcomed by religious women supposedly trying to be detached from possessions. Some of us tend to become great hoarders of things: holy cards, letters, photographs, ribbons and bows . . . "raindrops on roses and whiskers on kittens." Nobody had replaced the community bookbinder for years, but these sisters felt that one couldn't touch the room, just in case a bookbinder entered (preferably from Germany) who could also restore soles.

Since I had cleared out the room and made it the new Monastic Mediatatio Room, there were a couple sisters who would not cross the threshold out of principle. One sister in particular, Sr. Mary Boniface, wouldn't even speak to me unless she had to out of charity, which passed as politeness. I learned, again from Sr. John Dominic, that Sr. Mary Boniface had been very close to Sr. Hildegard and took scrupulous care of her in her last months. They spoke German to each other.

I suspect that Sr. Mary Boniface was one of my black beans when the community voted on me for solemn profession. All the solemnly professed sisters make up the Chapter, and vote *yes* (white bean) or *no* (black bean) when the Chapter comes together to admit a sister to solemn profession. It's a big step, you see, for not only are you binding yourself to God as a nun (as His bride) until death, but you're binding yourself to a community who accepts you in sickness and in health until death do you part!

The sisters vote the same way we did close to eight hundred years ago. There is a brown wooden box, looking like the coffee grinder at Shoemann's Deli. It has two drawers and a wide open chute at the top that falls into the drawer at the bottom. The top drawer is divided into white beans and black beans. A sister comes up, puts both hands into the top drawer, takes one bean only, and drops it in the chute. The sister being approved or rejected is not present. That was me on July 16, 1974—the feast of Our Lady of Mt. Carmel.

two

I remember sitting in the chapel, alone except for the sister making her hour of guard, who, like me, was not a member of the Chapter.

You go through a "Chapter vote" as a postulant to become a novice, and as a novice to make first profession, but this was the big one. You naturally think back on the past five years. I thought my little project of making an organized tape room would be seen as innovative, taking initiative, and a wonderful and practical service to the community—it would probably win me unanimous white beans. Funny, how we tend to judge ourselves according to what we do or don't do. The Chapter vote is secret, but certain things are apt to leak out, and that's how I knew I had at least two black beans. I was mortified! Instead of being grateful that I had ninety-nine percent white beans, I was fretting over the two who didn't want me. It is never revealed, of course—the sisters themselves don't know who drops the black beans in the box—but it took some time for me to accept that not everyone liked me. It really isn't a matter of the sisters liking or not liking you, but whether they in charity believe you can or cannot live this life. I learned later on that there is one sister who is scrupulous and unable to bring herself to vote *yes* in case it isn't God's will, so she never puts in a white bean. So that means really only one. That's how I deduced that it must have been Sr. Boniface. I also deduced that I probably wouldn't vote for me either if I were Sr. Boniface.

The blessing is that I had a high majority. I was going to make vows "until death." That's enough to scare you to death. The date was set for November 1, All Saints' Day. However, the bishop was unable to come, as it was a Holy Day and he was scheduled for Mass at the cathedral and a visit to Dunwoodie, the seminary for the New York Archdiocese. (He was Bishop of the Brooklyn Diocese, but some of our seminarians also went to Dunwoodie.) Mother arranged that the principal celebrant for my solemn vows would be Fr. Matthew Goldman.

And now I wanted to make the best retreat of my life. It didn't take me long in the lovely Mediatatio Room (*ahem*) to choose my taped retreat master; I knew exactly where he was shelved!

Ten years ago, Fr. Meriwether, O.P., had preached the community retreat on St. Dominic's Nine Ways of Prayer. And so I asked Mother Jane Mary if he could give me a directed retreat, as we had read an article about directed retreats in *Review for Religious*. But Mother said, "No, Sister, it is not our custom." She had that scary glare in her eyes as she shifted around in her chair. I never knew whether she was anxious or excited about being negative. But she wouldn't simply let it go.

"Sister, you must be careful about wanting exceptions to the rule for yourself." There it was again, the "old girl" and

14

her self-will manifesting itself. And I thought I had chosen the best time to ask her. It was right after the midday silence following the midday meal. At least I didn't ask her during the midday silence.

"I know, Mother, I'm sorry. I wasn't aware I was in the habit of doing that." Never a good line to respond with.

"Well, you do, my dear." A slightly scornful chuckle rolled out of her mouth and across the desk to my ignorant ears. "You've been given exception after exception since you entered. Your postulancy was shortened so your father could attend your clothing, and you were allowed to wear the old-fashioned wedding dress—I wasn't even allowed to do that."

I wanted to snap back, "I know, but the wedding gowns were reserved for virgins." Mother Jane Mary had entered as a widow after her son and husband had been killed. But I held my tongue. If I had learned anything in the last five years, it was restraint of tongue.

She wasn't done with her litany. "Your sister visited with you during Advent, and you were given a responsible charge while still a temporary professed."

"I know, Mother, you gave it to me." *Oops*, I thought. *Watch it, Baruch!*

"Yes, well, I was being efficient. And you've done a fine job reorganizing the library in such a short time. Of course, you had years of professional practice before you entered."

Mother was making it sound like I had practiced medicine or something. I had been a simple, but efficient—to use Mother's vocabulary—librarian at the New York Public Library on Fifth Avenue and 42nd Street.

"You wanted exceptions right up to three months ago when you asked to go to Father Goldman's ordination in Massachusetts. Now, you want your personal director to come from the Upper East Side of Manhattan every day to give you a private retreat."

"I think it's called a *directed retreat*." It slipped out before I could think. Restraint of tongue only works if for a second or two you think before you speak! I was beginning to feel hurt and resentful at the same time. Was Mother Jane Mary going to spoil everything for me? I had been a nun for five years and a grown-up for ten—at least—and hated being made to feel like a schoolgirl being reprimanded for talking in class or chewing gum . . . or unwrapping a Milky Way with one hand in my school bag without making a noise and taking a bite when the teacher was writing on the board.

My mind was drifting off in this flashback, and I didn't hear what Mother was saying.

"Directed, guided, or private—you're not having your personal chaplain come to see you. Father O'Mannion will be here for confession—are you listening, Sister?"

The elevated pitch in Mother's voice shattered my sentimental journey, where I had begun an interior debate over which was better: Milky Ways, Snickers, or Baby Ruth bars?

"Oh, yes, Mother, Father O'Mannion is coming today for confession, and I should probably go, and—"

"No, no, no. He's not coming today. It's only Tuesday. He will be here on Friday, as usual, and during your *private* retreat, you can talk to him on Friday. You don't need Father Meriwether."

I knew it was useless to try to change a prioress's mind, at least this prioress. I wanted to say, "Mother John Dominic would have let Father Meriwether come." But I didn't. I had learned by trial and error over the past five years to accept things as they were. One thing Greta Phillips once told me that I've pondered ever since is, "Expect nothing and be grateful for everything." Remembering that in the middle of the crisis was not always so easy. I wouldn't have been upset, hurt, or resentful if I hadn't expected Mother to agree with my plans and think the article in *Review for Religious* was applicable to my upcoming retreat. And I would be grateful I could listen to Fr. Meriwether's taped conferences.

"That will be fine, Mother. I just thought I'd ask, since it sounded so good in that article we read. It was so 'Vatican II,' you know." I hoped that didn't sound cynical. It was my acceptance speech.

I left Mother's office and went directly to the Mediatatio Room and took fourteen tapes and signed them out. We weren't permitted to take tapes to our cells, unlike books, but we could sign them out and leave them in our library drawers. Each sister had her own drawer that made up a cupboard running the length of the windows of the library, on the garth side of the building. The windows were not opaque like most of the windows in the house, thanks to which our eyes always kept the enclosure. (It was also canon law.) I didn't know if opaque windows were meant to keep us from looking out or people from looking in.

The library was on the second floor, above the infirmary, and had three large windows with ugly venetian blinds, which, when opened, allowed the afternoon sun to pour in. The other three walls were all bookshelves. There was a section for recent periodicals, with only Catholic publications, except for *Time* magazine, which was new. Mother Jane Mary thought the sisters should know what was going on in the world since we were praying for it. She had subscribed to *Time* in the "spirit of Vatican II." I was learning (we were all learning) that the "spirit of Vatican II" was a rather subjective scapegoat for changes. Pope John XXIII "opened the windows" and apparently replaced the opaque ones with clear glass, which showed lots of smudge marks when the sun shone through. I was playing with my own analogy, trying to accept that Vatican II hadn't changed that much here, but in ten years, I thought, probably every sister would be having directed retreats!

So I put Fr. Meriwether and Thomas Merton's conferences to his "juniors" in my library drawer, which was neatly labeled in Old English calligraphy: *Sr. M. Baruch.* I was grateful for our private library drawers, our own reserved compartments. In Benedictine monasteries, I learned, they had their own desks in the scriptorium where they would do their *lectio divina.* Our library drawer is the twentieth-century remnant. *Interesting,* I thought, *that, when living in a community where everything is held in common, one relishes her own cell, library drawer, place in the refectory, and choir stall.* Gratitude *did* have the ability to change one's negative mood. And I had so much to be grateful for. That would be a good theme for my private retreat.

There were two heavy wooden tables in the middle of the room with only a scattering of chairs with arms on them. I sat down in one and just looked around at this library, which was a far cry from any library on the outside but had a warm and secure atmosphere, which shelves of books always create. I was feeling grateful for the room and even what I had accomplished as monastery head librarian (a title only I used). By the door were the card index files, which still needed to be updated, but I knew I had lots of time for that. I wasn't going anywhere.

Next to the card files was the sign-out table where one merely took the card in the book, signed one's name, wrote the date, and placed it in the out-box. Books were not due in two weeks, like in a real library, but the date and one's name gave the librarian (*ahem*) all the information she needed. Every month I would go through to see what books were not yet returned. Nothing was said to the borrower unless the book was being requested by another sister; otherwise, a book could be kept for six months or more. There was another file box for short-term books—no more than a month. Keeping track of these was tedious work. This was all life before the age of computers, but I found it interesting to see which sisters were taking out what books. It did not help my struggle against curiosity, another hidden trait Sr. Trinity, my novice mistress, had charitably pointed out to me. What a life! I had never known so much about myself as I learned in those first five years. Fr. Meriwether was such a great help in sorting it all out and putting things in a larger context, as I could tend to get discouraged and down on myself. He was also my irregular confessor, meaning I would always go to him when we had our monthly or bimonthly meetings but also went to the regular confessor.

Fr. O'Mannion was newly assigned as our regular confessor. He was not a Dominican Father but a diocesan priest here in Brooklyn. He was a kind and affable priest who never seemed ruffled by any of my sins. When I once told him I had sinned by being overly curious about what a particular sister was reading, all he said was, "Well, remember, Sister, curiosity killed the cat."

I almost laughed right there in the confessional. *Curiosity killed the cat?* That's certainly a deep theological truth to be pondered. I wonder if St. Thomas ever asked: *Whether it was curiosity that killed the cat, or the salmonella poisoning from spoiled chicken?* There I was again, confessing my sins as honestly as

I could, becoming cynical about the whole thing right there in the box! It was all taken care of with three Hail Marys.

After that I never took much stock in Fr. O'Mannion's spiritual directives. But again, I wasn't a schoolgirl peeking at someone else's test answers, but a self-willed, cynical, and sometimes arrogant grown-up nun. Random thoughts in the library . . . why couldn't the windows of our soul just remain opaque?

My glance alighted on the carved crucifix over the sign-out table. Nearly every room in the monastery had a crucifix, but the library's was especially beautiful, and not at all gruesome like the bloodied ones in the cloister. The Lord's slumped shoulders portrayed His final surrender in death, and there was a trace of a smile on His face. It was one of the most beautiful and interesting crucifixes I had ever seen.

It prompted me—or my guardian angel prompted me—to "give it all to Our Lord," something grown-up nuns were good at. I was learning. Here I was, ready to vow holy obedience to God, the Blessed Virgin Mary, St. Dominic, and my prioress—until death. I realized that the self-willed part of me was being chiseled away, slowly but surely, and I didn't really know what new form it would all take. I also knew the self-willed part was still very strong in me. It was my blessing and my curse.

When I left the library, the stubborn self-willed part of me called Fr. Meriwether to tell him my retreat agenda was not granted, and would he come to see me on Saturday morning before I went on retreat? That was agreeable to him. He didn't seem too disappointed that he wouldn't be giving me a directed retreat. I was expecting him to be as disappointed as I was, but I was grateful I would see him before I began.

Maybe asking him to come down every day was a lot to ask. *Lord, help me to accept that.*

Next to the Mediatatio Room was another small room which served as a periodical room for the back issues, up to two years, neatly stacked on shelves with cubicles for each magazine. I had reorganized the room and added two wooden library chairs with arms and a low table like a coffee-table (without the coffee, unfortunately), where you could sit and listen to tapes, using earphones. It worked out well, except if you wanted to take notes; the table was too low. So I had Sr. Mary Joseph make a couple lap desks, which I never saw anyone using, but they were there, under the table. I probably wouldn't take notes either. I never really go back and read them.

I decided I could skip Fr. O'Mannion on Friday and go to Fr. Meriwether on Saturday. I realized I was full of distractions over details which probably shouldn't have been worrying me. But I simply wanted to review the situation, to meditate on what I was about to do, and hopefully let gratitude and the awesomeness of it all cancel out any worry, resentments, or anxiety.

Oh, how I missed Papa, whose presence had filled my clothing ceremony as a novice. Outsiders didn't come to first profession, but how Papa would have been proud of me on this day coming . . . my final vows. I knew he'd be here in spirit and see it all from Heaven. Maybe he could coax Mama into coming. In five years Ruthie was the only member of my family to set foot in our chapel. Mama wouldn't even be in New York, but in Boca with Esther Bellsey, her latest best friend, who just happened to have her own condo and, like Mama, was a widow. It's funny because Mrs. Bellsey, as I knew her as a child, had never been one of Mama's favorite people.

I guess we all make attitude changes about people as time goes by. I certainly had, just within these walls in five years. Sr. Catherine Agnes had been my nemesis when I first entered. She was postulant mistress, and I was convinced that she was out to get me. Sr. Anna Maria and I called her Scar for her initials—Sr. Catherine Agnes Russell—and because her words and looks could wound you, leaving a scar!

I'm grateful today for those scars, as I needed to grow a thicker skin, as Papa would say. I mean that, not just for my first five years in the monastery, but for my entire life. But by the time my solemn profession arrived, Sr. Catherine Agnes had proven to be a strength and a grace to me. She knew I had wanted to go to Fr. Matthew's ordination and was refused to go by Mother Jane Mary. I didn't know then that she had gone to Mother's office and tried to change her mind, knowing how much Fr. Matthew meant to me. I think there may have been an Ezra Goldman in her life at one time. She knew he was also my godfather, and she knew there was a precedent for going to family ordinations.

I also didn't know till years later was that it was Sr. Catherine Agnes who suggested to Mother to ask Fr. Matthew to be the principal celebrant at my solemn profession. There would be Fr. Matthew, Fr. Meriwether, Fr. Antoninus (our chaplain), and Fr. O'Mannion, who kind of invited himself. He had never seen a solemn profession. I guess he was curious about what happens.

My two best friends from the city would be there: Lady Gwendolyn, "with bells on" (knowing her, that might be literally true), and dear Greta Phillips, my former roommate, who took me in when I left the Feinstein apartment on West

79th Street. Greta was in my catechism class and was received into the Church a week before my baptism. She had been married to a Lutheran minister, and together they had served as missionaries in Africa. When she became a widow, she also became a Roman Catholic! At that time she was a librarian at the New York Public Library, and thus was my advocate when I needed a job.

Greta and Gwendolyn. I guess the three most influential people, not counting Ezra, in the early years of my conversion are all *G* names: Gracie, Gwendolyn, and Greta. Of course, there are also the most important three Persons who are the one God. Gracie, Gwendolyn, Greta, and God. Gosh!

But, of course, three men in my life also influenced me, and two of these were already with God: Papa, Ezra, and my brother Josh. When Josh was killed in Vietnam, something was awakened in me. I like to think it was a grace that came through him. It's easy to live on the surface of life, especially as an American teenager, and in the mid-1960s, it was almost exhilarating. It was the Age of Aquarius: long hair, wine fests, nudity on stage, rock music, and smoking pot. I wasn't exactly a flower child, nor did I join in the social upheaval over the war, civil rights, and the feminist movement. I was sympathetic to these, as much as a high school girl knows about all that, but when my own brother died, I was affected by it in a way I didn't even know at the time. It opened me up to the big questions, the serious questions about life and death and what it all means. Josh's sudden death had a greater impact on me, I think, than all we were learning about the Holocaust, which was devastating in itself.

I was open to see God in all of it or in none of it; I knew it couldn't be both. And perhaps I was on the brink of chucking it all, like so many of my generation, when my best friend in high school, Gracie Price, was struck down with a terminal illness. She was young, talented, ever so pretty, and slim, in a way only blond gentile girls can be. She was a devout Catholic, I knew, and so I was bold enough to go into a Catholic church to light a candle for her. And God was ready for me.

Whoever would have imagined in her wildest dreams that ten years later, sarcastic, slightly overweight, brown-haired Rebecca Feinstein would be laying down her life in a cloistered monastery, vowing to live by holy obedience until death? Incredible.

Greta had written a note when she returned her invitation card saying she would be here:

My dear Becky,

I am overjoyed at your upcoming solemn profession and will be so honored and delighted to be present to celebrate with you. Not a day goes by when I don't think of you and the few years we lived here and worked together, and best of all, went to St. Vincent's together for daily Mass and every novena and mission that came down the avenue! They have been such a blessing to me.

I lit a candle for you in thanksgiving this morning by the shrine statue of St. Vincent Ferrer, and I thanked him for his part in bringing you to the Lord and to His Church.

As I walked away, Becky, I swear I heard the bell ring once. It may have been a hidden draft somewhere, but I heard his bell, and I knew it was all a miracle. You are my miracle child.

Greta

24

It is all a miracle; if we all only knew that each of our lives is a miracle. And so I was happy in that miracle-mood, or miracle-mode, when I knelt before Mother Jane Mary on November 1, 1974 and vowed:

"I, Sister Mary Baruch of the Advent Heart, make profession and promise obedience to God and to blessed Mary and to blessed Dominic, and to the Master of the Order of Friars Preachers, and to you Sister Jane Mary, prioress of this monastery of Mary, Queen of Hope, and to your successors, according to the Rule of blessed Augustine and the Constitutions of the Nuns of the Order of Preachers, that I will be obedient to you and to your successors until death."

I then signed my vow formula, which was later placed on the altar, and knelt before Fr. Matthew for the solemn blessing over the newly professed.

How I wished Papa had been present to hear the Prayer of Consecration . . . and Mama, of course. The prayer says in part:

> *In the fullness of time You raised up the Holy Virgin from the stock of Jesse. The Holy Spirit was to come upon her, and Your power was to overshadow her, making her the Immaculate Mother of the world's Redeemer. He became poor, humble, and obedient, the source and pattern of all holiness. He formed the Church into His bride, loving it with love so great that He gave Himself up for it and sanctified it in His blood. . . .*

I wanted to look up and over at Fr. Meriwether at that point. He knew that I knew how God's love was made flesh in Jesus, because he taught me that. My poor heart was pierced with His love that Saturday morning when I edged my way, in slow motion, into St. Vincent Ferrer Church and found myself in the Real Presence of Christ for the first time, and I didn't even know it intellectually but I somehow did in the depths of my poor soul. The Sacred Heart of Jesus, the High Priest, in priestly vestments, touched me in a way that changed my life . . . that brought me to this day when I was espoused to Him forever.

. . . Father, we earnestly pray You: send the fire of the Holy Spirit into the heart of Your daughter to keep alive within her the holy desire He has given her. . . .

I'm grateful my gratitude didn't come flooding in on me at that moment. I would have collapsed right there and then. I've realized it takes a lifetime of surrenders to absorb the reality of those words. The holy desire given to me was to belong exclusively to Christ, to live for God alone, together with others who share that same desire, so we could hold each other up when the going gets rough, so we could help each other keep alive the holy desire.

. . . Lord, may the glory of baptism and holiness of life shine in her heart. Strengthened by the vows of her consecration, may she be always one with You in loving fidelity to Christ, her only Bridegroom. May she cherish the Church as her mother and love the whole world as God's creation, teaching all people to look forward in joy and hope to the good things of Heaven.

In those early years after my conversion, there were many people who taught me by their own love and joy how to be a Catholic, how to love God with all my heart, or at least strive to. It's part of the humility that comes with age to realize how much we forget who we are and Who calls us.

It is perhaps the virtue of humility that carries the grace of perseverance into the middle ages . . . for there would be moments when I would forget the consecration I made on this day.

three

Solemn profession was one of the happiest days of my life. Twenty years later I would sit in the same parlor with my same guests, in the same clothes I had worn for twenty-five years. Not literally the same clothes, but the same style—we call it our habit. We never modified our habit as many religious sisters did. Oh, we softened the guimpe around our faces and let go of the starch that could really irritate our faces, especially in the summer, but that's all.

My forty-two-year-old little sister Ruthie lingered behind on my jubilee day "parlor." That is what we call meeting with family and friends to chat. It was in the parlor, or literally, the "speak room." It was the one room in the house where we could speak to people, other than our sisters in community. Funny, because parlor was what Mama and Papa, and all of us kids, called the front room. I think today people call it the living room. In her British period Ruthie tried renaming the parlor the "drawing room" after the room to which the women would withdraw to chat while the men remained in the dining room for port, cigars, and conversation unfit for ladies' ears. Ruthie would quip, "They would probably have blushed port-red if they heard the chatter going on in the drawing room."

Ruthie once said that the parlor here was not the drawing room—the rest of the house was. When I would leave her to go back into the cloister I was withdrawing from the whole world. She didn't say that sarcastically or really very philosophically, just kind of sadly. She sometimes talked about my life—this life within the cloister—like it was sad. I suppose a lot of people feel that way when they think about the life of a nun. That it's sad. I used to think people, especially other women, who were married and deliriously happy and fulfilled, with half a dozen kidlings in tow, probably thought it was sad to be a nun. But Ruthie wasn't married—most of the time. She tried two times but was never deliriously happy over anyone; she always seemed "sad" to me when she would withdraw from the parlor and go back to her world. Ruthie was an actress, you see.

"I want to be a star," she announced to me when we were probably ten and twelve years old. We shared a bedroom through all of our childhood and saved our allowance money in an old Maxwell House coffee tin to buy Broadway show tickets, which we never really did, as we depleted our theater funds on movie tickets. Saturday afternoon matinees were great for kids, and when we got older, we could go together to earlier shows, if the "movie house," as Mama called it, was nearby. We had several movie houses nearby—but we considered a crosstown bus, or a downtown bus to Lincoln Center or Columbus Circle, nearby.

We both went through the "I want to be a star" phase; after all, we were New Yorkers. We knew the "silver screen" was a Hollywood thing, but the stage belonged to us.

All three of the Feinstein girls took ballet and tap lessons. Sally was never really swept up by it; Ruthie teased her about having two left feet, an expression she overheard Mama say to Mrs. Gutmann at the dance studio. Gutmann and Goldberg Dance Studio on Broadway and 88th Street was all the rage in the fifties. It was open on Shabbat (after services) on the excuse that learning to dance was not "work," but entertainment and "food for the soul and the sole." That's what it said on the storefront window. I had two years of ballet and quit. I loved the beauty of the music and that we learned the five basic positions and did them over and over a million times. But the shoes! Oy. Soft ballet slippers were lovely—I wish I had a pair now—but it was the toe shoes! Blisters and sore toes were the only food for my soles, and I wasn't buying it. Besides, I didn't exactly have the prototypical ballerina physique. When I split my tutu doing a *grand plié* and the class burst into a fit of laughter, I knew my ballet career had taken its final bow.

Ruthie, on the other hand, did both ballet and tap, and liked them both, though she preferred tap, which she excelled in. She couldn't stand *en pointe* on one leg and do a slow *arabesque* without falling over. But she loved the jazzy sound of metal heels and toes on a tap floor. She gave up ballet at Gutmann and Goldberg's and transferred to Michael's Dance Emporium when she was in junior high. With Sally and me retired from the stage, Papa said he could afford the Emporium, which cost twice as much as Gutmann and Goldberg but met just two evenings a week, and that excited Ruthie more than anything.

Ruthie showed great promise and had stars in her eyes for years. "It's not easy being a dancer *and* an actress in New York," Ruthie would lament, usually to get out of doing homework. Of all my family, I think Ruthie had a keener insight into our life; even if she thought it must be sad, she saw it as rather dramatic. The first time she came with Greta and stayed for Compline and saw the *Salve* procession—the whole community moving two by two in semi-darkness, chanting the ancient *Salve Regina* melody—she was moved to tears.

"It's beautiful to hear the nuns singing to Our Lady, isn't it?" Greta said to her afterwards. "Did it remind you of *The Sound of Music?*"

"Not really. It reminded me of 'The Kingdom of the Shades' in *La Bayadère*, the dancers making their way down the ramp almost in slow motion." Greta was amazed Ruthie knew this, but she didn't know our ballet history. Ruthie's love for the dance never ended. I knew that, and used it once when Ruthie was sitting in front of me, alone, in the parlor, in one of her isn't-this-life-sad moods.

"It must be so sad for you . . ." she half-whispered, as if she were thinking out loud.

I thought for a moment before speaking. It was almost like when we were girls and would chat to each other from our beds late at night. "It's all about Jesus, really. It's like a *pas de deux* with the Lord. It's not sad—it's beautiful. He's always holding on, looking into your eyes. He lifts you up, and He steadies you when you do an *arabesque*." I knew that would get to Ruthie. I could see the change of expression from a blank stare, looking at the bars of the grille, to a half smile, perhaps remembering the thrill and the beauty of it.

Ruthie also knew the discipline and practice it takes. "It takes years to do that without quivering or losing your balance. I could never do it so gracefully." And her half smile blossomed into a full-blown one.

"I never quite thought of it that way, but you're right." I could see Ruthie listening more intently. "It's like that with the Lord. You've got to let Him lead, but you keep practicing the steps over and over, and His grace makes it all grace-full." I was quite happy with my little analogy and secretly tucked it in my mind for a later meditation.

"Yeah, I guess you have to give up your whole life for it, if you want to be a *prima ballerina*." Ruthie was taking off on my analogy. "Or spend your whole life in the *corps*."

"That's not such a bad place to be, Ruthie. The *corps de ballet* makes it all beautiful too."

"Yeah, if everyone remembers the choreography . . ." and she stood up and bowed over, making the sign of the cross and bowing again, mimicking our singing the Divine Office.

"*Brava, brava.*" And we both laughed. Greta wondered what was so funny when she came from the chapel to join us.

When they would come to visit me, Ruthie would come to the parlor while Greta would go to the chapel first to make a visit, as she would say, which went completely over Ruthie's head. Then Ruthie would take a promenade on the promenade "to see your skyline" while I visited with Greta. I don't know what they talked about before or after.

But it was Gwendolyn who became close to Ruthie some years after I had entered. Gwendolyn always had a New York-London flair, which Ruthie was drawn to. Gwendolyn took an interest in Ruthie's acting career, and would always go to see any show she was in, which gave me great pleasure.

Ruthie was in an off-Broadway show uptown which was getting good reviews. *Ruth Steinway's supporting role as the sassy Mary Magdalene gives a whole new vibe to the lady in red,* wrote Bill Baranger, theater critic for the *Village Voice*. The play was called *Godspell* and was a modern version of the Gospel set to music and dance. It all sounded rather sacrilegious to me, but Gwendolyn said it was delightful, and Ruthie was superb. "Ruth Steinway is her stage name, you know." I didn't know, but it did not surprise me; she had at least a dozen while growing up. Steinway was nice (and who doesn't like a Steinway?). But besides that, the most extraordinary thing happened.

At the intermission, the audience was served little plastic cups of wine and were invited to greet each other, and who does Gwendolyn see but my mother. Mama didn't recognize her, Gwen said, as she had only met her once, at Papa's funeral, and Gwendolyn had been swathed in black then. But Gwendolyn recognized Mama.

"Mrs. Feinstein, I presume?" she had said, extending her hand with four bracelets all clinking at the same time.

"'Why, yes, do I know you?' Your mother was pleased but leery," Gwendolyn said, "and took me in from head to toe without making it obvious."

"How did she look?" I was all ears. I hadn't seen her in over ten years.

"Oh, she looked stunning, really. If she colors her hair, it's hard to tell, because she had beautiful silver threads and wheat-colored strands falling loose to her shoulders. She has your face, Becky—or rather, you have hers. The eyes are soft and twinkling with just the right touch of shadow."

"Oh, I'm not surprised. Mama was a disciple of Helena Rubenstein and always took care of her looks. So tell me more—what did she say?"

"Well, first I said, 'I'm Gwendolyn Putterforth. I have the English tea shop and am a good friend of Becky's, and of your dear late husband.'"

For a moment I was literally breathless, picturing the whole scene. And to think . . . Mama watching a show about Jesus made it all so much more fascinating.

"'Oh, of course. I didn't recognize you. Ruth speaks of you often. How nice of you to see her perform. Isn't she something? Such a blessing that one is!'"

Gwen sounded just like her. I was so happy they ran into each other. She went on. "'Oh, I know, you've got a very talented daughter,' I said. 'I wouldn't miss a thing she's in. I also see Becky, you know, on a regular basis. She would be so proud of Ruthie.'"

I could feel tears starting to accumulate behind my eyes, hoping Mama would say she was sorry she'd never been here to see me.

"'Oy, don't I know. Those two were so close growing up—Ruth still has the Comedy-Tragedy masks they had in their bedroom. They both loved the theater, you know. Such a blessing to live in this city.' She smiled slightly, staring at nothing, like when you're daydreaming or caught in a memory of the past."

And then Gwendolyn, God love her, had popped the question. "'If you would ever like to go visit Becky I would be more than happy to go with you. She would be so happy, you know—she thinks of you all the time and worries about you.'

"Then," Gwendolyn continued, "your mother cupped her hands over mine and said, 'That is so kind of you, dear. My Ruben often spoke about how kind you were, and I can see that now, may he rest in peace. I shall think about your offer. Here, dear, let's get another glass of wine. It's quite something they serve it free of charge, but they should serve us in such tiny cups?'"

Gwendolyn took her up on the suggestion without hesitating, waiting for her to say she'd come see me.

"Content for the moment with another swig of that terribly dry Chianti, your mother said, 'Such a play we're watching! You'd think they would serve Mogen David, but who's complaining? It's free, isn't it?' A 'sip' half-emptied the cup. 'How does my Becky look?'"

My heart stopped for a moment.

"'She looks radiant, Mrs. Feinstein, she looks radiant. She has your eyes, you know. And her father's laugh.' That made your mother giggle a bit.

"'I should know these things,' she said. 'They shared a sense of humor too.'"

I smiled. *She still doesn't know, does she?* My father had been secretly baptized. Gwendolyn and Greta were the only two who knew this, and Mother John Dominic, of course, who was my father's godmother.

"'My Ruben loved all his children, but his Becky always had a special place in his heart, even when, even when . . . well, you know even when what.'

"'I do,' I told her. There was a long pregnant pause. The last of the wine disappeared quickly. 'You must come up and see my little tea shop, Mrs. Feinstein, Ruthie will bring you up there. I know you have a weak spot for elderberry wine and raisin scones . . . and I have both.'

"'How did you know that?' Your mother blushed like a schoolgirl on her first date.

"'Becky told me,' I said. 'She loved my scones too.'"

And Mama laughed along with Gwen, and they gave each other a slight hug. The intermission bell sounded.

"I think I saw a tear or two roll down her pretty face before she turned away," Gwen told me, while a tear or two— or three or four—rolled down mine.

That was early on in Ruthie's career, but it was the only time Gwendolyn ran into my mother. Mama didn't come to visit me, but there was always hope that one day soon she would. And Ruthie's visits were farther apart than before. I prayed for her a lot.

O Lord, watch over my little sister Ruthie. She's moved away from home and lives in the East Village. She wants to get a water pipe, whatever that is. . . . O Lord, Ruthie is in an off-Broadway show, and is going out with the assistant director. She thinks she's in love, again. . . . Dear Lord, Ruthie is getting married and can't understand why I can't go. She came to mine, she says. . . . Dear Lord, Mama fell on the boardwalk in South Beach. She gashed her leg and sprained an ankle. She wants Ruthie to come to Boca to take care of her. Ruthie won't go. She's an understudy for a star on Broadway, which is news to me. Help Mama cope, Lord, and please move her heart to drop me a line. . . . Dear Lord, Ruthie got married on the beach at Coney Island. It would break Papa's heart if he were still with us. Ruthie had always wanted a grand wedding in Temple Emanu-El, under a canopy with at least two cantors. Gwendolyn went to the wedding. Mama wasn't there, nor were Sally or David.

Gwendolyn was the source of most of my news about the family. She had only met my brother David at my father's funeral, but some time later he went to Tea on Thames. Gwendolyn once told me the story.

"He was with a lady friend, a British gynecologist. I think he wanted to impress her that he was friends with the English lady who owned an English tea shop." Gwen sat close to the grille telling me all this, like the room was bugged.

"What was the woman like?" I was always curious about David's girlfriends. He rarely dated a "nice Jewish girl," as Mama would say. Poor Mama, going to Teflon parties in Boca Raton and no grandchildren photos to show off. "Was she impressed?"

"Oh, she was probably impressed because she ordered toast with Marmite, and was happily surprised that I had a jar. Your brother had never heard of it!"

Gwen was better than a journalist in remembering details. I think she also knew that I relished all the gossip, as we rarely had quite the same inside.

"She was from Lymington, near the New Forest, but went to school in London. She had an aunt from Leeds and visited there when a child. She loved Yorkshire and would even consider practicing there. I thought, 'Who's trying to impress who?'"

"And my brother?"

"He didn't say much. I think he was faking a taste for Marmite though. He made a mess of spreading it on the toast, and I think he almost choked on the taste." Gwen put back her head and laughed, her bobbing earrings swinging in every which direction. "'A bit salty' was his only comment. Philippa and I both laughed."

"Philippa was her name? I rather like that name," I said, in my best British accent. "Ruthie went by that once in one of her British periods. She was Philippa Persival, till Papa simply proclaimed, 'Too many syllables.'"

"Oh, speaking of Ruthie, M.B." (Gwen got in the habit of calling me M.B.) "You've got to pray for her. She's probably going to get divorced from Alex, that awful husband she married at Coney Island. And she's been hitting the bottle a lot—the two of them. I'm surprised it's lasted this long."

Gwendolyn's visits often left me rattled. I loved having news of the family, but the not-so-good news left me feeling helpless. I knew I couldn't say or do anything to help, except, of course, to pray. And that I did, mostly for Mama, whom I longed to see and whom I worried about, living half the year in Florida. The other half, she still lived on West 79th Street, thanks to David and a nice little pension she got after Papa's passing. And I prayed a lot for Ruthie. Her acting career never really made her a star, but it kept her in the whole New York theater crowd, where she was happy, or tried to be.

In my poor memory, cheap wine and marijuana was all the rage. I never smoked pot, although I wanted to try—I was curious about it! I think my older sister, Sally, used to, but then she smoked cigarettes all the time besides. Chesterfields. She gave me one once when I was a senior in high school when we had gone for a rare walk together around the campus of Barnard. I took one drag on it and held the smoke in my mouth and blew it out in one big clump, like a smoky hairball, and Sally said, "No, not like that. You have to inhale it, into your lungs, like you're breathing."

I tried again, turned blue, felt a terrible burning and light-headedness, and decided then and there that smoking would not be part of my persona, regardless of how sophisticated and grown-up it made me look.

Ten years in the smoke-free cloister (except for our lovely feast day incense) and I was hearing tales of disco clubs in Manhattan with hard drugs, like cocaine and speed and quaaludes. Ruthie was a part of this world, but I couldn't imagine it.

And who did Ruthie have to fall back on? She hid her life as best as she could from Mama and David. Sally was in Chicago, and I was "behind bars," as Ruthie would say when she was in a melancholic crying jag. Ballet, theater, or movie analogies just didn't work at those times.

She stopped coming with Greta, which I was sorry about, as I knew Greta was a kind-hearted soul Ruthie could talk to. Ruthie said once that she thought Greta looked like Princess Grace Kelly of Monaco. Greta let her hair go to its natural color, a silvery gray with strands of white highlights. I don't think Grace Kelly would have worn the half-moon glasses Greta sported with mother-of-pearl rims, but they looked quite smart on her, and betrayed the fact that she was a retired librarian. When she was received into the Church, she'd say she had "come into the fullness of the Faith." She did it all with so much grace that she could have been named Grace.

Greta was very much a spiritual mother to me without our ever calling it that. Living and working with her my first five years as a Catholic was the best formation I could have ever received. She always seemed to know just the right book to give me; we often read new books together, out loud, at night after supper and after watching the news. We'd also go walking together, east to York Avenue and then East End Avenue, along the promenade with its assortment of characters walking dogs, running, sitting alone on park benches looking at the East River or Roosevelt Island. We'd walk up to Gracie Mansion, the home of the mayor, to see if we could tell what event was going on there that night behind the high wall. Sometimes we'd quietly pray the rosary together, sitting on a park bench looking at the East River. Or sometimes our evening excursion took us west to Central Park. If we were really adventurous we'd walk all the way through the park to Broadway and uptown towards Columbia to Gwen's Tea on Thames. Gwendolyn was always thrilled when we did, and if business was slow, she would join us at the table for a "spot of her special brew." Her special brew was cognac or brandy served in a fancy teapot. We never gave it a thought that she could be in big trouble because she didn't have a liquor license, but she said she got around it, as the tea room was legally part of her home, and we were friends visiting her home—she didn't charge us for the "tea." I was always interested in what her latest concoction from the oven was. (And Gwendolyn would usually put half a dozen in a bag for me to take home. She knew how I liked a little snack before hitting the sack.)

Gwendolyn was my godmother, and Greta was my spiritual mother. It's interesting how over the years that reversed itself: I became Greta's spiritual mother and Gwendolyn's "prayer person." Greta would visit every several months and would make a weekend retreat at the monastery several times a year. Her faith never wavered—if anything, it became stronger with the passing of years and all the changes that were happening in the Church. It was her health that began to get weak, and she said she could no longer go on her long walks like we used to do.

Her visits to the monastery became less frequent too. She retired from the library, which I was happy to hear, thinking she'd be able to visit more often. Greta had always been very private, even when we were roommates. We shared a lot about a lot of things, mostly goings-on at work, at St. Vincent's, and at Lincoln Center. Greta was a great "patron of the arts," she'd say with a humble chuckle. She always had a subscription to the American Ballet Theatre, and I would often get a ticket at the last minute and go with her.

She was private about her personal life. She would speak about her deceased husband with much reserve and sometimes humor, usually recounting crazy things that happened to them in Africa. She had a son whom I never met and of whom she rarely spoke. And I tried not to pry, which was a real challenge—my "curiosity thing" again! He was born in Mozambique and was named Paul. Paul Martin Phillips. She told me once that she had chosen Paul after St. Paul, and her brother Paul who had died of pancreatic cancer when he was forty-seven. I thought that was strange, as her husband was also Paul, but she never said their son was Paul Junior. Paul Senior, the Lutheran pastor, had chosen Martin after "you know who"—she would wait for my answer before reacting. Clueless Becky said, "Who? Dean Martin? Dick Martin of *Rowan and Martin's Laugh-In?*" (That was our favorite Saturday night show.) "I know, Martini and Rossi vermouth, right?"

"No, no, and no, Becky. Martin Luther, of course!"

"Oh my, isn't that sad?"

And Greta would laugh. "Indeed! Today, I would wish he had been named for Saint Martin de Porres or Martin of Tours. But we thought Martin Luther was a good Lutheran name."

Greta was seventy-five at my jubilee, and I think she looked forty-five—Ruthie was right about the Grace Kelly look-alike. And so it was quite a shock to me when she visited a month afterwards and told me she was not well, and asked me to pray for her.

I didn't pry. I knew she would tell me what was going on when she was ready. I just hoped it wasn't anything incurable. Greta was my Rock of Gibraltar in the Faith.

It even prompted me to drop a note to Ruthie and ask her to go to St. Vincent Ferrer's and light a candle for me for a very special intention. I didn't even tell Ruthie what it was because—well, because Greta was very private, and perhaps a little of that had rubbed off on me.

You kind of learn that in the monastery too. We are not encouraged to ask too many questions about anything. It got a little more open as the years went by and we blamed or praised Vatican II for more openness in community. For us, it happened more at recreation than elsewhere. Sr. Boniface, my black-beaner, never came into the library if I was there, although I could see if and when she might have checked out a book. She was actually very comical, in a backhanded way. She complained a lot about everything, and didn't like any of "these changes being forced on us." That she could speak about all that at recreation or a community meeting apparently was not one of the "changes" she didn't like. "Ve used to have our special prayers and litanies every night after Vespers. Who said ve shouldn't have the Litany to Saint Dominic and Saint Joseph and Saint Catherine anymore? Saint Joseph is not very happy about all this." We all thought that was a riot. She'd say it all in her German accent, get all red in the face, and end by stomping her foot. "Good Pope John never saw this coming—he just vanted the Protestants to come back to the true faith. Now ve are singing Protestant hymns at Mass." *Stomp, stomp.*

Sr. Bertrand, sitting next to her, threw her hands up. "Oh, don't make such a fuss about it. Saint Joseph couldn't give two hoots whether we rattled through his litany or not!"

You could almost feel the gasp from everyone catching their breath. All eyes turned to Mother Agnes Mary, who suddenly realized she was supposed to say something to settle the matter and got all tongue-tied and flustered. It was her first term as prioress, and she didn't deal well with controversy.

"I think both our sisters have a point . . . and it's time for Compline." And that settled that. Everyone jumped to, as if it were a fire drill: knitting jammed into bags, rosaries clicking, chairs creaking, we filed out silently, relieved for the sudden resolution. I edged my way over to Sr. Boniface, who was huffing and puffing to get out of her chair, and I whispered to her, "I miss the litany to Saint Joseph, too."

After the initial shock, Sr. Boniface smiled at me. I think it was the first time ever—to me, that is! She didn't say a word, but the smile was worth volumes. Passing our statue of St. Joseph on the way to chapel, I winked at him and proceeded into choir wondering if he really gave two hoots or not.

I knew that would be a question I'd throw at Greta through the grille. She always delighted in what she called "theological conundrums." Sr. Boniface gave a half dozen hoots whether St. Joseph gave any. Her wise old "hooting" saved us from many a change, or at least made us think about why we were making certain changes.

four

After my twenty-fifth jubilee I decided it was time to clean out my drawers and cupboards and all the nooks and crannies one finds in one's cell to store things. Some of us, I admit, have a difficult time letting go of stuff. I had a shoebox full of cards and letters which I hadn't looked at in years, and thought that would be a good place to start. Fr. Meriwether once told me that getting rid of accumulated sentimentals was purifying for the soul. I suppose that's true, but it just seemed to bring on an avalanche of memories. I thought I'd start off with two piles: Throw Away Now and Save For Later, like when I'm old and will enjoy reading these again.

Nuns can be very talented women, I've learned over the years. We can create our own greeting cards, usually made up of cut-and-pasted other cards that wound up on the common table. Sr. Immaculate Heart used to make exquisite holy cards from discarded Christmas cards, Easter cards (once they became popular), and other things, like pressed

44

leaves and tiny flowers. This was all before the age of computers and a thousand fonts to choose from. She did her own calligraphy. Stupid me thought that she did it from her own talent, like she learned this in third grade when we perfected our penmanship learned in second grade. But Sister had a book on it and practiced it for months and years, I guess, till it became a wonderful skill.

I had lots of pretty cards with Sr. Immaculate Heart's calligraphy wishing me Happy Feast Day, Happy Anniversary, Happy Birthday, and even one Happy Passover. All the feast day and birthday cards went into the Throw Away Now pile. But Mother John Dominic's I couldn't part with, not yet.

It was her card to me for my silver jubilee. It was done in her own style of calligraphy. There was a colored photo of one of us (supposed to be me, I presume) standing in the cloister and looking out onto the garth. Below it said: *God Alone*. And on the left page inside she had the words from Psalm 73, which we pray at Matins on Mondays of the Fourth Week:

> *What else have I in Heaven but You?*
> *Apart from You I want nothing on earth.*
> *My body and my heart faint for joy;*
> *God is my possession forever.*

And on the right side in her own beautifully cursive hand:

My dear Sr. Mary Baruch of the Advent Heart,

I remember like it was yesterday when I opened the enclosure door and there was a young girl with long brown hair, tears streaming down her cheeks, kneeling on the floor. The tears broke their course by the most beautiful smile as we sang our welcome to you. It's hard to believe that was over twenty-six years ago. It has been a marvelous journey for me, and I thank the Lord every day that you have been a big part of it. May He bless you, our Sister Mary Blessing, in your next twenty-five years. Remember me, your poor and humble sister, in your prayers.

Blessings upon blessings,
Sr. John Dominic

It struck me, reading that again with tears and a smile, that although we are always close to our families when we enter the monastery (some more than others, I suppose), over the years the sisters really become our family. Some irritate us to no end and others drive us mad, but they truly become our sisters. I don't mean that in a sentimental way, but perhaps a deeper spiritual way. Mother John Dominic used to say, "We go to God alone together."

Those outside don't always get that. We all go to God alone, but we do it with others. I guess it's the going-to-God part many people don't get. And if they haven't that going for them in their own life, then our life seems like a big waste, or, as Ruthie thought, sad. And, of course, when we're just postulants kneeling at the enclosure door with tears and smiles, we don't know it either. There's a real leap of faith which carries us across that threshold. I thank the Lord it was Mother John Dominic who ushered me in.

There were lots of little crises for me in the early years, and I was ready to pack my bag more than once. But I stayed each time one more day. And it was Mother/Sister John Dominic whom the Lord used to hold on to me.

It was a beautiful card that I put in the Save For When I'm Old pile. Such a blessing she was at my jubilee. It was less than a week afterwards that she was in the infirmary again. But this time you could see she was weak and getting that drawn look from losing too much weight. I visited her one night before Compline and was shocked to see her hair, not quite covered by her night veil, grown white with age. I brought her a Dixie cup of vanilla ice cream, and she was as delighted as a six-year-old.

I asked her how she was doing, and she just smiled. She never liked to talk about herself. "Pull up a chair and visit with me before the bell rings. I think I missed the *Angelus* tonight—the nurse was in fussing over things when the bell rang. Would you pray it with me?"

"Of course, Mother." I still called her Mother when it was just the two of us, and she never objected. She only winced a little when schleppy me dragged the straight-backed chair over to the bedside. We prayed the *Angelus* quietly, and then she looked very serious and just a little sad when she said, "You know, Sister, one regret I have is that I never met your mother, dear Hannah of a Thousand Silver Hairs."

She remembered my calling Mama that. "I know, Mother, I do too. I would have loved for her to have met you, although she may have been a little jealous—my father loved you!" And that almost brought a giggle to her otherwise serious expression.

"He was such a gentleman, your father . . . my godson!" And we both smiled a big giggle. She was indeed his godmother. When he was privately baptized at St. Vincent's by Fr. Meriwether, Mother had gone by cab to the church to be his one witness. It was quite out of the ordinary, but then, she was an extraordinary woman, and an extraordinary nun.

"You know, Mother, you never told me what the two of you talked about when he brought me here on my entrance day. You were a good fifteen minutes or more in the parlor."

"It wasn't anything really so profound. I told him I admired his acceptance of your entering the monastery—of your becoming a Catholic, actually. And he smiled, not saying anything. 'You know,' I said, 'Rebecca is doing something most young women her age would never dream of doing. It reflects an integrity and courage she inherited from you and her mother. But when it comes down to it, Mr. Feinstein, she is giving her life to the Lord Jesus. And He's worth every heartbeat we have.'"

I could tell Mother was beginning to have trouble speaking, so I grabbed the water pitcher and gave her a plastic cup of cool water. She took her time swallowing and getting settled with the pillows at her back.

"Your father didn't say anything, but I could tell he was listening intently and taking it all in. I didn't know his fascination with *The Sound of Music*, which you told me about later, or I would have stood profile at the window and sung 'Climb Every Mountain.'"

That, of course, made me laugh, and Mother laughed, and together it resounded all around the infirmary like a laughing boomerang. She knew that line always made me laugh.

"And that's all you said to him? That Jesus is worth every heartbeat?"

"Yes, I believe that's all I said. But he did say back to me, 'This Jesus must be something else. But will my Becky be happy?'

"And I just gave him one of my best smiles. We sat for a minute in silence. 'You know, Mr. Feinstein—'

"'Please, call me Ruben.'

"'You know, Ruben, can any of us ever predict if we will be happy? But God made us to be so. And Jesus makes your Rebecca very happy.'

"'And you, Mother?'

"I leaned forward, close to the grille. 'Yes, Ruben, He makes me very happy.'

"'I should like to know this Jesus you and my Becky know.'

"Another sip of water, dear, thank you." I was so excited I kind of spilled the water all over the bed table. "My cup runneth over," chirped Mother, and we laughed again.

"Yeah, I'm sorry. It's only water." I got enough paper towels to dry the entire floor, soaked up the spill, and poured her another cup, plus one for myself in the empty Dixie cup. That didn't work too well, but I downed it before it collapsed in my hand.

"What did you say then, Mother?" I had never heard the full version of the story. Papa only told me he had had a very interesting conversation with the Mother Superior. He was using his best newly acquired *Sound of Music* vocabulary.

"I told him he could get to know the Lord if he simply began by talking to Him in his heart: 'Nobody has to know. You can read the Gospels, of course, but maybe the best way to get to know Him is to simply sit in the chapel without saying a word. Just sit there and look up at the altar.' That's all I said, because I knew our time was almost up. Oh, I did say when he was leaving that he could always come back and talk to me about Jesus: 'You won't get to talk to your "Sister Rebecca" but you can come and talk to me,' I said. He really liked that. I think maybe that was his *Sound of Music* moment."

I could tell Mother was really tired now. "Thank you, Mother, for sharing all that with me after all these years. Papa couldn't have had a better godmother in all the world than you." And I kissed her quietly on the forehead, returned the chair without a squeak, and almost tiptoed out of her room and tiptoed into Compline. Little did I know that that would be the last time I saw Mother John Dominic and that those would be last words she spoke to me.

Most of us didn't hear the EMTs clanging their gurney down the cloister hall to the infirmary; it was on the other side of the building. We didn't know till Chapter after Prime that Sr. John Dominic had suffered a stroke around four o'clock, after most of us had gone back to bed after Matins. I never got to say good-bye.

She lingered for a day, and the chapel was filled with silence and prayers all day. There was a tangible hush in the house; we all spent more time in the chapel begging for her recovery or for a holy death. A seven-day votive candle was lit in front of the statue of St. Joseph in the cloister, and a three-day candle burned in front of St. Dominic.

Sr. Paula, our youngest extern sister, had spent the night at the hospital. Mother Agnes Mary kept regular notices on the prioress's bulletin board, but there was no good news yet, only that she was in critical condition. Her whole left side was affected, and she could neither speak nor swallow.

The second day was much the same. I asked Mother if I could go to the hospital, and she said, "Not just now." A few of the cloistered nuns had gone that morning, but I wasn't one of them. I only rebelled a little interiorly; I offered it up instead and spent the morning in the chapel. I prayed to the Lord, to Our Lady, to St. Joseph, and to St. Dominic, but then I began my litany of non-canonized saints. I prayed first of all to Papa. I filled him in on the situation in case those in Heaven aren't *au courant* of these things. I told him about my last conversation with Mother and that she told me about their first conversation, which I would come to find out was not the one and only: he took her up on her offer and, before he couldn't do it anymore because of his health, he met with her every Friday afternoon for an hour.

I prayed to Fr. Meriwether, my latest friend in the communion of saints. He knew how much we all loved Mother John Dominic and how much she believed in my vocation, especially when I was having some serious doubts. He was there now with Papa, whom he had baptized and confirmed, and he knew how much Mother John Dominic did in preparing my father for that day.

I honestly didn't know how to pray or what to pray for. Did I want her to recover, to be miraculously cured, or to die a holy death and be with them and the Lord forever? Was it pure selfishness to want to keep her alive for myself, for all of us here who needed her? Didn't she tell Papa that knowing the Lord would make me happy? It made her happy, and isn't eternal life the ultimate happiness?

So I ended up just praying to the Lord that His holy will be done: *If this is the end of this life for Mother John Dominic, please, Lord, don't let her suffer. And protect her now from all the assaults of the evil one.* I prayed the prayer to St. Michael the Archangel, changing the pronoun to "her" instead of "us."

How many times over the years did Mother admonish or encourage me, "Think of our end, Sister, think of our end—eternal life"? Almost all our prayers remind us of that. I remembered my jubilee card and her quoting Psalm 73. I opened my breviary and found it quickly:

What else have I in Heaven but You?
Apart from You I want nothing on earth.
My body and my heart faint for joy;
God is my possession forever.

Mother John Dominic lived those sentiments without preaching them. She would remind us in her own inimitable way that our life is one of suffering and the cross, but it is our way of following the Lord. Our end is Heaven, where God will be our possession forever.

In our poor, limited way we create a heaven according to our own imagination. Mama used to talk about Heaven like it was a Thomas Kinkade painting, with cozy cottages bathed in light and smothered in flowers and spring breezes. She never knew of him, of course, but she had the same images. It would be like a perpetual Shabbat with family and friends and all kinds of goodies to eat. She never really described the Lord in this Kinkade Heaven, but I think she must have always been sad because I wouldn't be in the same cottage.

Others think of Heaven as the epitome of the ideal of their most pleasurable earthly experience. Sr. Beatrice told me once that her father thought Heaven was going to be a gorgeous but exclusive thirty-six-hole golf course. Others picture Heaven like attending a grand concert performed by the most talented and heavenly angels one could imagine. The Lord is the *maestro*, and if we're lucky, we will be in the orchestra or the chorus . . . or the *corps de ballet*. (That's us, if Ruthie's image is the real thing!)

I don't have an image of Heaven. I think it will be something beyond what we can even imagine. St. John himself says we don't know what we will be, but we will be like Him. We will be in the Son, because we are already.

Thinking such pious thoughts helped to pass my prayer time when I stopped praying for Mother's recovery and just prayed that God would bring her to Himself. I would miss her terribly—I already did—but we believe that we will be with our loved ones again. I can't imagine how incredible that will be.

The bell began to toll a half hour before Vespers. I jumped awake in my stall, clearing away the fog of where I was and what time it was. It wasn't the bell for Vespers; it was a toll. It was only tolled when one of us died.

I knew then. The bell summoned us to the Chapter room, where we all sat in utter silence. Mother Agnes Mary entered in silence, her hands hidden beneath her scapular, her eyes cast down carefully in front of her. We all stood when she entered, but she gestured for us to sit.

"*Laudetur Jesus Christus.*"

"*In aeternum,*" we responded with subdued voices, waiting for the news.

"Our dear Sister John Dominic has gone to the Lord. Sister Trinity, Sister Anna Maria, and I were with her till the end. We don't know if she knew we were there, but we prayed softly at her bedside, and she died very peacefully close to three o'clock this afternoon. We sang the *Salve* and the *O Lumen*. Let us now pray for the happy repose of her soul: *Eternal rest grant unto her, O Lord . . .*"

I don't think I heard anything after that. I remember the sisters didn't move from the Chapter room; we all just sat silently lost in our memories—at least, that's where I was. How many like myself would probably not be here if Mother John Dominic was not who she was when she was Mother?

I closed my eyes for a moment and was back to being a nervous and awestruck aspirant, sitting in the outside parlor and waiting for my first meeting with the Mother Prioress. I had gotten that far, so far, in my asking to enter the monastery. My initial interviews with the postulant and novice mistresses had gone well enough.

When she had come into her side of the parlor, I was surprised that she wasn't a big woman; she wasn't much taller than myself. But it was her face that captured everything. She had the warmest of smiles, which I would learn to take refuge in for many years. Of course, I didn't know that then.

"Blessed be God. Rebecca, I understand you would like to join us on the other side of this grille?" And her smile lit up the whole room and instantly put me at ease. And she certainly didn't hem and haw, but got right to the point, in a very nice way.

"Yes, Sister, I mean, Mother. I have been coming here for a couple years now and love being here . . ." I remember feeling like a blabbering idiot, tripping over my words. But she showed no reaction to my answer. "I mean, I never thought I would ever want to be a nun. I didn't even know there were nuns anymore, till I came here." *Slow down, Becky, you're just making it worse.* "I'm a convert, you know . . ."

"Yes, I know. Isn't it wonderful that you and Our Lord and Our Blessed Lady shared the same beautiful faith! I've often meditated on Our Lady's life as a faithful and pious Jewish mother, lighting the Sabbath candles on Friday night, closing her eyes as she prayed for her family—for her Son— and opened them on the Sabbath."

I was nearly speechless. "I think about that too. I can hear my mother's voice when she would pray the prayer, and then greet us all: 'Good Shabbos!' It's one of the things I miss most, I mean, when I think about it. My family was not too thrilled when I became a Catholic."

"I imagine not. And now a nun—my dear, it must be a real shock for them."

I wasn't sure if she was going to laugh or if she was dead serious. "I—er—haven't really told them that yet. Well, maybe I've hinted at it with my father. I can't really keep secrets from him . . ."

"Well, I'm sure it's a lot to take in, even for you, Rebecca. It's not the kind of life most young women your age are lining up to join." She giggled, kind of. It was a wonderful half giggle and half laugh I would come to know. It was Mother's way of being light-hearted while profoundly serious. "It's a life of sacrifice." And she paused, looking at me with a kind severity. "But it's a beautiful life. I think, in the end, we come to realize it's a calling from the Lord. Otherwise, none of us would persevere."

I knew she was talking about the "vocation" part—a new word in my Catholic vocabulary, at least when it was an arrow being shot at me. For years I'd heard prayers for "vocations to the priesthood and religious life" and hadn't given it much thought. I certainly didn't think my life as an assistant librarian was a vocation. My sisters and brother talked about their careers but not their vocations. Only Fr. Meriwether talked about vocation in the sense that Mother John Dominic now spoke the word, with a poignancy that was like an arrow shot to my heart, not by Cupid or any kind of angel really, but by the Lord Himself.

I wondered if Mother heard me swallow in the silence that fell on the room. But then she smiled again that all-embracing smile, and stood up. "We shall be praying for you, Rebecca, and for your family. May the Lord's will be made known to you, and may He give you always the grace to embrace it with fortitude and abandonment."

"Thank you, Mother." I stood up too. "Thank you for your prayers and for coming to see me." I felt like a radio host thanking her guest for visiting the show. But I think they were the right words, if there are right words or wrong words at times like that. I didn't meet with Mother again until she opened the enclosure door and welcomed me inside.

The bell for Vespers roused me out of my silent flashback. Only then did Mother Agnes Mary's words come back to me: "Sister Trinity and Sister Anna Maria and I were with her." Sr. Anna Maria! Why was she there? I had wanted to go; Mother knew that the night before! Why did Sr. Anna Maria get to go? I wasn't mad at her; she was still my good friend. *I'll have to find that out later*, I thought to myself.

Sr. Rosalina was kissing her scapular with great fervor, as I was blocking her way past me to her stall. I kissed mine in return, to say "I'm sorry." *I'm sorry I didn't see you standing there—my mind was at Mother's bedside, and Sr. Anna Maria standing there singing the* Salve *to usher Mother John Dominic's soul into eternal life. Oh, Lord, help me to turn this resentment into repentance for Mother's soul. How happy she must be now to see You face to face.* These thoughts filled my mind as we knelt to pray the O Sacred Banquet. We stood and turned to face the altar and the Office began: "O God, come to my assistance . . ." And life went on as usual, but there was a big hole in my heart as I tried to pray for the soul of my Mother John Dominic. It was only at the *Magnificat* that I opened my mouth and couldn't sing. I had to consciously hold back the tears.

five

Ruthie and Gwendolyn came together to Mother John Dominic's funeral Mass. I was very touched that they would both come, especially Ruthie. She was beginning to look somewhat haggard, which I would never say to her, of course, as it would send her off in a tailspin of anxiety. Gwendolyn, who was some fifteen years older than us, looked younger than she did. But I was so happy to see them both.

I wasn't able to see them right away, as they couldn't come inside the enclosure for the actual burial part, and then the two parlors were filled with well-wishers. But Gwendolyn got word to me through Sr. Paula that she and Ruthie would grab a bite to eat and return around one thirty. That would be perfect, as there would be a parlor free at that time; still, I put up a *reserved* note just in case.

"Thank you both so much for coming." My words were controlled but sincere, an acting technique held onto from high school, which I knew my dear actress sister, Ruthie, would recognize immediately.

Sounding almost Bankheadish, Ruthie responded, while taking off her sunglasses, "I know how terribly bereaved you must be, dahling, to have lost your second mother."

"Oh, Ruthie," the three of us laughed at her little performance, "that's just what I needed! The last couple days I thought I would never laugh again, and here you are . . ." and for the first time in years I instantly burst into a flood of tears, which I know had been pent up in me since Mother Agnes Mary gave us the terrible news.

"She was something else," chimed in Gwendolyn, and just the way she said it helped me to get a hold of myself. I blotted my face with a clean handkerchief and then blew my nose in it, which I rarely did. Linen handkerchiefs I thought should be used for blotting, especially if one began to schvitz; Kleenex were for blowing one's nose. But I wasn't thinking, and I didn't care.

"How are you two? I haven't really seen either one of you since my jubilee." Actually, I had seen Gwendolyn a couple of times—she was even here on retreat since then—but I said it for Ruthie, who hadn't been here for a long time.

"I've been in rehab." It was Ruthie now practicing her controlled-but-sincere voice.

"Rehab? What kind of rehab? Were you sick? Did you have an accident?"

"Drugs and alcohol, dahling." Her Tallulah Bankhead was back. "But we're all better now, aren't we, dahling?" Gwendolyn sat as calm and nonchalant as an English pickle.

"So tell me, tell me." I was sounding uncontrolled and anxious.

"It's nothing to sweat, Becky. I had a little too much a few times and kind of lost control, although I don't really remember. But I was sent to Smithers for thirty days. It's quite the place, you know, there are lots of actors there." Ruthie was sounding like she had just come back from a trip to Malibu.

"Are you okay now?" My controlled-but-sincere voice was back.

"Clean and sober." She polished an invisible star on her left shoulder. "But we're here to help you. What can we do? Could we put on a benefit memorial or something?"

I knew she wasn't kidding, but I couldn't help but laugh at the idea. "Of course not, Ruthie, but it's very thoughtful of you. We'll pray special prayers for her for a week, have another Mass in a month, and talk about her forever at recreation. That's our memorial."

"Oh, okay. I just thought I could get some of the guys down here and do a couple of numbers. I remember your saying how much she liked shows you put on."

"Oh, she did. They are done every year for the prioress's feast day, and we've got a whole house full of frustrated actresses in here." I knew it was a bit of an exaggeration, but Ruthie would have identified with it. *It's no wonder she drinks so much*, I thought to myself. She had been through two marriages and divorces, and her career never really took off beyond bit parts—there had been one hopeful soap opera, but she was eliminated after four episodes. And no talent scout from Hollywood or Broadway pursued her. But now she was excited about Gwendolyn's new adventure and very much a part of it.

Gwendolyn had a younger sister named Jacquelyn, who lived in London and owned and operated a small theater-pub in Soho. In all the years I had known Gwendolyn I had never known she had a sister. Well, a year before, her sister had called her from London to tell her their father had died and apparently left a sizeable inheritance. Gwendolyn was able to fly over immediately for the funeral. She had called and left a message on our prayer line: "Pray for a safe trip across the pond—my father died. Oh, and shoot up a prayer or two for him."

After the funeral in a small cemetery near Huddersfield, near Leeds in Yorkshire, Gwendolyn and Jacquelyn went to her flat in Soho. Again, Gwendolyn never shared anything with me about her relationship with her sister, but the trip apparently had been a time of healing and reconciliation between them. Funny how death can do that. Well, not funny really. After all, it's very Christian: the Lord's death brought healing and reconciliation for the alienated human race!

Jacquelyn, like her sister, was a businesswoman. She owned a building in Soho, which she had bought years ago when Soho, as she says, was "so-so." The main floor and the lower level became a pub with a theater theme. Lots of enlarged celebrity photos covered the walls, and a piano on a small corner stage hosted the likes of many would-be singers and West End stars. The first floor, which for us would be the second floor, was a large spacious loft once used by an artist. It may even have been a gallery at one time. Jacquelyn put in a small theater, holding no more than 150 people. Behind the stage was enough room for storage, sound equipment, and dressing rooms. On the top two floors were an office, a rehearsal space, and her own living quarters. So it was all quite compact for her. She said, according to Gwendolyn, that the piano player on the ground floor was most important. He or she brought in the customers, and eventually the theater angle caught on, and it became a thing to do in Soho.

Gwendolyn naturally was taken aback by the whole thing, though intrigued and entertained. She extended her stay there for another week, leaving Tea on Thames in the good hands of none other than Ruth Steinway! Ruthie had helped out there before and actually worked there for months at a time when show business wasn't producing. She still ran with the theater crowd, and Tea on Thames had taken on a more downtown feel from when I was a regular there drinking Earl Grey tea and eating raisin scones with Ezra Goldman—the "Catholic couple."

Gwendolyn flew back to New York full of ambition and dreams for starting her own theater-pub and a pocketful of money to do it with. She came to visit within the month and couldn't stop for a minute telling me all about it and asking me to pray that it would all happen.

I was a little befuddled. We are asked to pray for lots of things, and we do, mostly in a general way. Each of us had our own private prayers for special intentions, and that's where I put "Gwendolyn's project," as I called it. I was happy Ruthie was enthused about it too, and that she had a part to play in all of this. She could get so depressed at times when she wasn't working or her love affairs were not working out! What could I do? My own life seemed so out of touch with all that. I couldn't work up much enthusiasm for the whole thing, but I nonetheless promised I would pray. I was the "prayer partner." Even then, I wasn't so sure what I was praying for. I wanted Gwendolyn to be happy, and I thought Tea on Thames was enough to handle and would eventually take her right up to retirement. I was ever so grateful that she and Ruthie were friends. I think Gwendolyn may have filled in for an eccentric mother, which poor Ruthie didn't find in our dear Hannah Feinstein!

I kept it all tucked in the back of my veil. Nothing really happened immediately. In the meantime, my prayer life was not really what others, like Gwendolyn, thought it was. It became a lovely routine which I easily settled into and actually loved. Our life doesn't change much from day to day, but we pass through the liturgical seasons and big feasts and saints' days with great aplomb. That part never bored me, although my prayer wasn't always so fervent or simple. I could be distracted very easily by little things. I know there are times when we're in the middle of the fourth mystery of the rosary, and I realize I have not even thought about the Lord or Our Lady since we started. Little misunderstandings with another sister could be rehashed in my head all during silent prayer. We are admonished at Compline on Wednesday nights not to let the sun go down on our anger. I wish St. Paul had included our resentment, our fears, our worries, our obsessing over something, and even our fantasies, which are not always so savory or easy to be rid of before the sun goes down.

I told Fr. Wilcox once in confession that I lacked joy and gratitude and carried a bunch of resentments and mistaken judgments about others to bed with me. He told me, "Have some warm milk and say five Hail Marys." The whole time he was giving me absolution I was thinking, *Warm milk? What's he think, that we live on a farm or have free access to the kitchen?* Then I left the confessional and forgot what my penance was, so I just said ten Hail Marys. I hope that still makes for a valid and good confession. I missed my confessions with Fr. Meriwether. I knew he really listened and seemed to see things beneath all my regular collection of venial sins. I sometimes wonder if Fr. Wilcox is reading a book while we routinely go into our weekly or biweekly confession. I wanted to bring that up to him in confession, but didn't think it was right, nor did I know how to word it correctly. I was usually in and out in three minutes, while some of the sisters seemed to linger much longer.

Sr. Anna Maria and I would occasionally kibitz over tea and cookies in the infirmary kitchenette. It was during this time that I was both the librarian and one of the assistant infirmarians, which was usually nothing more than babysitting, although that probably isn't nice to say. We always have a sister present in case of emergencies. It gives the real infirmarians a break. Sr. Anna Maria would bring over piles of towels, washcloths, handkerchiefs, and anything else one could fold from the laundry and leave them in the folding room (an unoccupied infirmary room) with two or three sisters who took great delight in having a job and would chat quietly among themselves. I know remembrances of Mother John Dominic filled the room for weeks.

"Wasn't the funeral Mass sad?" Sister began before we even settled into our straight-backed chairs around the round table covered in the most hideous plastic and felt-bottom table cover. Its design depended on the season. It was presently an ugly mix of yellow and aquamarine flowers in a kind of fish aquarium.

"It was one of the saddest days in my life here. But I hope Mother John Dominic was happy with our poor chant. The *Requiem* is so beautiful, and I think really joyful, but I think our souls were all filled with sorrow, you know?"

Without asking if I wanted any, Sister had gone into the freezer of the small fridge and brought out a half gallon of mint chocolate chip ice cream and two bowls. "I know, but it's really a blessing she didn't linger and suffer for a long time." Sr. Anna Maria was sounding very knowledgeable of these things.

We blessed ourselves silently before diving into the mint chocolate chip. "I saw that your sister and Gwendolyn were here yesterday. Anything going on?" So before I could delve into why she was at the hospital when Mother died and not me, I told her all about the new project.

"I'm not so sure it's a good thing for Gwendolyn—I think she should just keep Tea on Thames until she retires—but it will be good for Ruthie, I suppose. She, ah, seems to be having a problem with drugs."

Anna Maria said, not really shocked by what I said, "I think your sister has had a problem with it for a long time."

That kind of surprised me, right in the middle of a spoonful of mint chocolate chip. She had never mentioned this before. Sister knew Ruthie and my few friends that visited me. I tried to include her at times because she had even fewer visitors.

"She hasn't had it easy, my Ruthie. Two failed marriages, one which didn't help the situation at all, and her career never hit the big time."

"Yeah, but booze can mess up your head even in good marriages and celebrity careers. My father made life pretty miserable for us growing up. So what's the name for the theater-teahouse?"

"I don't know. Gwendolyn is all excited about a loft she found on Barrow Street in the West Village. She thinks this will be it. I hate to think of her closing Tea on Thames."

"Well, maybe she'll just sell it, or rent it out to another manager, and if the theater thing doesn't work out, she can fall back on it."

64

Sr. Anna Maria was always so good at analyzing things and having practical solutions. "You're right! That's what I'm going to pray for. Anyway, you never told me your father had a problem." *And why were you at the hospital and not me?* I added, only in my head, of course.

"Oh yeah, you know, the 'Irish virus,' I think they call it. He died a drunk when he was fifty years old. I don't know if my mother ever got over it."

We were just getting into our second scoop of ice cream when we heard Sr. Gerard give out a scream. I was sure Sr. Amata had had a heart attack or collapsed or just passed out—she was prone to doing that. We literally ran into the hallway and down the hall into the folding room. Sr. Amata and Sr. Benedict were hysterical with laughter. Sr. Gerard uncovered a huge black spider in one of the towels and was sure it was a black widow or the devil himself out to get her.

We assured her the spider was just a spider. Sr. Anna Maria said the laundry room was full of them, which wasn't very helpful information. "So you might want to shake out the towels before you fold them." And everybody thought that was a riot, except Sr. Gerard, who then and there retired from the folding career, got up, and returned to the ongoing jigsaw puzzle in the infirmary sitting room. The other two dutifully took up the shaking advice with great gusto.

I never got to ask Sr. Anna Maria about the hospital, and we never got to finish off the ice cream. Sr. Mary Boniface's call bell went off, and, being the only so-called infirmarian, I started off towards her room to attend to whatever she was ringing for. It was not unusual for her call bell to summon whomever was on call: poor Sister needed help to go to the bathroom, to get in her chair, to get out of her chair, to get into bed, and so on. She was in her nineties and suffered from dementia.

She was also very sweet to me, which was the fruit of old age or the dementia, I don't know. She would often speak to me in German, and I would just smile, and nod, and once in a while throw in a "*yah*," which could be dangerous, as I didn't know what I was saying *yah* to!

Some weeks before this incident, I had been on the late shift from after Vespers to Compline, which was uneventful but active. Supper was served to the few sisters in bed who couldn't really go out to the infirmary kitchenette and sit at the round table. There was an audio speaker in the kitchenette so the sisters could listen to the reading in the refectory. But Sr. Mary Boniface was in her chair in her room when I brought in her soup and about fifteen saltines. She loved saltines, which probably shot her blood pressure sky-high but were one of her last enjoyments in life. She also loved pretzels, which I would often bring to her, as I loved pretzels too and it gave me an excuse for eating some between meals. She liked the hard pretzels, which were not my favorite, but the monastery had them by the caseful.

I got her soup and saltines all settled on the TV table in front of her, and she began speaking to me in German. She leaned down by her side, picked up an old book which had become loose from its binding, and handed it to me. She was pointing out the loose binding when it dawned on me that she thought I was Sr. Hildegard, her old German crony who was the community bookbinder.

Without blinking an eye, I assumed the role of Sr. Hildegard; it was a performance that Ruthie would have been proud of. I spoke in broken English in my best German accent, telling her I would take care of it, and now she should eat her soup before it gets cold. Sr. Boniface beamed. She was so pleased. In a very ladylike way she ladled a spoonful of soup from bowl to mouth, without spilling a drop, and *mmm-mmmed* it like a Campbell's commercial.

I sat with her while she ate all her soup, which now included five saltines crumbled up in it, and she neatly wrapped the rest in a paper napkin, I knew for her late night snack. I went to take the tray, and she grabbed my hand and kissed it. I thought, *If she only knew these are the hands that dragged Sr. Hildegard's bulky ugly bookbinding equipment out of the library annex.* But I smiled, and leaned down and gave her a peck on the cheek. She was very happy. I left quietly, tray and book in hand, promising I would get her book back to her all mended.

I wasn't Sr. Mary Hildegard every time I'd visit her room; most times I was just another sister whose name escaped her. My face was familiar enough now that she didn't show any fear. I don't know if she always knew where she was. And she was not always so obedient, and her German stubbornness was still hidden beneath her newly acquired mellowness.

So I took my time getting to her room to answer the call bell, making sure first to remind Sr. Anna Maria to pray for Gwendolyn and Ruthie's adventure and that she hadn't told me about Mother's dying yet. She told me she would do both, and joined the folding sisters to speed them along. "They don't have to be folded so perfectly," she'd tell them. But you can't tell an old nun to do it differently. All the corners had to be lined up perfectly with each other.

When I arrived at Sr. Boniface's room, I was expecting to find her in her chair, but she was in bed. She was very still and didn't turn to look when I walked in.

"Sister Mary Boniface? It's Sister Hildegard." I thought that would rouse her or get a reaction at least. "Sister Boniface? Sister Boniface?"

She was gone. I could see it immediately on her face: her eyes were still partly opened, and her mouth was agape, but she was not breathing. And she was an ashen white. I immediately ran out of the room, crying, "Anna Maria, Anna Maria!"

Sister shot out of the folding room in an instant. "Heavens to Betsy, Baruch, what is it?"

I was instantly riddled with guilt that I hadn't run into her room the minute the call bell sounded. Maybe she was crying for help, maybe I could have saved her. But Sr. Anna Maria knew all about death and dying, didn't she? She would know what to do. That's probably why Mother Agnes didn't ask me to the hospital—she knew I would be a mess.

"She's gone, Sister Boniface is gone." I was out of breath.

Sr. Anna Maria slapped me hard on the arm. "Calm down, Sister, show me." And we returned to Sr. Boniface's room.

"Yep, she's gone." This was the observation of my death-and-dying expert?

"What should we do? Dear me, I should have come in right away."

"Don't be silly, Sister, she would have died anyway. We should call Mother first. I'll go do that."

"No, I'll do it, I'm on duty here, and not doing a good job of it." I thought for a moment that I would bring up my mint chocolate chip, my stomach had turned sour. But I rushed to the infirmary office, called Mother on the phone, and in a panicky voice hollered, "Sister Boniface is gone!"

68

"Gone where?" Mother replied rather impatiently, no doubt a bit miffed that I was calling her.

"She's dead, Mother, she's dead. I just found her in her bed. Sister Anna Maria confirmed it." As if that would settle any doubts on Mother's part.

And Mother immediately became motherly. "Calm down, Sister Mary Baruch. I will be right there. Try not to panic the other sisters." That was always an unwritten rule in the infirmary. But my excited voice reached the ears of every sister who had her hearing aid on or didn't need one. Everyone was heading for Sr. Boniface's door, except old Sr. Gertrude of the Sacred Heart, who didn't hear a thing and slept through the whole commotion.

Mother Agnes Mary arrived shortly afterwards and calmed everyone down, and led us all in prayer. I admired her for her soothing presence. It did calm us down, and we were able to pray. Only Sr. Benedict cried in front of us, and we let her, of course. She and Sr. Mary Boniface had become close in the last year. She knew a bit of German and would sit in Sister's room and read to her. Being librarian for so long, I noticed what books they were reading: *The Imitation of Christ*, by Thomas à Kempis, and the latest Agatha Christie murder mystery. (This was one of the more interesting changes that came in the spirit of Vatican II. We could actually read novels and biographies that were "clean." Murder mysteries were the most popular.)

So our little community of infirmary sisters prayed. We didn't sing the *Salve*, but recited it instead, to the chagrin of Sr. Lucy Marie, who had been chantress for years. The doctor and our chaplain came in with Sr. Paula, and Father said he would still anoint her, since she had just passed and we don't really know when the soul leaves the body. That was news to me! Looking at her body, I would have said that soul was long gone, but nobody asked me, thank goodness. Nobody asked if there was a sister present when she passed. And Dr. Campbell pronounced her dead. Mother bid me to get the other sisters back to their rooms while they took care of things. The old sisters liked me, I think, and would do anything I asked. So I coaxed them all into their rooms with the promise of a cup of tea and some cookies. I spent a little time with each one and asked for their prayers for my sister Ruthie, whose career they had followed over the years. I thought this would take their minds off Sister's dying so suddenly. I popped in to see Sr. Gertrude too and told her I'd be bringing tea around, and she was pleased. She probably thought it was four in the morning rather than four in the afternoon. She prayed for Ruthie all the time. Sr. Gertrude was our retired showgirl who tap-danced her way into our hearts into her late sixties.

That all being done, it was close to the time for Vespers, and another sister would take my place. I quietly went back to Sr. Mary Boniface's room. The body was still in the bed, not covered up, but like she was asleep, her hands folded with a rosary in them, waiting for the funeral director to arrive. I'm glad they didn't cover her face with the sheet. I peeked in the top drawer of her night table to see if there were any books I should take back to the library with me. There were none. The only thing were four paper-napkin-wrapped packages of saltines. So I kissed her forehead and smiled. *"Auf Wiedersehen, Schwester.* Rest in peace."

six

"Things happen in threes!" announced Sr. Gerard, whom I was pushing in a wheelchair the day after Sr. Mary Boniface's funeral. I was taking her to the library for a change of scenery and to give the other sisters in the infirmary a little peace and quiet. Apparently Sr. Gerard thought Sr. Mary Boniface's death and her finding a black spider were *not* a coincidence. "Mark my words, Sister, there will be another funeral within three weeks. Sister John Dominic, Sister Boniface, and who?"

I knew where this was going; the other sisters had filled me in more than once. Sr. Gerard was sure she was marked out to be behind door number three.

"Sister Boniface was from Germany, where Hitler was from, and what did the swastika look like? A black spider. So the German sister dies right when the swastika leaps out from the towel I was folding. Of all the towels and all the sisters, it was me who got the swastika."

I thought that, following her logic, I should be the swastika, being the only Jewess in the community, but I didn't mention it. Sr. Gerard had enough complications on her plate. But she was probably right about things happening in threes. That didn't always come true, but who was I to say?

I didn't want to think about it. It seemed like we had just finished our suffrages for Mother John Dominic and now we were beginning them for Sr. Mary Boniface. Sr. Mary Boniface of the Blessed Sacrament was her full name. She had entered many years ago as a lay sister. She was a hard worker, according to the other sisters who knew her when. She never complained about any of the menial jobs she had to do, and she did them all with great gusto.

She was from Upper Manhattan, in what we call Yorkville. I think she lived on 87th Street and Second Avenue. Her father was a cabinet maker and, as a result, she was handy with all kinds of tools herself. Her family immigrated when the Black Spider was spreading across Germany and Poland and Austria. They settled in the large German section in the Lower East Side—they used to call it "Little Germany"—but eventually moved uptown. My own great-uncle Sol, the Talmudic scholar among the Feinsteins of Austria, came to America by way of Germany, but that was twenty years before Hitler came to power. It must have been so devastating for them.

Sr. Mary Boniface became a choir nun after Vatican II and our new Constitutions eliminated the lay sisters. She was still a workhorse, however, and was the sister in charge of maintenance for many years, up until she got sick. Sisters would say she took care of the boilers and Sr. Hildegard with equal devotion. She was never infirmarian, but when Sr. Hildegard moved to the infirmary, Sr. Boniface visited her faithfully every morning, afternoon, and between supper and Compline. When Sr. Hildegard became more seriously ill,

Mother dispensed Sr. Boniface from common meals and recreation. She became Sister's unofficial full-time nurse, as it were. It was ideal, as they spoke German together, and Sr. Boniface had a knack for making Sr. Hildegard feel like she was in charge—that she still had a purpose—and that they should pray for the salvation of the world. With Mother's permission, Sr. Boniface moved a lovely statue of Our Lady of Fatima from the cloister into Sr. Hildegard's room. Many rosaries were prayed in German. And Sr. Boniface was there, holding Sister's hand when she passed.

Poor Sr. Boniface went through a terrible depression after that and lost interest in all the things that kept her going (including the boilers!). I wished now that I had waited to move Sr. Hildegard's bookbinding stuff out of the room. I also wished that I had run into her room when the call bell sounded so that I would have been there to hold her hand. But we can't go back and redo the past.

I don't know how much I like the middle ages of life. I guess there's a lot of letting go of things, and that's good, but a lot of the letting go includes loved ones dying. So I didn't want to hear any more about things happening in threes. I parked Sr. Gerard in the Mediatatio Room, put large earphones over her ears, which were already covered by the infirmary veil, handed her a stack of tapes from conferences given on various theological topics, and told her I needed to eliminate the ones nobody would like, to make room for those they do. This gave her an air of authority, that I trusted her judgment in these matters, which was partially true—in any case, it was good child psychology. This would be her project for weeks, and it sure beat folding towels. She would invariably fall asleep listening to the tapes, but that was okay.

Sr. Gerard was a convert from the Episcopal Church. She grew up in the Kips Bay section of Manhattan. I told her I thought that must have been exciting being so close to Midtown, and near the U.N. "Yeah," she said, "and I grew up in the shadow of Bellevue Hospital where all the crazies were." "Oh, that's right. I think my brother worked there for a while." It was hard keeping up with my brother, David, the doctor. "Being a psychiatrist, he probably did an internship or something there." I hoped I wasn't sounding too snobbish.

"What's his name?" Sr. Gerard suddenly became knowledgeable of New York psychiatrists.

"David Feinstein," I announced.

"Doctor Feinstein? Nope, I don't recall the name."

Of course, Sr. Gerard had been in the monastery for twenty-five years before David even began medical school, but I let her think she was impressing me. To my surprise, we had something in common: we both had brothers who were doctors, and hers was once a resident at Bellevue. "Doctor Rutherford, may he rest in peace." She blessed herself. "He loved helping the crazies. He thought I was crazy when I came here." And we both laughed.

"My brother did too—still does. He tells people he's got a sister who ran away to the nunnery."

Sr. Gerard kept laughing. "Oh, so you're Sister Ophelia!"

I picked up on the reference right away. "That's right, I'm one of the crazies." And I left her there laughing and ready to dig into her work, forgetting about the doom of death that she thought had settled over the monastery. *Please, Lord, don't let any spiders be nesting among the tapes! Amen.*

That night in choir, after Vespers, in the wonderful half hour we have for silent prayer before supper, I thought about how unique each of these sisters is, and that we don't really get to read the entire book, as it were. We only have snatches from chapters, but each would be a wonderful novel if it were ever told.

I usually felt guilty for wasting my meditation time, but that night I didn't. It wasn't often that I'd have a wave of gratitude sweep over me, and so I was going to ride this one. It was getting too depressing otherwise. Sometimes I felt that there was such a lack of joy in the community, that visitors were given such a wrong impression, thinking we were all so joyful. We had our moments, of course, but most of the time it was just life being lived day in and day out. There is a kind of hidden, spiritual joy. And that pervades things in the community, but it's not a giddy hee-haw-like joy.

I didn't quite know how to pray for this new venture of Gwendolyn's, so I just called it "Gwendolyn's thing." The Lord would know what I meant. I had to wait two months till I got more news, when Gwendolyn came by herself to visit.

Gwendolyn was close to sixty-four, but she looked in her early fifties. Not a gray hair to be found among the ash blond with platinum blond streaks. Usually pulled back in a French twist, today her hair was loose, almost shoulder-length and held back on the sides above each ear by a penguin barrette. Bobbing earrings dangled over an azure blue silk scarf loosely tied around her neck. She wore a blue-and-white blouse and navy blue slacks.

"We're all set to go!" were her first words as I was quietly closing the door on my side of the parlor. "Ruth says to tell you we need opening night prayers. She's directing the entire musical revue . . ."

"Slow down," I got in edgewise. "I haven't heard a word since you were debating about a loft in the Village."

"I bought it. You should see it, M.B. It's fabulous. There are two workable floors. The ground floor is huge—that will be the tea shop in three different rooms. The Abbey will have heavy wooden tables, and the waiters will dress in modified Franciscan robes, and we'll specialize in sandwiches and cheese trays. The Tower will be darker, with torches on the wall, the waiters all in a modified Beefeaters uniform. Soup and salads only, with a variety of breads, of course. And the Penguinham Palace is the main room, looking much like Tea on Thames but expanded. The waiters will be dressed like peasants, or perhaps palace waiters—we haven't made up our minds yet. There's a full-size kitchen, and I've hired a real British chef. Well, he's actually from Wales, but who would know? The upstairs is the theater, with small tables for two or four people, surrounding the stage on three sides. A high tea will be served an hour before the performance if one wants a package deal. Otherwise one can eat downstairs at the regular prices, which, my dear, will be a bit more dear than Tea on Thames. We're calling it a tea pub."

"A tea pub? I never heard of such a thing."

She laughed, her earrings clinking and bobbing in every which direction. "Nobody has—that's what's unique about the place. I thought of applying for a liquor license, but it was too expensive and had too much red tape attached, so I'm sticking with a British theme, but calling it a pub. Of course one can still get my penguin tea cakes and scones, the usual stuff. You would love the Tower and the Abbey— they're totally awesome."

"Awesome? Such a place should look awesome?" I was sounding more and more like my mother.

"Yes, it's cozy and intimate, and different from a dinner theater, and different from a cocktail lounge. It's a British tea shop with entertainment."

"And what's my Ruthie doing in this? You said a musical revue—is she singing and dancing? Oh my, I hope she's not doing any ballet." We both laughed.

"Of course not, she's too old for that. She's directing the revue, which will be made up of already-popular Broadway musical numbers. She's assembled a cast of eight: four blokes and four birds." And I laughed. She was putting on Ruthie's British accent for me, and knowing I would get it. *Blokes and birds. What a riot*, I thought.

"She introduces each act, and does a little stand-up routine herself. She's very funny, you know. . . . She ends with a little soft-shoe to 'Me and My Shadow.' The audience will go crazy."

My goodness, I was thinking, *Gwendolyn looks fifty and is talking like she's twenty-five!* But I was happy to see her so excited about it, and Ruthie being a part of it.

"Where *is* Ruthie? She didn't want to come with you?"

"Oh no, she couldn't possibly. She's rehearsing everybody to death, but it will pay off in the end. She knows a lot of talented but unemployed singers and dancers and actors. We could've had twice the people we hired, but we couldn't afford it."

"The blokes and birds," I said, causing the earrings to bob up and down. I loved watching her earrings and had a momentary fantasy of all of us wearing long bobbing earrings. I smiled back at her, grateful we still wore the guimpe that covered hair and ears!

"Is Ruthie doing okay?" I kind of slipped that in amidst the merriment. "You know, is she behaving herself." I didn't know how else to say it.

Gwen got serious for the moment. "Well, you know Ruthie. She's doing okay, I'd say . . ."

"But?"

"But, well, she's not going to her meetings. She says she doesn't have time, and that besides, she wasn't getting anything out of them. Too much Higher Power talk."

"Higher Power?" I asked. All these new words making their way through the ancient grille!

"It's what they say instead of 'God.' God is the Higher Power."

"Oh . . ." I thought about this for a moment. "I wonder why they just don't say 'God.' Maybe Ruthie just doesn't like the words. You know how she is about language."

"Yeah, maybe. But, well, between you and me, she's drinking again. Just a little wine, she says, the doctor says it's good for her heart and her nerves. I haven't seen that she's overdoing it, but then, I don't see her when she leaves for the night. She's kind of dating one of the blokes."

"Oh my, I hope that's okay. Poor Ruthie. Tell her I'm praying extra hard for her. The sisters are all praying for you too, you know. By the way, what's the name of the place? The sisters have been asking me for weeks, and I think Sister Gertrude is making a novena when she hears when opening night is."

Gwen's serious face took on a lighter air. "Well, we had a bunch of names at the beginning. Tea on Thames Downtown . . . but that wouldn't mean anything to everybody downtown. I wanted to include my penguins, of course."

"Of course."

"We went through Penguin Place, Penguin Palace, and plain old Penguins. Penguin Tower or Penguin Abbey didn't quite fit. So we—well, I—came up with Penguin Pub. And in smaller letters underneath: 'Teatime is Showtime.' Neat, huh?"

"Awesome!" I wouldn't let her out-jargon me.

"And guess what? You're gonna love this. Ruth invited your mother, and she's coming along with a handful of Hadassah ladies."

"Oy vey," I crooned in my best Yiddish. Gwendolyn's earrings went wild with that!

"Can you imagine? I just hope your mother isn't scandalized by Ruth's humor—she can get rather, how do you say . . . blue."

"Oh, I wouldn't worry about that, Mama and her generation grew up with Milton Berle and Lenny Bruce, of all people!"

I momentarily got lost in another flashback. Mama and Papa would go to Grossinger's at least once a year when we were old enough to be left alone. I could still hear the ad on the radio: "Hello, I'm Jennie Grossinger, and I have an invitation for you." Mama could imitate her to a tee. Grossinger's was famous as a Jewish resort for stand-up comics. "I'm sure Mama will love the show," I said.

"Oh, I wish you could be there, or at least come by and see the place. You'd love it. And you know what stands at the entrance."

"Ah, I know . . . Ruben the Penguin."

"That's right, he's my good luck piece. He's looking a little worn for wear now, but he still greets everyone coming in. He's inherited a little black bow tie and a tiny pair of rimless glasses."

"Oh, that's perfect. Papa would be so pleased. I wonder if Greta knows about your place? I haven't heard from her in ages. I hope she's okay."

"You don't know, do you?" Gwendolyn's words made my blood turn cold. Our happy, light, exciting chatter about Penguin Pub suddenly froze and I stared at her, unable to say anything, unable to even blink. "What? What don't I know?"

There was a long silence. Gwendolyn's earrings were as still as my heart. "Greta is dying from lymphatic cancer. They thought they had caught it when she was diagnosed with breast cancer and she had her mastectomy, but it has spread throughout the whole lymph system. I'm sorry, M.B, I thought you knew. She told me you were praying for her."

"I was, I was, but I didn't know how serious it was. Where is she? At home? In the hospital? Did you see her?" I couldn't believe my poor ears.

"She's in a lovely place called Saint Rose Home on the Lower East Side, I think on Water Street, just off the FDR Drive."

"I know the place. It's run by Dominican sisters, the Hawthorne Dominicans. We've had a couple sisters go there when we couldn't really take care of them. The Hawthorne sisters were so wonderful, and that's all they do—care for the dying—and it's totally free. Greta must be so happy to be there—well, not to be there, but you know what I mean."

"She's in a lovely corner room with a view of the East River. I was there just the other day, and she spoke of you like you knew all about this. That's why I didn't mention it right away. There's a bookcase with about three shelves, and she's got your picture there, a very nicely framed photo of you from your first profession. You still look the same, if I may say so!" I just smiled. "She's got a group photo of herself with other missionaries—one I presume was her husband."

"The Reverend."

"Yes, not in a minister's collar but a kind of African shirt. Very colorful. There was one young minister, or maybe a priest. He was the only one in a cassock and collar."

"They were missionaries in Mozambique." Of course, Gwendolyn knew all that, but she humored me.

"There was a picture of a young man too—do you know who that is?"

"I suspect it's her son. She has a son named Paul Martin, but I never met him, and Greta never spoke about him."

"Oh, and the weirdest thing—she has a photo of a rocking chair! Isn't that weird!"

I couldn't speak for a moment. "That was my rocking chair. I left it for her when I entered. It's the only piece of furniture I brought with me when I moved in with her. We named it Squeak, because it . . ." I couldn't get the rest of the sentence out. I felt so foolish, getting choked up over a rocking chair.

"It squeaked," said Gwendolyn. "Greta told me. It was sitting in the corner by the window, but she also had a photo of it. Weird."

She let a couple minutes go by while we sat in a kind of uncomfortable silence. She had to pass me a Kleenex from her side of the grille.

"She looked very good, considering. She's lost a lot of weight, and her hair . . . well, it's beginning to grow back. I always remember how beautiful her hair was."

"How beautiful she was. Ruthie thought she looked like Grace Kelly."

"That's true, Grace Kelly should have lived so long. And she was in pretty good spirits, I'd say. She said she didn't know how much longer she had, but she suspected it wasn't much, and she was ready to go. She said she was actually looking forward to it."

I smiled. "That's Greta for you. She always knew what was most important.

"One of the sisters came in while I was there and brought her fresh water and said she'd be back with tea and biscuits, and would I like to join her. I of course accepted and made a mental note to bring a boxful of raisin almond scones next time. Greta told me that only sisters take care of the women patients. They don't have any lay nurses. All the sisters are either nurses or nurses' aides. And really, you know, it didn't seem like a hospital—it sure didn't smell like one. And Greta's room had flower-print sheets, plants in the window, and a beautiful picture of Mary with child. She also had her own little telly, which was like being on an airplane. She told me she receives Communion every morning, and they pray the rosary and the *Angelus* over the PA so she can pray along. And on Sundays they take her to the chapel for Mass."

I was sad but at the same time content to hear this. Greta, of all people, deserved the best care. "I wonder if she can read."

"Oh yes, she had a few magazines and one or two books on the night table. She had her crazy looking specs hanging from a ribbon around her neck. I had a lovely cup of tea with her and what passed as a biscuit, and left her. I could see she was getting very tired. I told her I'd give you her regards, that I was coming down here on Thursday."

"Tell her I'm depending on her prayers."

"She never mentioned that you didn't know she was there. Maybe she thought she had, and doesn't remember."

"Maybe. Did you tell her about the new place and opening night?"

"Oh, of course. She was quite interested in it all, and regretted she couldn't be there and told me to tell Ruthie to break a leg."

Gwen and I ended our visit on an upbeat note, despite this sad news. I promised I would pray that opening night was a huge success. And that they ran out of tea.

Gwendolyn's earrings were back to bobbing as she gathered all her stuff. She left a box of goodies for me on the turn, put her finger through the grille so I could squeeze it, and she was off.

"Love to Ruthie!" I half-shouted as she fluttered through the door. "And tell Mama I love her . . ." But I don't think she heard me.

My meditation that night was full of memories of Greta, from when we first met in Fr. Meriwether's instruction class to my moving in with her during the week following my baptism. It was going to be only temporary till I found a job and a place. It went on for five years. And she was the one who found me a job, with her, at the public library. They were all good memories. I don't think we ever had cross words with each other, and looking back, I certainly gave her a lot of frustration.

We were being given permission to leave the enclosure for more things than ever before—in the spirit of Vatican II. So I decided I would ask Mother permission to visit Greta at St. Rose Home. After all, it was just across the river. I could almost walk there. Kinda. (*Catholic nun seen walking across Brooklyn Bridge.*)

Mother Agnes Mary was not like any of our four prioresses before her. She was proving to be more sympathetic and a really good listener, and I knew she liked me. You can tell those things. So I was pretty confident she'd let me go, although she didn't let me go to the hospital to see Mother John Dominic. The "rule" about visiting the sick seemed to apply to immediate families, but Greta was like a mother to me, or a lovely spiritual aunt. Maybe I should call her "Aunt Greta," but no, that would be lying. And I didn't want to confess to Fr. Wilcox that I had fibbed to Mother. I once confessed that I had fibbed to Mother, and he said, "You mean you lied to the superior?"

"Not really lied, it was just a little fib. Maybe you could say it was a white lie."

"What do you mean? Did you lie or not?"

He had never been so adamant about any of my sins before. Maybe he was having a boring day, or maybe lying struck a chord in him.

"I told Mother I liked her Chapter talk. But I really thought it was dull and redundant. She went on and on about silence in the cloister and . . ."

"I don't need to hear the sermon, Sister. Try not to lie anymore to Mother or to anyone."

I said, "Yes, Father," which was probably a white lie in itself. I knew I would fib about things—sometimes it's the charitable thing to do. But I didn't want to get into a theological discussion in the confessional. Anyway, Fr. Wilcox isn't a Dominican. Like diocesan priests don't know how to make distinctions. I knew that wasn't true, but I was spoiled, having had only Dominican priests for my teachers in the faith. And Ezra, of course. And Greta. I had come full circle in my meditation.

If I had learned anything in the last twenty-five years, it was not to presume permission for anything. So I just prayed that I would be able to go see Greta and that opening night for Ruthie was a smash. *Please, Higher Power. Amen.*

seven

Mother Agnes had a note on the prioress's bulletin board:

I am leaving for the prioresses' meeting tomorrow morning immediately following Holy Mass. I shall return on Sunday.

I knew she would be pressed for time, and I don't think she liked going to meetings. She once commented that they all leave the enclosure to go to a meeting to discuss enclosure. We all accepted it in the spirit of Vatican II. I think it was good for her to get away for a few days, and that they all talked about the life in their monasteries was good. But we kept our fingers crossed under our scapulars. We were still resistant to a lot of the changes other monasteries seemed to embrace very openly.

My dilemma, however, was whether I should wait till she came back to ask permission to visit Greta, or to ask the subprioress, Sr. Dominica, who wasn't keen on granting extraordinary permissions. I once asked her if I could go to the funeral of my great-uncle Sol. Of all my family, he used to write to me and enjoy talking to me about God. He was a great Talmudic scholar, according to Papa, Uncle Sol's favorite nephew—at least that's what Papa said.

I had been professed ten years in the monastery and hadn't really asked any special permissions for anything, except a few things for the library, which were more business than personal. Mother Mary of the Trinity said no. And that was that. "We may now go to funerals of immediate family, but great-uncle is over the limit."

I remember being disappointed more than hurt. It wasn't so much Uncle Sol as it was that I would have seen my family. I would have seen Mama, and Sally, and David. But I accepted her refusal. I had had fifteen years of practice.

That was all some ten years ago, but I still hesitated to go to her for permission. I could wait a few days for Mother Agnes Mary to return. *Maybe she'll be so happy to be home that she'll be effusive in giving permissions*, I thought. *Anyway, it's all out of my hands. The Lord knows what is best.*

In the meantime, I sorted out more of my shoeboxes of stuff. First I put my note from Greta into the Save pile. It was Greta who had first brought me here. I'll always remember our first weekend retreat here and how I was in awe of everything. I think I must have thought the nuns all walked two inches off the ground. They kind of glided along. I knew I could never be a nun because I just can't glide. I learned soon enough that the nuns have their feet on the ground. There are days when I've kind of glided, but they are few and far between.

It's an interior kind of thing. Maybe better than "gliding," one gets into the rhythm of the life. Maybe it's the chanting of the psalms like we do: the psalm tones and the chant itself, with its highs and lows and pauses and rests, and you let yourself glide along with the neumes.

Greta was always tuned into this interior gliding more than a lot of the exterior things which hold it up, especially when you're interiorly skidding to a halt. That's not an original thought. I remember Sr. Gertrude of the Sacred Heart used that analogy in a Chapter talk she gave when she was subprioress.

Sr. Gertrude was a born-and-bred New Yorker from the West Side of Manhattan, I think around 54th Street. She was baptized at St. Paul's. She also studied ballet and tap, and, like Ruthie, abandoned the ballet and concentrated on modern dance and tap. She was from a theatrical family. I think her parents may have even performed together in vaudeville.

She said she called herself the queen of auditions. "If you want to learn how to cope with rejection, envy, resentment, jealousy, and perseverance," she once told me, "audition for the chorus of a Broadway musical. I would get a couple callbacks, and that would soar my hopes to the rafters, and then I'd get rejected in the end. 'Too tall, too short, legs are too fat, legs aren't long enough, sloppy hand work, didn't smile enough, smiled too much.' Oh, I'd get a few parts, mostly in off-Broadway shows, which were terrific, but I never landed the big one on Broadway."

"What kept you going and kept you from throwing in the towel altogether?" I meant it sincerely, because I understood what she was saying, and I was thinking about Ruthie. This was ten or fifteen years ago.

Without a moment's hesitation she said, "My faith. You had your Saint Vincent's up there in the la-di-da East Side, I had my Saint Malachy's."

I laughed. "Oh, I knew Saint Malachy's. If my sister ever went into a Catholic church it would have been Saint Malachy's."

"The churches were all unlocked in those days, and it was nothing to go in for a visit, usually before an audition, but many times afterwards too. And you never knew whom you'd be kneeling next to or watch lighting a candle! I've seen Perry Como and Spencer Tracy praying in there."

I knew the theater world boasted of many Jewish actors, comedians, musicians, singers . . . but I learned mostly from Sr. Gertrude of a whole slew of Catholic actors and entertainers. They call St. Malachy's the Actors' Chapel. It's still going strong too. It's on West 49th Street between Broadway and Eighth Avenue. I remember it well. Ezra and I made a visit to the Blessed Sacrament there every time we were hanging out around the Theater District.

"I used to go to the eleven o'clock Mass on Saturday night," Sister kind of lisped out. I think she had left her bottom plate on the night table. "It spilled over past midnight, so it counted as your Sunday Mass. Pat O'Brien used to serve Mass sometimes."

"What's the other popular church in the Theater District?" I knew what it was, but I had Sr. Gertrude on a roll and let her run with it.

"Oh, that's Smoky Mary's." She saw me grinning, so she added, "Well, it's really Saint Mary the Virgin, you know. It's Episcopal," the *p*'s being prominently pronounced in her explanation. "It was high-church Episcopal, well, probably still is. They used so much incense at their . . . services . . . they called it Smoky Mary's. I peeked in once with a Protestant friend on our way to an audition, as I recall. We were blocks away from Saint Malachy's, and she said, 'Let's go light a candle in Smoky Mary's.' I think she thought it was a Catholic church. It looked it." And she was lost in a personal flashback. "A candle is just a candle, but I guess where you light it makes all the difference . . ."

I was lost in my own candle-lighting flashback. Some days I blamed the whole thing (my becoming Catholic and then becoming a nun) on that candle I lit for Gracie Price.

Sr. Gertrude came around. "Yes, my dear, a candle is just a candle, but the Real Presence is the Real Presence, and it wasn't at Smoky Mary's. I went to confession after lighting a candle in there. Years ago, you know, it was a sin to go into a Protestant church, or at least to attend a Protestant ceremony."

"I didn't know that. Amazing, everything you've got to learn when you become a Catholic."

"Yes, but the choreography's great!" Sr. Gertrude loved that analogy and used it more than once. "I may have learned that line from the Actors' Chapel. They had great priests come and preach on a regular basis. And Bishop Sheen used to preach there. He was a great draw, you know, and a television star himself."

"*Life Is Worth Living,*" I said.

"It certainly is . . ."

"No, that was the name of his show: *Life Is Worth Living.*"

"You're right, I forgot that." Sr. Gertrude giggled. "He was on at the same time as the *Milton Berle Show*. Uncle Milty and Uncle Fulty." She laughed at her own joke. "I think it was Bishop Sheen who planted in my head the idea that Jesus wanted to dance with me, that I was His own special ballroom girl." And she actually blushed an eighty-three-year-old blush. Even her voice got a little softer and little-girlish. "I wanted Him as number one on my dance card . . . so I came here."

"Well, we're certainly glad you did, Sister. And you know, the dance ain't over yet."

She smiled a big little-girl grown-up smile. "I know, darlin', and the music keeps getting sweeter and keeps going on . . . till we waltz into Heaven." There was that quiet, serious silence that falls upon our conversations every once in a while. Both of us were lost for a second in our thoughts.

Sr. Gertrude laughed, "Speaking of Smoky Mary's," as if we hadn't said anything in between, "you know there's a Tallulah story about her and Smoky Mary's—have you heard it?" I had, but I didn't want to deprive Sr. Gertrude of the joy of telling it, so I said, "No, I don't think so." There I was again, Sr. Mary Fibber.

"Well, Tallulah Bankhead was noted for her vulgarity, especially if she'd had a few too many. So early one Sunday morning on her way home she goes into Saint Mary the Virgin and falls asleep, like passes out, in a rear pew. Hours later she comes to as the grand procession is coming up the aisle, and the deacon is swinging the thurible with billows of smoke coming out. And Tallulah shouts at him, 'I love your drag, dahling, but your purse is on fire!'"

We both burst out laughing so hard, Sr. Gertrude got a fit of coughing and turned red in the face. I ran to get her some water, and we were still giggling our heads off when I brought it back.

There were one or two other would-be actors among us in the monastery, but Sr. Gertrude was my favorite. She redirected the passion for the theater into a passion for the religious life, and she knew the choreography well because she loved the choreographer. She was one of the most prayerful nuns I've ever met. She could spend hours in the chapel mumbling over her rosary. And when she'd chat with you, like at recreation, she'd talk to you like you were the most important person in the room, or like you had been her best friend forever.

She came to the parlor several times to visit briefly with Ruthie. I really wanted Ruthie to meet her. When she did, she was duly impressed, which caused the monastic life to shoot up on her scale of "happy things to be." She told Sr. Gertrude about our Comedy-Tragedy masks we had in our room growing up, and that she still had them in her bedroom. And she actually asked her, "Would you like to have them for your cell? I'd be very happy to give them to you. We both would, wouldn't we, Beck—Sister Baruch?" I was surprised and delighted at Ruthie's generosity and detachment. She loved those masks.

"Oh no, thank you, dear, that's very kind of you and Sister to offer them to me. But I have my own Comedy-Tragedy mask already in our cell."

I think Ruthie and I both said at the same time: "You do?" That was certainly news to me, and apparently quite delightful to Ruthie.

"Yes, it's a lovely picture of the Sacred Heart of Jesus. It contains all the happiness and all the sorrow in the world in that divine heart surrounded with thorns and on fire with love."

Ruthie sat speechless, her mouth a little open in that unladylike facial expression. I knew that meant she was "processing it all," as they say today. I was moved as well. I had never heard Sr. Gertrude say that before, and it gave me a whole new meditation on the Sacred Heart, which was my most interior devotion too.

Ruthie was very kind to her every time they met and always asked her to pray for her, I think, more than she ever asked me. I think she knew somehow that Sr. Gertrude's prayers were more powerful than mine; after all, she gave up the lights of Broadway for this.

Now Sr. Gertrude was settled in the infirmary, and she still had her Comedy-Tragedy masks in her new cell there. She was still able to go to the chapel with a walker, or better, a wheelchair. And she was also content to sit in the infirmary by the large picture window looking out on the back property with its rose bushes and hydrangeas. Off to the right you could see the monastic cemetery with our stone crosses at the head of each grave. I don't think it was planned that way, but the view gave the sisters in the infirmary something to meditate on.

Visitors (other sisters, that is) could sit with a sister looking out on the lawn. I was sitting there with Sr. Gertrude the afternoon after Gwendolyn's visit and news about Greta. We were talking about various things. And I mentioned that I thought she had been a wonderful subprioress and hoped that she would have been elected prioress.

"Oh, my dear, no. That was not for me. I was content to be the understudy, but I didn't want the lead role. Not today, my dear. Now, you, Sister Mary Baruch, you should move from librarian to novice mistress. You'd be wonderful with the young women." She paused and caught my expression. "Auditioning today."

"Well, I certainly wouldn't kick them out of the chorus line if they didn't know their steps." We had recently received the album, *A Chorus Line,* which was a Broadway musical playing at the Shubert. We would never listen to such things at recreation or when we'd on occasion play music in the refectory; it was always sacred music or classical music. But in the infirmary there was a small audio room with great new stereo speakers, a record player, a tape player, and a few earphone sets, like in the Mediatatio Room. Sr. Gertrude and I listened to *A Chorus Line* at least a dozen times. We loved the music by Marvin Hamlisch, and the tap numbers were better than a blood transfusion for Sr. Gertrude. It had made its Broadway debut in 1975 and was so far the longest running musical on Broadway. In its first year it received twelve Tony Award nominations and won nine.

"Being the understudy can be very demanding too." I was trying to distract her from thinking of me as novice mistress.

"Yes, but as an understudy you deal with all the grown-ups, whereas as the novice mistress you're forming the newcomers, just teaching them the steps. You didn't have an easy novitiate, as I recall, and so that would make you even more qualified. Mercy doesn't come to us from reading about it in books."

"Yes," I sputtered. "But I'm still battling my own self-willfulness."

"And the young girls in the novitiate are not? 'Mercy I seek, not sacrifice.'" We both stared out at the stone crosses. "Now, tell me more about Ruthie's theater and all about this Penguin Pub thing."

So I filled her in on all the details as Gwendolyn had told them to me. Sr. Gertrude was skeptical about the Tower and the Abbey rooms; she thought it was overkill and would work better as just a British tea shop. But she loved the theater part and that the stage was three-fourths surrounded by tables. She also loved the idea of a revue of old Broadway show tunes and hoped we'd get a program or playbill or something listing all the numbers.

"Tell Gwendolyn and Ruthie that I'm beginning a novena to Saint Genesius and the Sacred Heart, in that order."

"Saint Genesius is the patron saint of actors, right?" (See, I was still learning!)

"Oh, yes, but more than just actors. He's the patron saint of dancers, musicians, clowns, comedians, converts, printers, and lawyers."

"Whoa, I had no idea. I had never even heard of him till I came here."

"Yes, we had a Sister Genesius once, but she didn't persevere." Sister paused for a minute, remembering, and then said, "She got through the audition alright, but fell apart in the first act. Poor thing." We both kind of giggled. I knew what she meant. She got through the novitiate and took vows, but left before solemn vows.

Sister looked at me, and in the quietest of voices, but with perfect pitch, sang, "Kiss today good-bye and point me toward tomorrow. We did what we had to do. Won't forget, can't regret what I did for love, what I did for love." A *Chorus Line* show-stopper.

I love the older sisters, both inside and outside the infirmary. They take the life all in stride and don't get upset over too many things. They love to share stories about the past without regret—all that they did for love, and still do. They're wonderful, because they don't have ambition driving them anymore.

So I confided my sadness over my friend Greta to Sr. Gertrude and knew she would put her in the Sacred Heart of Jesus along with all the other "prayers, works, joys, and sufferings of each day."

I left her in her infirmary easy chair watching the sun go down. I hurried off to the chapel for my hour of guard before the Blessed Sacrament, knowing this was not an actors' chapel but that we were for real. Oh, we may seem in some people's minds to be playing a role, that it's all somehow phony—but we're for real. We may wear lovely thirteenth-century costumes, but we carry the hopes and dreams, fears and wonderment, sorrows and joys of all human beings in our hearts, under our scapulars and veils that in many ways hide our womanhood and allow us to belong to Him alone, together. We may know the "choreography" of liturgical prayer and common living, but we know with whom and for whom we dance.

We may retire to our cells at night, where the comedy and tragedy of life confront us in silence and solitude, in the desert of the human heart, and we may live behind bars called an enclosure, until death, but we are the most free women in all the world. "Like burning incense, Lord, rising up to You as an evening sacrifice." That's what we do for love.

Maybe, like Shakespeare says, we are just poor players who strut and fret our hour upon the stage of life, and so it is. And on our best days, perhaps, and our not so best, we know it's all been just the overture. The house lights go down gradually, dimly, and the curtain rises on the third day. . . . *Alleluia.*

eight

Mother Agnes Mary returned on Sunday in midafternoon. She put up a note that she would talk with all of us at recreation and perhaps more formally at the month's Chapter. She assured us that there was nothing urgent or pressing.

Vespers began in its usual way, with Mother reciting the O Sacred Banquet and the hebdom intoning the introductory verse. Sr. Anna Maria had begun her week as heb last evening. The choir assignments—hebdom, chantresses, reader—all change at First Vespers of the Sunday, on Saturday evening.

Sr. Anna Maria has a pleasant voice, which can be at times just slightly off-key, and sometimes Sr. Henry's organ playing is a little off . . . but it carries us through very nicely. I like being chantress when my turn comes, but I still get nervous right before my antiphon is to be sung. I can make myself laugh—not out loud—when I think, *Baruch, you are not the cantor at Temple Emanu-El on Yom Kippur*. But I love singing to the Lord and Our Blessed Mother. I've grown to love

Vespers as one of my favorite hours of the Office. It really ushers us into the evening time, which is slower and quieter than the rest of the day. I love it especially in winter, when it is already dark when Vespers begins.

Someday, as I've told myself a dozen times, I will research how our Divine Office is derived from the Temple prayers of the Jews at the time of Jesus. I wish I had paid more attention to the psalms and chants we sang on Friday evenings at synagogue, but we didn't go that often really. Ezra used to talk about it, and I usually pretended I understood what he was saying, but I didn't.

We were encouraged to add our own petitions at Vespers after the formal ones in the breviary. This was one of the changes Sr. Boniface liked. She always had some newsworthy cause to pray for. I thought I should pray out loud a few times "for my friend, Greta, who is dying of cancer." But I had never prayed out loud for anything or anyone yet, and I didn't want to use it as a way to finagle Mother's permission for me to go visit her. No, I would simply go see Mother tomorrow morning. Of course, I rehearsed it all during Vespers, and I almost let it slip out at the petitions. Sr. Gerard used to pray for the conversion of Russia, Sr. Beatrice for "a special intention," which used to get on everyone's nerves, I'm sure . . . we all had special intentions. Old Sr. Mary Raymond would pray "that the Dodgers win the pennant." That used to get a smile from half the community, and frowns from others who were praying for the Yankees. I don't think retreatants or visitors who had come to Vespers could hear our freelance petitions (this was probably good).

Anyway, I silently made my "special intention" and hoped for the best.

98

We had chocolate chip pancakes for supper, which were one of Mother Agnes Mary's favorites. It was our way of saying "welcome home." She seemed very happy to be home.

After dishes we had a good half hour before recreation, so I headed for the library. I thought I should take a picture book of some sort with me to show Greta. We had received a beautiful coffee-table book on scenes from Africa. She would like that. I passed Mother's office on the way, and her light was on. She was in her office, probably checking her mail or reviewing her notes for whatever she was going to share from her meeting.

I stopped, started to walk again, stopped, walked back three steps, and knocked lightly on her door.

"Enter."

I opened the door with my best smile. "*Laudetur Jesus Christus*," I said as I stepped inside.

"*In aeternum*. Good evening, Sister Baruch. You're looking like the cat that ate the canary."

"Good evening, Mother, and welcome home. We missed you."

"What may I do for you? Is everything alright?"

"Oh yes, Mother, everything's fine. I had a visit last week from my friend Gwendolyn—you know, my godmother Gwendolyn." Mother smiled. Everyone knew Gwendolyn—the English lady who's a pastry chef!

"She had very sad news. Our dear friend, Greta, with whom I lived before entering here—it was Greta who brought me here for the first time. Well, she's dying of cancer. I knew she was sick, but I didn't know how serious it was. Greta is very private." Mother sat without saying a word, listening.

"She's now at Saint Rose Home, run by the Dominican Sisters of Hawthorne. You know them—I believe Sister Valerian died there." Mother nodded.

"Would it be possible for me to go and see her? I know it would mean the world to her." That was it. I didn't say any more. I sat there across from Mother with my head down.

"Sister Mary Baruch, of course you may go."

I could feel the tears starting to flow. I wasn't counting on that. Why was I crying? Mother went on, "I never met Greta, but I remember seeing her when she was here. She was . . . what? Distinguished-looking, elegant in a virtuous kind of way."

I didn't care that Mother could see the tears running down my cheeks. I looked at her with such gratitude for her kindness.

"Sister John Dominic would speak of her, I remember. She was a generous benefactor to our poor library. But more than all that, she was like family to you. Indeed, you should go, you must go."

We both sat in utter silence for a minute. I think I muttered a "thank you, Mother." I don't remember, I was still stunned by it all. After another minute, Mother broke the silence.

"I think tomorrow afternoon would be best. You may be excused from dishes. Stop by here tomorrow morning and I will give you money for a cab. I don't want you walking or taking the subway. And what could we send with you?" She paused again. "We can arrange a bouquet of flowers from our garden, and this lovely, small icon of Our Lady." She opened her desk drawer and pulled out a five-by-seven print of Vladimir's *Virgin of Tenderness* mounted on wood.

"That's perfect, Mother, Greta will love it. I can't thank you enough." And I broke down right there in front of her. That had never happened before, even in front of Mother John Dominic. Mother came around from her desk and put her arm around me.

"That's alright, Sister. You just cry as much as you want. Remember, our dear Lord wept too at the death of His friend. Now, listen, you are excused from recreation tonight as well. Go to the chapel or go tuck in the old sisters in the infirmary. They love you, you know."

No one had ever said that to me here. I could feel my shoulders shaking, and I sobbed one big sob and then stopped. I stood up and hugged Mother and thanked her. I was fidgeting all over the place in my tunic pockets for a handkerchief. Mother handed me hers and whispered, "Keep it, it's from the common pile." I presumed she meant the community pile.

I hurried off to my cell to splash cold water on my face; I must have looked like a wreck. *I'll do both*, I thought. *I'll go to the chapel first and thank the Lord for the tenderness of Mother Agnes Mary. Then I'll go tuck in the old sisters in the infirmary— except for Sr. Gertrude, I'll wheel her into the kitchenette and fix us each a cup of chamomile tea, and we'll listen and pray Compline together over the PA. She'll love that, and I can share with her my upcoming visit tomorrow to St. Rose Home.*

"Such a blessing"—Sr. Gertrude was imitating me. She was delighted for me: even though it was a sad business I'd be on, it would be a blessing for both of us. I thought I could also call Gwen tomorrow morning. It would be wonderful if she could meet me there. I would call St. Rose Home after Mass and get the exact address to tell the cabbie. Others had mentioned to me that New York had a whole new genre of cab drivers.

Needless to say, I didn't sleep well. I usually could go immediately back to sleep after the Midnight Office, but I was restless all morning thinking about Greta and preparing myself not to be shocked at her appearance. *I'll be fine*, I told myself, *after all, I'm the big sister of Ruth Steinway.*

I would use the time for praying rather than for fretting. An early morning shower would be delightful too. I was looking at my hair after my shower, surprised at how much grayer it had become. Hair: in the world it's a million-dollar business and the concern of every young girl and woman. Mama loved to get her hair done. She had tried those Toni Home Permanents maybe twice, but it wasn't the same. And it stunk up the whole apartment. I think the fact that Papa complained more about the smell when he got home than the result on Mama's head was the reason she gave it up. Anyway, it was a whole ritual going to the hairdresser.

I never had a perm. My hair was still thick, although it was shorter than a boy's haircut—like a crew cut. I thought once that in my position as community librarian I got to see what every sister was reading, but Sr. Barbara got to see everyone's hair. Sr. Barbara was our barber—Sr. Barbara the Barber. And we have a kind of barbershop: there's a swivel chair with arms for the "client" and a counter with combs, scissors, and the electric clipper with attachments of various sizes. You can always do your own head if you prefer; there is a large mirror behind the counter. I have done that several times, but there's something relaxing or soothing about getting your hair cut.

Some sisters keep their hair a few inches long. I did that for nearly a year after receiving the habit, but when summer came, I told Sr. Mary St. John (she was the barber then) to "take it all off." I was shocked when I finally opened my eyes and dared to look in the mirror. I immediately thought of Edith Stein, and offered it up for the poor souls in Purgatory.

I didn't need to have my hair done before going to see Greta, but I did have a freshly washed and ironed habit and veil. I broke the morning silence talking to Sr. Anna Maria in the laundry room, telling her about my meeting with Mother and how kind she was, and that I was taking a cab into Manhattan that morning to go to St. Rose Home.

"Maybe you can get some pretzels when you're there," she said. This was her most profound response, but I knew she was being funny. She knew my penchant for New York soft pretzels.

It hadn't crossed my mind at all till then that I would actually be in Manhattan. I was just another cab ride away from Tea on Thames, or West 79th Street . . . wouldn't that be a shock to Mama and a surprise to Gwendolyn! I shook my head, knowing it was indeed a temptation. But I would never do that. I was grateful enough just to be going to see Greta; that's all that mattered.

"Earth to Baruch . . . earth to Baruch." Sr. Anna Maria brought me back from my fantasy. "Where were you?" she inquired while throwing a load of linen napkins into a small washer.

"I was . . . on the corner near Saint Rose's looking for a pretzel vendor. Thanks for the temptation!"

"Oh Seesta, take-a two pretzels, there be no-a charge for you." I guess Anna Maria thought all pretzel vendors were Italian. But she made me laugh.

"Thanks, Luigi, I'll take one home for our laundry maid."

And I was off. Mass was in a half hour and I wanted to pray a rosary before. There was a note at my place in choir, which was very unusual. We always put notes in a sister's mailbox.

Sr. M. Baruch,

Please come to my office following Holy Mass before going to breakfast.

Mother

That was kind of Mother. She probably wanted to give me the money for the cab or to pick out some flowers for the bouquet.

Mother always stayed in chapel at least five minutes after Mass, so I didn't rush out. I waited for her to leave, and two minutes later I was knocking on the door.

She opened the door.

"*Laudetur Jesus Christus,*" I said.

"*In aeternum.* Come in, Sister, and have a seat. I wanted to wait till we had been to Mass before seeing you. I usually check the answering machine for any messages overnight, and there was one from a Sister Bernadine from Saint Rose Home, asking me to call her when I received this message, and she gave me the number. I called her right away. This was around five thirty this morning."

I think I had entered into a state of suspended animation. "Yes, Mother, and what?"

"Sister Bernadine was very kind. She told me that Greta Phillips passed away early this morning around two thirty. It was very peaceful, and there was a sister by her side praying the rosary when Our Lady came to take her to eternal life."

"She passed away . . ." I somehow muttered.

"Yes, my dear. I'm so sorry for you to have missed seeing her. Sister Bernadine said that Greta had left our number with the chart papers to be called when she passed, and for you to call Sister Rita Mary, the administrator, when you were able. She also said that the funeral arrangements were made in advance and that her body will be going to New Jersey, there will be no wake, and she will be cremated and laid to rest with her husband's cremains."

"No Mass . . ." I said. *Poor Greta, no Mass.* I sat there, lost in that thought. I didn't cry, and I wasn't overcome with grief or disappointment. It wasn't meant to be for me to be there, that's all.

"Now, here's the number for Sister Rita Mary. Give her a call after breakfast. And we will have Mass said here for the repose of Greta's soul. Shall we say a few prayers for her right now?"

I nodded. Mother pulled a chair over next to me and took her side rosary in her left hand, and we prayed a decade of the rosary quietly together.

I wandered around in a daze for about an hour. Eventually I just sat in the chapel before the Lord, enthroned in our beautiful weekday monstrance. I was terribly disappointed—not because I wouldn't be setting foot in Manhattan, but because I didn't get to say good-bye to Greta face to face. That lovely Grace Kelly face. I tried thinking about Greta meeting the Lord face to face, whom she loved so much, and that made me smile. *She knows and sees it all now. Dear Greta.*

I went and had coffee and a big slice of Sr. Simon's homemade bread, smeared with peanut butter and drizzled with honey. It's high on my list of remedies for sadness. Then I went to our little private phone room and settled in the chair next to the table with the phone on it. The room had acoustic tiles on three of the four walls. The plain wall had an old-fashioned and faded wallpaper design of roses in variously shaped vases.

I called the number Mother gave me, and a lovely voice answered, "Saint Rose Home." I asked for Sr. Rita Mary. Three seconds later, a voice came on the line: "Sister Rita Mary."

"Good morning, Sister, my name is Sister Mary Baruch. I'm from the monastery of Mary, Queen of Hope in Brooklyn, and a friend of Greta Phillips."

"Oh, Sister, I am so happy to finally talk to you. Greta spoke of you all the time. I am so sorry for your loss."

"Thank you, Sister."

"Greta was a dear heart, as you well know, I'm sure. We will miss her very much. She added a certain—what shall I call it—unobtrusive intelligence to the floor. I think she had read more spiritual books than I have in my forty years in the convent." She gave a slight guttural giggle while listening for my reaction. So I giggled back, "I know what you mean."

"Now, Sister, you know how organized Greta was. She had everything taken care of before she got to when she couldn't. And she almost had that timed to a tee. She only really took a turn for the worse last week. She spoke of you often to me. I tried to get in to visit her every day and was able to feed her supper the last two weeks. Well, she had five things set aside for you, literally with your name on them. I think she was hoping her son, Paul, would deliver them to you, and he said he would if and when he got around to it. Fortunately, I was in the room when he said it, and I told him not to worry about that, I would be happy to take them to Brooklyn Heights for his mother, since I often went there.

That was a bit of a fib, but I didn't want him to change my mind."

Another fibber in the convent; I liked her instantly. "That was very kind of you, Sister. I've never ever met her son. She rarely spoke of him when we were roommates. I only knew he was born and grew up in Africa. I would be curious but very uncomfortable meeting him, I think."

"Yes, and 'if and when' is not very reassuring. Well, it just happens that my day off is this Wednesday, the day after tomorrow, and another sister and I were planning to visit the Maronite cathedral there in Brooklyn Heights, and we would be happy to drop off her things for you. Maybe we could visit with you for a few minutes in the parlor?"

"Oh, Sister, that would be so wonderful. I'm so happy I called. You've pulled me out of the doldrums. I will tell Sister Paula, our extern, to keep an eye out for you. You'd be most welcome to have some lunch as well."

"Oh, that won't be necessary—part of our day-off treat is eating out! We will be there by midmorning on Wednesday then. Greta loved you very much, you know."

"I know, Sister, I know." I was surprised I could get it out. We ended our call, and I went back for another slice of bread with peanut butter and honey.

nine

Since I wasn't going into the city after all, I had the afternoon free. Sr. Anna Maria was not free, however, as it was "sheets day," and that took the entire afternoon, right up till Vespers. She invited me to come fold the sheets with her, but I really wasn't in the mood. It was too distracting with the dryers going full speed, and, honestly, it was too hot in that room.

So I decided to go to the infirmary and try to organize a card game. I should have known that two thirty in the afternoon is not a good time for alertness among the infirm! A jigsaw puzzle was a better choice, and there were presently two going, on separate card tables. Sr. Amata was leaning over the latest one, a thousand pieces of ten kittens, all different colors, playing with balls of yarn, all different colors, while the white-haired knitter lady was dozing in her chair. I wondered what this poor woman was doing with ten kittens, for Heaven's sake! But the puzzles aren't not meant to raise such questions; the challenge is getting the pieces to fit.

Sr. Amata was good at it. Sr. Anna Maria and I used to say her glasses looked like the bottom of Coke bottles, but for all that, she had good jigsaw eyes if she didn't doze off herself, which is what happened. She was leaning on her elbow, she fell asleep, the elbow gave way, and she nearly went *splat* on the table, coke-bottle glasses and all, but she jerked awake and banged the table with her other arm, sending half of the thousand pieces flying. That sent Sr. Benedict, who was doing the other jigsaw, into a fit of laughter, which can be contagious among the infirm. The elderly sisters were easily entertained by the smallest things.

Picking up the pieces became a project for Sr. Gerard and Sr. Benedict. Neither could lean over far enough to pick them up by hand. Sr. Gerard, sitting in her chair with roller wheels, tried leaning down, but the chair rolled backward and she landed—*bang!*—on the floor, scattering the jigsaw pieces in all directions. By this time, Sr. Amata, who was the cause of all this, got caught up in the humor of it all.

I didn't know what to do. I certainly couldn't lift up Sr. Gerard, even with the help of the other sisters. Sr. Bernadette, the infirmarian, was not there, so I went to the intercom phone and phoned the subprioress, who was there. She told me Greg and Paul, our two maintenance men, were just in the next corridor replastering part of the cloister. She would page them and send them immediately to the infirmary; in the meantime, I should keep the sisters calm.

When I returned, they were throwing pieces of the puzzle up in the air. Sr. Benedict was saying, "Here, kitty, kitty," which they all thought was hysterical. Soon the audio room door swung open to the booming recording, "There's No Business Like Show Business," and out came eighty-three-year-old Sr. Gertrude with a top hat on over her veil and a white-tipped cane, doing a soft-shoe across the infirmary floor. She literally stopped the show, and we all applauded her as she came to a crescendo ending. I was laughing and crying at the same time. It was the strangest thing! Greg and Paul arrived as Sr. Gertrude retreated into her "dressing room." They got on either side of Sr. Gerard, and with a heave-ho she was on her feet, very grateful indeed for their assistance. She then politely asked if, while they were here, would they pick up the puzzle pieces and put them on the card table.

I got them settled down at their respective tables and promised them lemonade with shortbread cookies, at which point Sr. Benedict checked her blood sugar for the okay signal. They were something else.

In all the excitement (or entertainment) I forgot my grief and thanked the Lord for this interlude of comedy and tragedy, like those masks Ruthie and I had, or like Sr. Gertrude's picture of the Sacred Heart.

Sr. Gertrude! I quickly prepared another lemonade, a tall one, with a piece of lime, and went into the audio room, praying I would find her there sitting up and enjoying a record and not sprawled out on the floor. She did her little soft-shoe without a walker or a cane, except for the white-tipped one.

There she was, sitting up with the earphones on, her top hat back on the shelf, enjoying a record. She waved at me. "Ethel Merman's greatest hits." She was ever so grateful for the lemonade. "That Ethel has some voice—never took a voice lesson in her life, you know." I knew. She was one of Mama's favorites too. I did share with Sr. Gertrude my news about Greta. I guess she had forgotten I was supposed to be at St. Rose's that same afternoon. But she was most sympathetic.

"Dear Sister Baruch, it's a sign of getting old when you begin to lose your best friends. In a way, I can't wait to go to Heaven. I have more friends there now than here."

We toasted to Greta Phillips and clinked our glasses. It was like an old ritual between friends. "She's my number three," I said.

"Number three?"

"Yes, Sister Gerard kept saying deaths come in threes. We had Mother John Dominic and then Sister Boniface. So Greta is my number three."

"Well, that's for you—but she's not my number three. Maybe I'm number three."

"Don't speak like that!" Then, in my best Tallulah Bankhead, I said, "Drink your cocktail, dahling, it doesn't get any better than this."

That evening at recreation Mother Agnes Mary very kindly shared with the community Greta's passing. Most knew of her from my talking about her. One of the good changes that came with Vatican II was that we shared more about our families and friends.

Many sisters came over to me afterwards and expressed their sympathy. I was deeply moved by it all. Sometimes we take each other for granted, but that night I knew these women, these sisters, were my family. *Maybe*, I thought, *this is a grace sent my way from Greta.* She knew there were times that I felt alienated from the community, that maybe I didn't belong, that nobody cared. But tonight I knew they did. I was especially moved by Sr. Catherine Agnes. She waited till the sisters had filed out of the community room on their way to Compline, and then came over and hugged me without saying a word. I don't think ol' Scar ever hugged anyone, let alone me.

She held on to my arm. "Help an old nun into Compline, will you dear?" Sr. Catherine Agnes was close to seventy-eight now, and still as faithful as ever, but she didn't terrorize the novices anymore. She was very prayerful and would spend hours in front of the Blessed Sacrament, her hands hidden beneath her scapular, holding onto a pocket rosary and making the rounds of the mysteries.

"We shall keep Greta in prayer with our dear Mother John Dominic." That's all she needed to say, and I knew she would. And we went into chapel together, arm in arm.

The next day, a few more notes and verbal condolences came my way. I was able to call Gwendolyn on the phone. She was very saddened by the news, but not really surprised. She was also happy with my getting permission to visit her, even though it never happened.

"I don't suppose, in the spirit of Vatican II, they'll let you come to opening night at Penguin Pub?"

I laughed. "No, that will only happen after Vatican III. How's it going? Please give Ruthie my love and tell her about Greta. I don't suppose she's there right now?"

"Ruthie? Oh no, I don't think she's even up yet. She'll roll in around four in the afternoon, an hour before rehearsals. They're sounding very good though. The opening number is 'Try to Remember,' from *The Fantasticks*."

"*The Fantasticks*! I think that was the last show Ruthie and I saw together."

"It was. She's told me, more than once."

"Well, tell her Sister Gertrude is making a novena to Saint Genesius, the patron saint of actors and comedians."

"I will, if I remember how to pronounce that. It sounds like a sneeze. Oh, my only other news is that I think my sister Jacquelyn is coming over for the opening. She'll be surprised to see the place, I'm sure. If she doesn't behave, I'll lock her up in the Tower." I thought I could hear Gwen's earrings jingling when she laughed.

Late in the afternoon, I checked my mail cubby hole and there was a card. It wasn't handmade but store-bought. It was a beautiful sympathy card: *At the Loss of Your Friend*. It was from Sr. Jane Mary. I had noticed at the end of the previous evening's recreation that she did not come over to express her condolences. I wasn't expecting her to, really. We had not always sailed on smooth waters, shall we say. Like Sr. Catherine Agnes, she was in her mid-seventies, maybe even eighty. She served two terms as Mother and, to her credit, held things together after the initial blast of changes came from Vatican II.

Unlike Sr. Catherine Agnes, she didn't seem to have many friends in the community. She was always faithful, as all our elder sisters are, but also seemed to lack a certain joy that the others seem to acquire. Sr. Mary of the Trinity once told me that Sister had a difficult time expressing emotion. "She was an excellent administrator, you know. And she was very intelligent—well, you know that from her marvelous Chapter talks—but she had a difficult time bringing all the head stuff down and out through her heart, if you know what I mean."

So I was rather moved that she took the time and care to send her very best. It was a Hallmark card. Inside she had only written:

My prayers for your dear friend, Greta, may she rest in peace.

I left a little thank-you note in her cubby hole too. I guess sometimes that's how we best express ourselves. I remembered Greta's words to me so many years ago: "Expect nothing, and be grateful for everything." I was grateful.

Nonetheless, when Friday came I was anxious to meet Sr. Rita Mary and wondered what Greta could possibly have left for me. I knew it wasn't any of her jewelry—at least I hoped it wasn't! Maybe it would be that beautiful mother-of-pearl rosary she had.

I put on my newly pressed coif and veil for our visit, the one I had been planning on wearing to St. Rose's. We were coming out from Terce when Sr. Paula signaled to me that there were visitors in the parlor.

I quietly slipped into the parlor, where two Dominican sisters were standing together by the grille.

"Sister Mary Baruch, I'm Sister Rita Mary, and this is Sister Rafka. I'm so happy to meet you. Terce was so beautiful. We got in right as it was beginning."

"Please, sit down. I'm so grateful you've come. Your congregation is such a blessing for the Church. Mother was telling me about how good you were to our sisters who died there, and to Greta . . ." It got caught momentarily in my throat. *Get a hold of yourself, Baruch, you're not going to cry!*

Sr. Rita Mary didn't miss a beat. "It is a blessing, indeed. We are still living out the charism given to Rose Hawthorne, our Mother Mary Alphonsa. It is such a blessing to be with people at the most important and most precious moment in their life."

She said it without being sentimental or sounding rehearsed. I could see she meant every word of it.

"Sister Rafka is Maronite, and she's been promising for years to show me the Maronite cathedral here and the shrine to Saint Sharbel."

Sr. Rafka just sat, very quiet and attentive. She had a beautiful complexion, and without a dab of makeup. Mama would have killed for skin like that.

"Now, we don't want to keep you, but as I said on the phone, Greta had everything planned and even labelled, so there would be no confusion."

I could only smile at that, thinking how Greta had once wanted to label all the drawers in the kitchen, and I talked her out of it.

"She spoke of you often, as I said. And she had a small framed picture of you on her shelf by her bed. I suspect she often spoke to you when no one else was around. The photograph, she told me, was from your first profession. And on the back was a little tag: *To be given to Gwendolyn.* Do you know who that is?"

"Oh, of course. I was just speaking to her yesterday. She visited Greta last week and was the one who told me she was there. Gwendolyn is my godmother, and is the owner—well, used to be the owner—of Tea on Thames on the Upper West Side. She's now running her tea shop on Barrow Street in the Village. It's called Penguin Pub. It's going to be like a tea shop and theater together. You could go there for tea and sandwiches." Here I was, sounding like Gwen's press agent.

"Does Gwendolyn come here to visit you?"

"Yes, at least once a month or so. She's just opening this new place with my sister Ruth."

"Oh, well that's very nice. If I may, then, I'll leave your little photo here with you and you can pass it on to her. Would that be alright?"

"Yes, that would be fine. She'll be thrilled to think Greta left it for her."

After that she held up two envelopes. "These are for you. Shall I put them here on the turn with the photo?" This she did, before I could answer. The envelopes were followed by two neatly wrapped packages, which I was sure were books. That didn't surprise me at all—that would be the obvious gift Greta would leave.

"Okay, Sister." Sr. Rita Mary nodded to Sr. Rafka, who got up and left the room.

"Now, this last item may be a bit of a surprise, and I'm not sure what you will do with it, but Greta insisted we give it to you and only you." Leaning into the grille with almost a whisper she said, "That's another reason I didn't want to leave it with her son, ha! Okay, Sister!"

And the parlor door opened, and Sr. Rakfa came in backwards pulling . . . a rocking chair.

"Squeak!" I shouted. "My old rocker from 79th Street. I don't believe it! You won't believe this, but you could almost say I came to the faith sitting on that rocker. That's where I first read the Gospels and fell in love with the Lord." That was it. My voice cracked, and my grand Feinstein composure fell apart right there. I managed to get out, "It was the only thing I brought with me from my home when I moved into Greta's."

"And it was the only thing Greta brought with her to Saint Rose's. We usually don't encourage patients to move in furniture, but it was small, and it fit nicely by the window looking out at the East River. And she sat in it every day and read, and prayed, and watched the boats go by. And it squeaked!"

"Thank you, Sister, so much, for bringing this to me. I hope you didn't come by subway!"

"No, we do have a couple cars. It was easy. But now it's yours again."

We chatted for maybe ten minutes more about Greta's last days and how to get to the Maronite cathedral, and they promised to light a candle for me for Greta by the shrine of St. Sharbel. It was a wonderful visit, and Sister promised to come back again sometime.

I went to Mother's office immediately, grateful to find her there, and told her about my visit and about Squeak. "Maybe we could put it in the infirmary by the picture window, so the sisters could enjoy an old-fashioned rocker," I suggested. Mother could see I was excited about it.

She didn't say anything, but sat there, thinking. She always put her right index finger between her nose and upper lip and rested her chin on her thumb when she was thinking. I hoped she wouldn't think my suggestion was frivolous.

"It's very kind of you, Sister, to suggest we put the rocker in the infirmary, and I'm sure some of the sisters would love it, but I think . . ." She paused again, finger to upper lip. "I think . . . Squeak should go in your cell. If you get rid of that old brown chair, your rocker would fit very nicely in the corner. And I think your friend would be very happy to know it's back home again with you."

These last couple days were going to do me in! Mother was so caring towards me. I didn't know what to say.

"Also," she added, "I am touched that you first offered it for the sisters in the infirmary. You were not thinking of yourself. When the day comes that you move into the infirmary," she smiled, "you can take old Squeak with you then. For now, you keep it in your cell." And that was that.

Sr. Paula managed very easily to bring Squeak to my cell. We moved the brown chair out. And I stood there for a silent five minutes just staring at it. I couldn't believe that after all these years my old rocker was here in my cell. Now, it may seem silly, but I decided I would wait till that night, when the day was done, to sit in old Squeak and open my letters and packages from Greta. It was kind of making a ceremony of it. Maybe it was just my way of saying good-bye and thank you to Greta. I decided that this would be my prayer chair. It was ideal for *lectio* and spiritual reading. Of course, I had always used Squeak for this, at home on West 79th Street and again at Greta's.

I lay down on my bed. It was our regular siesta time. I was suddenly very tired, and it didn't take any effort to drift off into a deep sleep. The bell for None woke me, and I groggily dragged myself down to the chapel for the Office. I smiled to myself when I realized that after all these years it had become my way. None, the ninth hour, is at two fifteen. The light in the choir then is different from all other times. There are usually fewer nuns present, as some are dispensed because of work or being out (though the latter is rare). It's kind of like the transition Office from the morning to evening. A work period follows, and then Vespers. I know that many active communities that pray the Office—now called the Liturgy of the Hours—only have one of the "little hours" (Terce, Sext, and None), which they call Midday Prayer. I'm glad we've kept all the little hours. They become a natural part of the rhythm of the day. I had a lot to pray over those last few days, so I lingered in the chapel after None.

Sr. Micah and I were the only ones there. She was keeping her hour of guard. She was one of the ones who had made a point of coming over to me after Mother told the community about Greta. She's always struck me as being very shy. I was probably ten years solemnly professed when she entered. We don't really get to know the postulants and novices, but she and another postulant were sent to the library twice a week to reshelve books. And if that didn't take the whole time, I had other little projects of reorganizing the shelves. She was very quiet and worked better alone than with her companion, who tended to be chatty. They reminded me of Sr. Anna Maria and myself when we used to chat folding sheets.

The chatty one—I forget her name—didn't persevere. She received the habit, I remember, but after a while she said that the guimpe and veil were too restricting, that she couldn't wait to take them off at night. I only know that because she shared that sort of thing with Sr. Micah in the library. (The library was supposed to be a place of silence, but she found that too restrictive too.)

Sr. Micah has persevered and seems very happy; the life fits her, as it were. She's still rather shy and blushes if you tease her, but she's a good sister.

I sat back in my stall and just kept my gaze on the Lord in the Eucharist, always so silent and always so present. I prayed for Greta and the few friends we had at the library, wondering if they knew she had died, wondering if they were still alive themselves. And I prayed for my family, sad that they didn't know the Lord in the Eucharist and how loving He is. Mama was still very active between New York and Boca, keeping her tabs on Ruthie and, I suppose, on Sally and David.

I wondered what their lives were like now. I would only get bits and pieces from Ruthie whenever she visited, and that had been a long time now too. I prayed she wasn't over-doing it with running this show. She had told me that Sally had given up a marvelous career as a journalist to operate a dog grooming salon with her "partner," Ruthie called her. I wasn't sure what that was. I presumed she meant a business partner.

And Dr. David Feinstein lived in one of the new high rise apartments near St. Vincent's. He has a private psychiatric practice which has made him quite rich. So many people have complexes that he can afford a duplex. He is married to his career and never to Miss Right, although I know he's tried. Maybe he tends to analyze his dates. I guess all couples do that in a natural way, but sometimes you've just got to let God surprise you. My family . . . we all went in such different directions. *What makes their lives tick*, I wondered, *what purpose do they hold onto to make sense of it all?*

Lord, I pray that all would come to know You, and to know that there is an eternal life, and that when we belong to You, dear Lord, that life has already begun to live in us. How incomprehensible are Your ways. Dear Mother of God, watch over Mama and keep her safe from harm and any anxiety she may meet. Bring her to know you and your Son. She is a good woman. Such a blessing she was to me growing up! I hope she knows that. Please tell her for me. And say hello to Papa. I hope he's keeping an eye on Ruthie. Amen.

On my way out of the chapel just before three o'clock, I patted Sr. Micah on the shoulder and whispered, "Say a prayer for me, Sister." She nodded and blushed.

I could have used a couple postulants then, as I had to reshelve the books myself—not my most enjoyable job. But the library was empty, and there were only about fifteen books to be reshelved. I wondered what books Greta had wrapped up for me and what had happened to all her other books. I know she gave a slew of them to St. Vincent's when they wanted to have a parish lending library. And she mentioned once sending boxes of books to Zimbabwe and Mozambique. They certainly got good stuff from her! I hope they can read English.

Reshelving books can be mindless, especially with our system, so I thought about how kind the sisters were in offering their condolences, and it dawned on me that Sr. Anna Maria hadn't said anything to me. Of all people, I thought she would have been the first. *Something's going on here*, I thought. *She's probably preoccupied with the new dryers being installed in the laundry.*

I reshelved all fifteen books, dusted the shelves, changed the liner in the trash can, shut off the lights, and headed for the infirmary.

Sr. Benedict was asleep in the La-Z-Boy facing the picture window, her book nearly falling off her lap. Sr. Amata and Sr. Gerard were each at a separate card table, poring over the jigsaw puzzles. The kittens were nearly assembled. I checked in Sr. Gertrude's room first, as she often took a late afternoon nap before Vespers. She wasn't there. *The audio room* . . . sure enough, there she was, sitting with the earphones on, her eyes closed, tapping her foot. I flashed the ceiling lamp so as not to frighten her. Her eyes popped open nonetheless, and she smiled and waved hello.

"I'm listening to Ethel Merman singing 'Everything's Coming Up Roses.' It was recorded at the Waldorf in the mid-seventies, shortly after she retired from Broadway, and she's still got it!"

I laughed and joined her, and we listened to it again together, twice. I think Mother Mary of the Trinity envisioned this audio room would fill the infirmary with sacred music, and at times it does. But thanks to a generous benefactor and Vatican II, we inherited a little library of Broadway show tunes and popular singers, probably from when recordings began. It brought great joy to the likes of Sr. Gertrude. I'd even say it was very spiritual, because it touched something deep in her soul, in her life, which was good and had actually brought her to the monastery and was now re-sparking in her that passion. I've seen Sr. Gertrude listen to a record or tape and clap her hands together, not in applause but in prayer. For many a year she brought joy and laughter and applause into the monastic feast day celebrations with her tap dancing and her own version of "Everything's Coming Up Roses."

I told her about my visit with the Hawthorne sisters, and the things Greta left me, which I hadn't opened yet, and the biggest surprise, Squeak. Sr. Gertrude thought they had given me a pet mouse till I explained it was my old rocking chair and that Mother Agnes Mary insisted I keep it in my cell.

"Well, I never. A rocking chair in your cell! How perfect is that?" She put on a big smile and said, "Such a blessing, that Mother Agnes Mary." She sounded just like Mama when she said it!

I laughed and repeated, "Such a blessing!"

"I wonder if she'd let me move Ethel Merman into my cell?" And we laughed more.

The door opened and Sr. Gerard appeared. "What's all the racket going on in here? Come on, Gert, we're about to do our rosary." This was something new for the infirmary community. The hour before Vespers and supper, they sat together with the statue of Our Lady of Fatima, lit a candle— presently a pumpkin-spice-scented one—and prayed the rosary, beginning with a litany of intentions.

Sr. "Gert" promptly got up, right on cue, and headed toward the door. "Everything's coming up a rosary for you and for me." And off they went.

I would have joined them, but I knew this was their thing to do, so I checked the kitchenette, washed up the used teacups, glasses, and plates, and made my way back to the chapel.

ten

My night habit was washed and ironed, and I put on a fresh night veil and my soft penguin print slippers. (I think they were meant for children, but they were a gift from you-know-who.) I was ready. The gooseneck lamp from my tiny desk was angled to shed light on the rocker corner.

I sat down in Squeak for the first time. Greta had replaced the cushions probably twice—not too thick, and a plain color, a kind of soft burgundy. I rubbed my hands along the well-worn arms and rocked backward, and then—*squeak*—forward. It was still there. I could have just sat there and let the memories flood my mind for hours, but I said a prayer first, asking the Lord to give sweet repose to His servant Greta, and I commended her again to the Mother of God, as I had done less than a half hour ago at the conclusion of Compline. My *Salve* was for Greta.

Greta's gifts to me were on the side table. I took the thinner of the two envelopes and slit it open with a letter opener, and a hundred-dollar bill appeared, all new and crispy-looking. It was folded in a single sheet of paper with the note:

Dear Sisters,

Enclosed is a $100 stipend for twenty Masses for the repose of my poor soul. They may be offered at any time on any day, but at your community Mass, please. If the stipend has increased to $10 then ten Masses will also suffice. My spirit was always uplifted whenever I was at the monastery for Mass. It is a comfort to know that with this it will not end for a while.

Greta Phillips

I smiled, thinking Greta may have surmised that her family was not going to have anything to do with the Catholic Mass, so she took care of it herself. I put the note and the money back in the envelope and would pass it on to Sr. John of God, who was in charge of Mass stipends. I opened the other one, which was thicker, and knew immediately what it was—a letter from Greta.

Rocking back and forth, I closed my eyes for a minute before reading it. The letter was handwritten, in Greta's hand, just a little shakier than I remember.

My dear Sr. Mary Baruch of the Advent Heart,

When you are reading this I will have entered upon the great adventure that we would sometimes speak of. My poor body has finally given up and is ready, I think, to let me go. I have had a wonderful and full life, and I have only a few regrets, for which I beg the Lord in His love to have mercy on me.

I have been blessed, as you know, since my childhood with knowing the Lord Jesus, and when I was in college the Lord introduced me to a wonderful, zealous young man who would be my husband, Paul Phillips. I thought it was an arrangement made in Heaven.

Paul was a devout Lutheran and was studying for the ministry at Emmitsburg. After he was ordained and we were married, we settled in a small parish near Trenton, New Jersey. I had gotten my BA in English Lit., but I wanted to go on for a Masters in Library Science. I almost completed it, but Paul volunteered us for a mission outreach post in Mozambique. And so began our lives as Lutheran missionaries in Africa.

I was so homesick my first couple years, really. But I couldn't let on to Paul how miserable I was. And I loved the beauty of the country, and the people were so lovely and welcoming to us. My greatest joy in all that time was my small class, teaching children and many adults how to read. Learning and speaking Portuguese was certainly a challenge, but we were young and quick to learn.

"Pastor Pao," as they called him, was more zealous for Christ than he had ever been in the States. I think people's absorption of and need for the faith make a big difference. He would often be gone for a week at a time, going by jeep to the mission outposts the main mission also ran. Our own relationship suffered from this, I am sorry to say. It was not entirely Paul's doing; I was also taken up with lots of projects and organizing things for the women and children.

After five years, Paul's absences were longer and longer, and my loneliness became more painful. I turned to the Lord in prayer as best as I could, but I was often left dry, and I felt abandoned.

It was near Christmas when we met a newly arrived Catholic missionary priest. He was from Brazil and spoke perfect English. I'll call him Padre John, although that's not his real name. We both took a liking to him, as he was very personable and wanted to do great things. Paul would be away on his trips, and I would have Padre John over for supper. He really took an interest in my work, and we could sit for hours on the straw mat on the porch talking about authors and books. He was very knowledgeable.

Dear Sister, I don't want to shock you or scandalize you, but I have carried this in my heart all the years I have known you. You were so innocent and in love with the Lord and His Church that I couldn't say anything to injure that. John and I had a—what shall I call it?—a romantic fling. I was by this time so lonely for affection, which Paul was not able to give to me. When he would come back for a week or so, he was either so exhausted or wrapped up in a thousand things to do, that he hardly had time for me. Padre John also began to absent himself when Paul was home, which was good, as we were both afraid that he would suspect something. John was so caring, and, I suppose, so needy too. He said he never expected celibacy to be such a cross. He had never been with a woman, he told me, and was afraid, and didn't want to sin against his vows, and he said I had the loveliest face and hair he ever saw. He told me I was more beautiful than all the women in Brazil. You can imagine what that did to my already-deflated ego.

Paul announced to me that the Lutheran Mission Office was calling for him ("for us") to come back to the States for three months. We had not been home in seven years. He didn't want to go, because of all the work "we" were doing; we couldn't just abandon the schools and mission outposts.

By this time, I dreaded the thought of three months alone with Paul, putting on airs of the devoted and happy pastor's wife. I had no one to turn to for advice. The other ministers' wives were few and far between, and much too busy with their own work. So it was decided that I would stay and mind the fort. Paul would go on our home leave and, if he had time, also visit my family, which I knew he wouldn't do.

Paul was actually kind of sad and caring for a moment, saying how much he would miss me. It was all a bit too much to take, but I played along and assured him I would be fine, that the school moms would look after me.

John invited me to visit his mission church to do something to set up a library of sorts. He had a house larger than ours, actually, so I had my own room and bath. But we spent every night together.

After a week, I needed to return to our own mission. The summer break was nearly over and there were lots of things to do.

Now, I don't know how to put this into words that you would understand. John became so remorseful about our committing adultery that he began to talk of leaving the priesthood. I was also remorseful, but it was different from his. He spoke so poignantly about the heart of Christ, and His forgiveness, and mercy, and transforming grace, that I begged him not to leave the priesthood for me. We both knew what we had to do: we had to end our little affair and ask the Lord's forgiveness. But he seemed to have a way to attain that, or to believe in that, that I didn't have. I was feeling desperate and wretched. My marriage was on the rocks, my affair was on the rocks, and I had nowhere to turn. It was the one and only time in my life that I thought about taking my life. But I knew I couldn't do that. My faith would get me through, I hoped, but I saw in John's faith something more real. His contrition was for the right reasons; he was as wretched a priest as I ever saw, but he believed in God's love and mercy in a way that had never touched me. I was mostly feeling terribly sorry for myself.

I realized that my poor Christian life had been all very shallow, routine, by the book—whatever book that was. And I think above all else it was John being able to break from it all, with true contrition, and carry on, that made me look at Catholicism differently. Lest it sound like I'm canonizing him—I'm not—he was devastated by it all too. But he never passed over into the kind of despair I was feeling. And, I learned, he also had help. He went to his superior and confessed the whole thing, and the result was that he would be transferred to one of their other missions in Zimbabwe after a home leave and a rest. He came to see me the night before he left. All the old emotions stirred up in me, and saying good-bye to him was the most difficult thing I ever did. In the nights and weeks that followed, I realized his strength—that his love for the Lord, for his faith, and for his priesthood were greater than the love (or lust) we experienced.

Paul's home leave was extended by two more months, which he was sincerely apologetic for, as if he had made that choice himself. He missed me terribly, he said, and would be home at our mission hut, as he called it, for Christmas. I was grateful for the extra months to get a hold of myself and prepare myself for what was to come.

Paul wasn't expecting the Christmas gift I had for him. I was five months pregnant. It's the only time I think I saw my husband cry. It was a cry of dismay, mixed with anger, and hurt, and all the emotions someone goes through whose marriage bond has been betrayed. Paul had also felt terribly guilty for years, I learned, that we had not had any children of our own.

*But he had always thought it was my fault, and he hadn't
wanted to blame me. And then the work took over the romance.
It's a terrible thing when you lose hold of your initial love.*

*Paul was outwardly forgiving in a necessary, pastoral way.
He didn't ask questions other than whether it—the affair—was
still going on. And I assured him that it wasn't . . . and that I
would not be having a black baby. I knew that that was in his
mind and he was afraid to ask. I don't think he ever suspected
Padre John, because, well, because he was a priest. There were
always lots of Protestant missionaries passing through. When
Paul Martin was born, Paul accepted him. I think he loved him
as best he could. I don't really know what was going on in his
heart. He was as cold as ice with me, and when we were alone
he would verbally abuse me for being a hypocrite and a wanton
woman. The only consolation I had was my son, and at times
that caused me great pain and guilt. I never saw John again. He
doesn't even know that he is a father.*

*Young Paul grew up in Africa. We offered to send him to
school in the States, but he was happy "at home." He was a bit of
a rebel, however, like so many ministers' sons. This caused great
dismay to Paul Senior. He was always afraid Paul Junior
would bring scandal to our mission. And I used to secretly wish
that he would. I didn't want to be the only hypocrite parading
around the mission pound.*

*My marriage with Paul never got better; his look tore me
apart at times. No matter how many times I told him I was
sorry, I knew he never forgave me. Maybe I was more of a hypocrite than he knew. I wasn't really sorry for the weeks I had
had with John. And John's faith haunted me.*

*My refuge has always been books, as you know. And so I
began to study the Catholic faith on my own. Reading the early*

Church Fathers opened up a whole new world to me. Like everyone, I loved Good Pope John, and I fell in love with his Journal of a Soul. I remembered Padre John's contrition, and it brought me closer to Christ. I carried the guilt of it all for many years. I hoped it didn't rub off on Paul Martin. I blamed myself for his rebelliousness. And I prayed for the grace of true contrition—to be sorry, not because I had messed up everything and ruined my marriage and my own happiness, but because I offended God, because I had cut myself off from His divine friendship.

Paul Martin left home when he was eighteen. Well, you know the story from there on out. Pastor Paul and I returned to the States and settled again in New Jersey. We had left word in Mozambique for Paul Martin; he would be able to reach us if he needed to. He only did so once, to tell me I was a grandmother. Paul took sick and passed away. He had gotten old and bitter. It was all very sad, but, at the same time, it was a great relief, in a way. I felt a great weight lifted from my shoulders.

I sold the house in Jersey and moved to Manhattan to begin a new life. I had a wonderful job at the public library, and that wonderful apartment on East 79th Street. And one evening I met a priest at intermission at the Metropolitan Opera. He was wearing a Roman collar, standing by himself and reading his program. He looked very distinguished. I swear it was my guardian angel who pushed me over to him, and I said, "Good evening, Father, are you enjoying the opera?"

"Indeed I am, Madame, and I hope you are too."

I smiled. "I am. My name is Greta Phillips, and I want to become a Catholic. Can you help me with that?" Can you imagine, right there on the third tier of the opera house. I just blurted it out like a deranged street person.

"Indeed I can. My name is Father Aquinas Meriwether. I'm from Saint Vincent Ferrer Church, on 65th and Lexington. Do you know it?"

"Oh, yes," I said. "I go by there all the time."

"Marvelous. I'm beginning an instruction class next Monday night in the priory at seven o'clock. You're most welcome to join us, and we'll see how things go from there."

So I went to the inquiry class. And that's where I met Rebecca Abigail Feinstein, the only inquiring Jewish girl in the class. Meeting Fr. Meriwether at the Met . . . You know, we've talked about that scene a million times, but you've never known the Greta behind the scenes. I suppose you always had me on a kind of pedestal, and I didn't want to fall off it. But before I go to meet our dear Lord and maker, I wanted to share with you my true self and my wretched past, because I know you will pray for me when I am gone.

I wanted so many times to call you, Becky, to tell you how beautiful and peaceful it is at St. Rose. But to my utter amazement, one day Paul Martin appeared at my door. He had been contacted by a sister here who had a knack for doing those kind of things. I was so happy he came. He's grown up into a handsome middle-aged man with a strong Portuguese accent. I am the grandmother of his three sons and one daughter. He told me that I would be very proud of them; they're all avid readers. His daughter is named Greta.

I was afraid then to call you because I was afraid you'd meet him and not understand. Isn't it awful to carry our fears right to our deathbeds! But now I am also presuming that if you are reading this letter then you have met Paul Martin. He doesn't know this story as I have told it to you. Paul Phillips is his father, for all he knows. I've told him all about you and hoped that

*he would deliver my little gifts to you, especially the Mass sti-
pend—well, especially Squeak, who has missed you for over
twenty-five years. I know you won't be able to read the book I
sent, but perhaps the other will be used when you are rocking
back and forth.*

*Becky . . . Sister Mary Baruch. The time has come for me to
say good-bye. Knowing me as you now do, I hope you will find
it in your heart to forgive me, and to pray for my poor soul. The
years that we shared on East 79th Street have been the happiest
years of my life; they were a time of healing and strength and
such joy to share with you our beautiful Catholic faith. When
you left for the monastery it was one of the saddest days, but one
of the most beautiful. I have cherished these years having you as
my own very dear sister, Mary Baruch, a cloistered nun. You
will never know, until we merrily meet again in Heaven. Such
a blessing you have been.*

My love and prayers,
Greta

The silence in my cell was profound. I had stopped rocking pages ago. I felt my hands go numb as I hung on to this
letter. *Greta.* I was filled with a deep sense of regret that she
had never shared any of this with me before. Why hadn't she?
Was I that fragile or innocent? Then my heart was filled with
such a pain of shame and guilt, like unto that which Greta
must have known all those years. I was shocked, but not
scandalized, by her love for this priest. I could understand it.
It struck me, right there and then, sitting in my rocker, that
I had loved Ezra, and I knew that he had loved me. But our
love for the Lord had transcended that and we had never
touched each other in an impure way. Poor Greta; I could
understand. And, if it's possible in the spiritual life, I felt her

pain and guilt. I felt her regret and loss. I felt all of these things, all rolled into one. And all I could do was silently offer them to the Lord. It felt like a stone, a rock, was stuck in my soul.

I couldn't move from my chair. I realized for the first time why we must pray for our priests. Oh, I knew sisters who did it routinely, who included it in their spontaneous intercessions. And I routinely prayed for Fr. Matthew—Ezra—and even for Fr. Wilcox, and always for the soul of Fr. Meriwether. But I thought of the soul of Greta's Fr. John and what he must have gone through. Our priests need our prayers to protect them from the assaults of the evil one, to save them from the demons of lust and loneliness. We need to pray that they never lose sight of who they are, sacramentally conformed to the person of Christ, to act in His person, to make present the sacrifice of forgiveness and healing. The life of every priest is incomprehensible, and it is given to us "in earthen vessels."

Why didn't Greta tell me all this before? Did she think I wouldn't forgive her? Was it really her shame or her pride that didn't want me to know that she had sinned? Are we not all sinners in need of forgiveness and mercy?

Her husband Paul was so wounded by her betrayal, and it sounded like he was never healed, he never forgave her. I realized I had little pockets of unforgiveness in my soul. *Dear Lord, I don't want to carry these to my deathbed.* The prayer came without prompting:

Soul of Christ, sanctify me.
Body of Christ, save me.
Blood of Christ, inebriate me.
Water from the side of Christ, wash me.

Passion of Christ, strengthen me.
O good Jesus, hear me.
Within Thy wounds hide me.
Never let me be separated from Thee.
From the malicious enemy defend me.
In the hour of my death call me
And bid me come unto Thee
That with Thy saints I may praise Thee
Forever and ever.
Amen.

I heard Sr. Veronica walk by on her way to the eleven o'clock guard. I'd been sitting here for over two hours. I wasn't paralyzed, just kind of numb. My spiritual life changed that night, for I now knew what it was to pray for others, to pray in their place and carry the weight of their shame and guilt and place it before the merciful heart of our beloved Jesus. I now knew that His love is indeed infinite and beyond what we can even imagine, and in our "schleppitude" He lifts us up and holds us tight and rocks us back and forth. . . . *squeak . . . squeak . . . squeak . . .*

eleven

I couldn't get Greta's letter out of my head. Her two packages were left unwrapped on the top shelf of my little bookcase. I couldn't imagine Greta being the woman she had described in her letter. I had always thought her marriage had fairy-tale happiness, and that her life as a missionary was like being married to a Dr. Dolittle. It was like her letter was about somebody else. *How could Greta commit adultery? And with a priest! How could a priest* . . . oh, I couldn't think about it. We'd read articles about how many priests were leaving to get married, as if celibacy was the big problem. But Greta wasn't a celibate. Marriage wasn't a magic solution to loneliness. I want to say the Lord is the solution—and He is, of course, but both Greta and her priest friend loved the Lord. I've got to believe that. I know Greta loved the Lord; she had said so herself ever since I had known her. But she still fell into sin.

I searched my own heart and wondered if I had ever really fallen into mortal sin. I know I am full of self-love, and my pride trips me up around every corner. I know I can be gluttonous and envious of others' gifts and even their looks—vanity of vanities! And I know loneliness and staring into the emptiness that can surround me. I missed Mama and the comfort of her love and feeling that she was somehow proud of me. Why didn't she visit? Did my becoming a Christian hurt her so much? Did she feel it was a betrayal, as Paul Phillips felt Greta's sin was? Did Mama think I had sinned? I had thought these things over and over for more than twenty-five years, but maybe never in the context of Greta's revelation.

Do we all have a shadow side that's dark and secret and plagues us all through our lives? If we do, I thought, *what's mine? I can have all kinds of dark thoughts that I wouldn't want to share with anybody, but I don't act out on them. Sometimes people think I'm so funny or so sweet, and lots of people think we're all living saints and sing like angels. I guess that's the community's dark side.*

That's one of the rude awakenings every new sister faces eventually. We don't live the life perfectly or as ideally as we fantasized before we entered. People can misjudge us. And if I'm honest, I have my own hidden judgment about other sisters, which may just be based on my own prejudices, fears, or silly taste. I often don't accept all those splinters of the cross that are offered to me each day, usually in the form of another sister or a service I'm asked to give. Having hurt my family is probably my biggest wound, if it is a wound. Or maybe I did put Greta on a pedestal which kept her from feeling she could unburden herself on me. That could have been her own spiritual pride or fear of losing face. I suppose we like to be on a pedestal once in a while. *But who am I,* I thought, *that I should know everything about everyone? Don't we deserve to have our little secrets and wounds? And doesn't the Lord's mercy heal us? Don't we pray for that all the time, or are we just mouthing words?*

I held everything in, of course. I didn't share a word with Sr. Anna Maria or Sr. Gertrude or Mother Agnes. I just kept my secrets. Greta's memory deserved my confidence, even after death. And I could stoically keep that. I was good at keeping secrets. I had a flashback to Ruthie sitting in the parlor that afternoon, polishing her invisible star. *Do I do that, Lord? Does my spiritual pride keep me on my own complacent pedestal?*

The sisters who knew asked what my "inheritance" was, and I just said it was the rocker and something Greta had written. I couldn't even call it a farewell letter.

I also wasn't morose about any of it, nor did I think Greta was a wanton woman, a liar, or an evil person in any way. I certainly didn't love Greta any less; if anything, I loved her more in her sharing her weakness with me. I tried to understand the anguish she must have gone through, and how devastating it must have been for her, and her husband . . . and Padre John. I wondered if he was still alive: did he move on from his early sins and become a holy priest, or did he leave the priesthood and get married? It seemed to be happening more and more. And this, of course, made me think of Fr. Matthew. . . . *Ezra.* I hadn't had a word from him in more than six months.

I resolved to pray even more fervently for him. Greta and Gwendolyn had known Ezra from the beginning, and how much we had shared in the time before my baptism and then the years afterward, till he went off to join the Passionists.

I remember my surprise visit to his monastery in West Springfield, when Fr. Meriwether, the other woman from the parish, and I drove up together. Fr. Meriwether gave the nuns conferences, and Whatshername and I stayed in the nuns' guest rooms and made a kind of retreat.

Ezra had always been my rock and pillar. It came back to me in a sudden flashback, Gwen telling me that Fr. Matthew was in the tea shop with Whatshername. And when I acted surprised, she was surprised that I didn't know they were friends. *I wonder if Gwen has kept other times a secret from me? Like Greta kept her past a secret from me. Why do people do that? Do they think I have to be protected from what's going on in the world, or in their lives in particular? I know we don't live in the ordinary climate of the world and the pop culture, but we're not inoculated from feeling the hurts and pains and scandals of others, especially those we love. If anything, we feel them more intensely, as we don't have the normal escapes to take away the pain.*

My meditation after Vespers was swamped with a playback conversation I had had with Ezra almost ten years before. He had been on a kind of mission band where he and one or two others would go to a parish for week and have a parish mission. It was usually focused on the mysteries of the faith, like from the rosary, but with a Passionist emphasis on the "redemptive mysteries." I remember wishing he would come to Queen of Hope and give us the mission. He was always such an eloquent speaker, and he spoke with passion about the Lord.

We were sitting in the parlor. I was noticing that his temples were beginning to turn gray, and I hoped he would let his hair grow out like when we were young. *Such thoughts I should have? He's talking about the Paschal Mystery, and I'm wondering if his hair is still naturally curly. He should let his side locks grow out like real* payos . . . *the Jewish priest.*

"I've been at our retreat house in Riverdale for over five years now. It's been great because I've gotten into the city a lot. I get to see Aunt Sarah—who sends her regards, by the way—and I always try to stop in at Tea on Thames for an Earl Grey!"

This was a nice nostalgic moment, I recalled, and I smiled when he mentioned our old drink, Earl Grey tea. I had always pictured him sitting at a little round table by himself, but apparently Whatshername had often been with him. She had been working as a dental receptionist in Yonkers.

"Things have changed quite a bit. A lot of our men have left the Order and the priesthood. It would seem we have to bring the Church into the highways and byways."

"What are you telling me? You aren't thinking of leaving, are you?" We had read the articles about the great exodus of both nuns and priests. We had a subscription to the *Catholic Reporter* in the library, and the headlines alone used to depress me.

I never had the experience of Catholic school like most of the sisters in the monastery did, and I didn't share in their tales of growing up Catholic. I entered here at a time when the renewal among active sisters was just taking off. The Immaculate Heart of Mary Community in Los Angeles had been a huge congregation of teaching sisters. Sisters here said some of their classes in Catholic school were forty to sixty students. I learned later that many of the teachers were not even college-educated; after novitiate they were sent for summer workshops and put into a school to teach in the fall. Apparently the Cardinal Archbishop of Los Angeles, Cardinal McIntyre, insisted that more and more sisters become full-time teachers and "follow his rules," as one paper put it. The sisters rebelled, and something like ninety percent of them left with the superior, Anita Caspary. They were all dispensed from their vows and fired from the schools.

Fr. Matthew went on, dodging my question. "You wouldn't believe how things have changed. Most of the Dominican sisters we knew are now in secular clothes. Many, of course, simply left. Others are no longer teaching but doing social work and living in their own apartments. The latest thing, you know, is not to have superiors but 'local coordinators.'"

I had heard such things. We were pretty much immune from the details, but they got in. Sr. Catherine Agnes used to say, "They get to us through cracks in the enclosure wall!" And we all laughed and thought that was hysterical. But we saw it happening. Few sisters came for retreat anymore. The prioresses would have their meetings and come back and share what other monasteries were doing. Many had modified their habit: a softer simple veil with a little hair showing, no more guimpe or bandeau or full sleeves. Many had abandoned the night habit for regular nightgowns or men's pajamas. The Midnight Office was also dropped in many places, and Matins was now the Office of Readings and could be done at any time: noon, before Compline, first thing in the morning. A number of our monasteries stopped using the title "Mother" for the prioress, claiming that the first sisters never did that, or that it was not Dominican but Benedictine. The biggest change was that the Divine Office, which for hundreds and hundreds of years had been chanted in Latin with Gregorian psalm tones, was now being sung in English with a kind of adapted English chant. Hymns were also allowed at Mass. Sr. Anna Maria called them "parish hymns." Some of these hymns were even Protestant, which shocked many of the sisters. Some of the sisters refused to sing them.

Many of the really radical changes didn't affect me as much as the older sisters. I didn't fully get why they could be so upset or emotional over these waves of change—at least, not until that afternoon, sitting in the parlor with Fr. Matthew. He was my godfather, my mentor, my closest priest friend, and there he was, telling me he may leave the priesthood.

"Is there a woman?" I blurted it out without thinking. But we knew each other; we used to blurt things out at each other all the time. I read a lot of the articles in the Catholic periodicals and papers that talked *ad nauseam* about the new ministries and relevant strides to bring the Church up to date. There was a whole spirit of dissent spreading across the American Church (the *American* Church?) in protest to Pope Paul VI's encyclical *Humanae vitae*. And the whole feminist movement, which had been stirring in the sixties with the birth control pill and the right to kill your baby before it's born, had now spread even into convents and large sisters' motherhouses. They wanted to be called "women religious." They spoke a different language. Some of us just looked at each other when we read their articles in the refectory; we didn't know what they were talking about. Fr. Matthew, when he was Ezra, used to laugh and say, "It's all a new vocabulary, Beck." And we'd laugh. I'd say that to Sr. Anna Maria after one of the new relevant articles about the renewal of religious life—it's all a new vocabulary.

I looked him square in the eye and repeated, "Is there a woman?"

Fr. Matthew was always honest with me, I could count on that. "I'm not thinking of leaving because of anyone, and honestly, Becky, I'm torn apart by all this. I don't know what to do." He put his head down, staring at the paneling under the grille, and in a softer voice said, "I am seeing Barbara Parker off and on."

Barbara Parker! I screamed to myself. *Barbara Parker, that's Whatshername! I was with her when she first met Br. Matthew in West Springfield. And we even had dinner a couple times afterwards, and I introduced her to Tea on Thames—oh, I should never have done that!*

All that went through my head before I could speak. "I remember her," I said, slowly. "Gwen has mentioned you've been with her a few times at Tea on Thames. But I thought you were just—"

"We are just friends . . . or were. I think she would like it to be more."

"I thought she was thinking about entering the convent somewhere."

"Oh, she inquired at a number of places, but when she visited she was turned off. Nice middle-aged ladies in polyester pantsuits watching Jeopardy together."

"Yeah," I added, "The local coordinator probably left the prayer life up to them."

Fr. Matthew chuckled. "Oh, I see Rebecca Feinstein hasn't completely lost her cynical witticism."

"Cynical witticism? What are you talking about? I have an insightful sense of humor. Remember, Ezra Goldman, I'm Jewish. Barbara Parker wouldn't be caught dead in polyester. For such a meshuga you're going to abandon the priesthood? Oy."

Only to Ezra could I talk like that. And he loved it. He laughed the old laugh I used to love to hear.

"My dear, dear sister, how I've missed our chats! You must pray for this schlemiel, okay?"

"I pray for you all the time, you should know that. Leave the Passionists and become a Dominican." I blurted this out too, not seriously, but not entirely joking either.

That was all ten years ago. I not only prayed, I fasted. And for me, that's a real sacrifice. It's too much like dieting, which was always the bane of my youth.

Fr. Matthew did not leave the priesthood. He did leave the retreat house in Riverdale, however, and volunteered for one of their missions in Africa. He would visit me every time he was home in New York, but I hadn't seen him in over a year nor heard from him in six months. All of a sudden I thought of Greta's letter. *Africa. Ezra's in Africa. Dear me, dear me*, I said to myself.

I went to Office, but nothing sank in. I'm not sure I even thought about God once the whole time. It was like a dark cloud was forming out there on the horizon and heading in my direction. I suppose I was a little depressed. Three deaths in a single year, two of whom I loved dearly, Mother John Dominic and Greta Phillips. Even old Sr. Boniface—she black-beaned me, I'm pretty sure, but I white-beaned her into Heaven. I guess my cynical witticism is still with me.

The Lord has His own strange way of showing us He loves us. Supper can sometimes be one item, like tapioca pudding, or soup, or homemade bread and cold cuts. But that night it was four varieties of bagels, made fresh here in Brooklyn, and three varieties of cream cheese: plain, veggie, and raisin walnut. *There is a God*, I thought.

Needless to say, I didn't settle into Squeak that evening on an empty stomach. It was a free night, which meant we didn't have a common recreation and could do what we liked. I often went to the infirmary on free nights, but that night I went to my cell. The two unwrapped packages from Greta were waiting patiently.

144

I knew the wrapping paper was not Greta's choice. She would never wrap anything in such tawdry, cheap-looking paper; but she was not really "at home" when she wrapped these.

I opened the thinner one first. I knew what it was immediately. It was a beautiful book journal. My first gift ever from Greta was thirty years ago after my baptism, and it was a beautiful journal. Not as beautiful as this one, but she knew how much I liked to write. This one had a metallic-looking cover, gold with speckles of red, green, and black. I named it right then and there Greta's Journal. I would only fill it in on very special occasions.

I unwrapped the larger package, which was a book and a note card. The note card read:

Dear Sr. Mary Baruch,

If you recall, my first book to you was Dietrich Bonhoeffer's The Cost of Discipleship. *I could only imagine the "cost" it was to you and your family for you to enter the Church, let alone the cloister! I'm sure it has not been easy these past twenty-five years. Perhaps there are days when the "cost" seems to have sky-rocketed. But you have persevered beautifully.*

This is one of my prized possessions, a first edition of The Cost of Discipleship *in the original German. Perhaps it could begin the Rare Books section of the Queen of Hope library. Blessed be God.*

Greta

The book was beautifully bound, with the single title, *Nachfolge,* which I oddly knew was "Discipleship." Greta and I used to refer to Bonhoeffer's book whenever we felt the sting of sacrifice. Until now I had no idea how pertinent it must have been in her own life.

I rummaged through my shoebox of cards and found one I had saved from my first profession. It was a Greta original, and inside she quoted from Bonhoeffer:

> *Costly grace confronts us as a gracious call to follow Jesus, it comes as a word of forgiveness to the broken spirit and the contrite heart. Grace is costly because it compels a man to submit to the yoke of Christ and follow him; it is grace because Jesus says: "My yoke is easy and my burden is light."*

I sank into my rocker. The light depression was not really lifted, as I once again thought about Greta's past and how painful it must have been. Why hadn't she shared it with me? I thought I was trustworthy and wouldn't have judged her or have been scandalized. Was she afraid that my esteem for her would be lessened? I felt so empty and unworthy to be anyone's friend. *Has my being a nun alienated me from my friends? I know it has from my family. I always knew that was my "cost of discipleship." But what good has any of it done? Is being a nun our invisible star we polish? Isn't this life supposed to let us take off our false faces? Or does it just become one more big mask to hide behind? Such thoughts I should have? Should I have never come here? Was I just a naïve, overly zealous or overly romantic girl who didn't really know what life was about? Was I escaping from the real world? If I had been married twenty-five years ago, I would probably be a grandmother now. Mama would have had half a dozen grandchildren spilling out of her wallet's picture section. She would have been so happy and proud of me. I could have helped Ruthie with all her problems, but I ran away from being her big sister to being a sad lady behind bars who could never come out and enjoy life. I don't even know if I've been a good nun, whatever that means. I've never really held any big positions in the monastery. I've been told over and over that I'm a spoiled child always wanting my own way. Not in those exact words, but that's what I've felt like at times. I don't even know if my so-called spiritual life has gotten any better. The thrill and fervor of prayer I had when Greta and I used to go to daily Mass before work disappeared years ago. I think I waste a lot of time thinking about myself or others, but not about Our Lord or Our Lady or my favorite saints.*

Greta's letter was on the table next to me. I read it again. She was about my age when she made a complete turnabout in her life. And that's when it hit me: *Maybe I should leave and start over. I could move back with Mama and take care of her. I'd even go with her to Boca every winter. Gwen would probably give me a job at Penguin Pub. I could keep an eye on Ruthie. Does the Lord want me to start over? What about my vows?*

I felt so alone. I had no one to talk to. Mother John Dominic would know just what to say, but she was gone. Greta was gone. Ezra was far away and no doubt fighting his own demons (*if there are demons*, I thought). And my dear Fr. Meriwether—oh, how I missed him that night.

I took off my veil and guimpe and ran my fingers through my chopped-up hair and scratched my poor head. *I'm becoming an old lady*, I thought, *whose life* . . . whose life, what? I didn't dare verbalize it. Fear, I guess. Fear that it had all been a waste of time, a waste of a life, all a big delusion. I crawled into my bed without a night veil. And when the bell rang calling us to the Midnight Office, I just stayed in bed. I couldn't pray anymore.

twelve

I was wide awake and feeling just a tiny bit guilty. I never missed Matins unless I was really sick and was told not to go. I dragged myself out of bed and began my routine. I mumbled the morning offering I prayed every morning, but I don't know if I meant it. It was just words. I had an hour before Lauds. I usually had breakfast and spent at least a half hour in chapel before Lauds. That was my routine, and thank goodness for routine. I didn't have to figure out what I was going to do. For a brief moment I wondered if this would be my last day here, but brushing my teeth distracted me from dwelling on that.

I was dressed and ready to go. I routinely blessed myself, kissed my scapular, and stepped out into the hallway and then into the cloister leading to the refectory. I felt guilty passing the door to the ante-choir, so I stopped and turned and went in. It almost felt like something or someone else was moving me into my stall. Sr. Albert was at the *prie-dieu* near the grille. She looked so peaceful, so caught up in her prayer. Her face was buried in her hands, and I wondered if she was meditating on a mystery of the rosary or thinking about breakfast? Was she happy and at peace with the Lord? Or was she battling her own temptations and wrestling with her own fears and doubts? How do we know what somebody else is going through?

I knelt and blessed myself. Routine. And I looked up at the monstrance facing us in its niche above the tabernacle. The Lord. I wish I could say that I was filled with light and a flood of consolation that washed away my darkness and cleared away all my doubts and temptations. But I wasn't. I knew, maybe just from the routine of being in the Real Presence, that I was being called to surrender. I nearly choked on the word, spoken silently inside my head: *surrender*.

"Lord . . . Lord. Yeshua." I couldn't say anything else. I only felt empty. I slipped out of my stall, genuflected, and quickly fled the chapel and headed for the refectory. I passed sisters moving along their side of the cloister, keeping perfect silence and custody of the eyes, as if invisible. I passed the hallway leading to the infirmary and momentarily thought of Sr. Gertrude and wondered if she ever felt sorry that she stayed. Did any of them?

I was grateful for the silence in the refectory. A few sisters were sitting quietly nibbling on toast. I never understood or got the nibbling habit. There was an aspirant too, making a little too much noise and not realizing it, trying to be nonchalant about everything, but nobody paid any attention to her.

I did something I've never done in all my years here before or since. I had half a mug of coffee, and, while drinking it, I got a bagel and a schmear of cream cheese, cut it in half, wrapped it tight in two paper napkins, and put it in my tunic pocket. I finished the coffee and, instead of heading to the chapel, I went outside by the infirmary door and went to the cemetery. Mother John Dominic's grave was still a mound of earth; there were a few leftover flowers, but no engraved cross yet. I just stood there, with my back to the monastery. If anyone was watching they'd think I was praying—which I was, in a way—but I was having my bagel and cream cheese and talking to Mother.

"Hi, Mother—oh my, I mean, good morning, Mother. Please forgive me for being so informal. I'm having my breakfast with you this morning, as I hope you can see. I miss you so much. I'm going through a terrible time, and you're not here to tell me what to do. It's been so difficult here without you, and now with my dear friend Greta's passing . . . I hope you've been able to welcome her to eternal life. I know she will be much consoled to see you again. Oh, Mother, I don't know what to do. What would you tell me to do?"

Now, I don't have mystical experiences or locutions of any sort, interior or exterior, and it may have been the wind rustling through our beautiful crepe myrtle tree, but I thought I heard, "Two weeks." It startled me so much I turned around expecting to find a sister sneaking up behind me, but there was only the wind and a chipmunk more startled than I was, who literally jumped behind a stone cross.

Two weeks. I remember one other time when I was feeling down and out, convinced, I think, that the Lord wanted me to be a teaching sister, like Edith Stein had been before she entered Carmel, or to go off to the missions, probably to Africa. (Ha!) I had been fantasizing about packing my shabby suitcase, and knew I should go to Mother, even if it was just to say good-bye. And I remember exactly where we were, sitting together in the infirmary in front of the picture window, looking out on the cemetery.

"Do you remember that, Mother? I poured out my heart to you, and you listened without interrupting. When I was done and probably expecting that you would say you'd help me pack, you simply said, 'Just stay for two weeks more. We can't act on our feelings, because they are always changing, aren't they? We are such fickle women at times. But our faith is not a feeling. And our vocations are not based on feelings, or we'd put in a turnstile instead of an enclosure door. You see, Sister, Our Lord allows all kinds of trials to purify us even of our fickleness. He is our foundation and our strength. And of course, He gave us our biggest helper, Our Mother of Perpetual Help. I know you know her well. Go to her like you've come to me, and give it two weeks.'"

And that's what I had done. I still had the novena booklet I had "borrowed" from the Redemptorist church when Ezra took me to my first novena. I had been so distraught over Gracie's wake that I ran away from the funeral home. I wasn't even baptized yet, and I felt like I wanted to run away from everything religious—there were those fickle feelings again. And Ezra had introduced me to Our Mother of Perpetual Help. And I grew to love her. Like Ezra, I used to call her "my other Jewish mother." But actually it wasn't really Ezra who had introduced us; I had met her silently at Gracie's apartment on New Year's Eve, when we all prayed the rosary in the living room before an icon of Our Mother of Perpetual Help. I prayed really hard that night for Gracie. She was my friend, and I didn't want her to die.

Now here I was, in a cemetery, distraught again, pouring out my heart to Mother John Dominic, and I somehow heard her tell me, "Two weeks." It stirred in me a little hope. I knew I wasn't alone, even in my loneliness.

Mother used to compliment me on my "lovely voice." I was never house chantress, but I was always one of the weekly chantresses. So I swallowed the last of my bagel and wished I had brought some water with me. Nonetheless I decided to sing the *Salve* for Mother. Quietly. Not in full voice. Softly.

Salve Regina, Mater Misericordiae: vita, dulcedo, et spes nostra, salve. . . . I couldn't get any further. My throat was all dried up, but the words watered my soul. Mary is Mother of Mercy, our life, our sweetness, and our hope. Our *hope*. We pray this every night. I had prayed this thousands of times. For Heaven's sake, I was living in a monastery named Mary, Queen of Hope! Where were my faith and my hope? Were they all dried up?

I knew I could give myself and all I was feeling, all I carried, to Our Mother of Perpetual Help—my Mother of Perpetual Help—my life, my sweetness, and my hope.

The darkness didn't disappear; the burden I felt over Greta was still weighing on me. But I knew, or I hoped, it would pass. I would not pack my bag today. I'd wait for two weeks.

I heard the ten-minute bell calling us to Lauds, right on time, too, as the sun was just peeking at us from the horizon. I whispered, "Thanks, Mother," and blew her a kiss from my open hand. I turned and made my way to the chapel and moved into my stall, knelt down, and blessed myself. Routine—such a blessing.

* * *

Mail was usually delivered and sorted and put into our cubby holes before the bell for Sext—that is, around eleven fifty. I hardly ever got mail, so I was surprised to see an envelope sticking out from my mail slot. It was a number ten envelope with a return address to Gwendolyn Putterforth on Barrow Street. I didn't open it, but folded it instead and put it in my tunic pocket. It could wait till I went to our cell for siesta. No one asked me if I was okay; maybe no one noticed I wasn't at Matins. Even Sr. Anna Maria didn't say a word.

It was probably just as well; I didn't want to explain anything to anyone. I was still thinking about my breakfast with Mother John Dominic and dug out my old prayer to Our Mother of Perpetual Help. I wanted a sign, but I didn't ask for one. I just needed to know I should stay. Even that didn't sit well with me. I was solemnly professed, for better or worse. That should be sign enough. For better or worse— maybe this was just the "worse" part. *I'll pray every day for two weeks*, I thought. *I'm not expecting a sign . . . but I wouldn't object if there were one.* I remembered the Lord's words: "An unfaithful generation seeks a sign, but no sign will be given it except the sign of Jonah the prophet."

The envelope in my mailbox was thicker than a typical letter, and Gwen wouldn't be writing me anyway. I opened it in our cell, and was delighted to unfold a half-page ad from the *Village Voice*:

PENGUIN PUB PRESENTS
Puttin' on the Ritz:
A gala evening of Broadway melodies and memories,
hosted by the inimitable Ruth Steinway
Start the evening with high tea and complimentary scones
with homemade preserves and clotted cream
Two shows opening night, October 1:
7:30 and 10:30 p.m.

There was a picture of the theater on the bottom, and covering the entire right side was Ruthie, wearing what looked like a modified version of a gown Queen Elizabeth I would have worn and crooning into a microphone. And on the entire left side was Ruben the Penguin King, wearing a little golden crown. *Papa.* In small print below were the names of the singers, groups, and dancers, none of whom I recognized. But what did it matter?

"Thank you, Gwendolyn," I said out loud. "I love it." *October 1, that's just a week from Friday,* I thought. I made a mental note to take the ad to Sr. Gertrude. I fell asleep in Squeak and woke up when the bell for None rang, with a crick in my poor neck that didn't go away for days.

Sr. Gertrude not only hung the ad in her cell, she made copies of it, and distributed them to all the cells in the infirmary. Apparently, she had the whole infirmary praying for opening night.

"We're all preparing for *our* opening night, you might say," Sr. Gertrude confided to me as we sat together in front of the picture window overlooking the cemetery. It was during that quiet time after Vespers. The September sun was setting behind us, casting long shadows across the cemetery.

"Sister?" I leaned in toward her good ear. "May I ask you a personal question?"

Sr. Gertrude chuckled. "You can always ask. You may not always get an answer." She giggled again.

"Are you happy you have stayed here, or have you ever thought about leaving?"

She didn't respond immediately, as if she were thinking about what her response would be. I wondered if anyone had ever asked her that.

"When I entered, many years ago, Mother Rose"—she gestured towards the cemetery—"told me to remember the words of Our Divine Lord to His disciples: 'You have not chosen me; it is I who have chosen you.' It is, when all is said and done, a vocation, a calling, a being chosen. But for what?" She paused again, perhaps to let her words sink into my poor head, or to gather the next ones together in her own head first. "Chosen to be one with Christ on the cross. Why do you think the largest image in our chapel is that larger-than-life crucifix? When we are one with Him there, conformed to Him, we are truly transformed. It's an invisible play going on, and we are chosen to be so identified with the lead Actor, that He lives now His death and resurrection in us."

I didn't say anything. I was listening and trying to understand this. Certainly I had heard it before, but with different ears.

"That's the real stuff going on," Sr. Gertrude continued. "Think what life without Christ must be for people. I think, my dear, that it all comes down to the question: Who is Jesus to you? Is He truly God, who has taken human flesh and come among us, and has taken all the sins of all the world for all time upon Himself out of love for us? Or is He just a nice man whose cause was thwarted and then picked up momentum thanks to His followers?"

"Yes, I know. You're bringing me back to my very beginning. It was coming to know and believe in Him that I sacrificed everything, although I wouldn't have used those words then."

"That's right, my dear. And you know, it's for the salvation of our souls and those of others that we are chosen. How many people never give God a thought, never pray or thank

Him, never think about why they are here on this earth, and whether there really is a Heaven and a Hell?"

My silence spoke for me.

"To answer your question: yes, there have been times when I wanted to chuck it all. Everybody goes through those times—I'm sure even married people go through those times. I discovered myself, I think, that when I was going through those times of trial or just the ordinary acedia which comes and goes, I was usually not praying very much. Really praying, I mean. Interiorizing the words, even the prayers we say over and over, to pray them like it's the first time. That's not being phony—sometimes we have to act as if we mean what we say. But the deeper prayer where we touch the presence of God, or He touches us, that's usually what's missing. So I pray more. Even if I don't feel like it, even if I don't get anything out of it. I pray."

There was a profound silence for a least a full minute. Then Sr. Gertrude quietly said, "Sacred Heart of Jesus, have mercy on us."

"You could've been a star." I said it thoughtfully, not teasing her or meaning to compliment her. We all knew how talented she was, and how much she loved the theater, and that she probably would have been a Broadway star.

She smiled. "My dear Sister Baruch, don't you see that I am a star? Not on Broadway—the lights of the Great White Way are passing. We've been chosen for another Way—not Broadway, but the Narrow Way. There's no applause, and no Tony Awards to envy, but the show must go on. It does go on, day after day. You're a little star yourself, you know. We all are. Because we have been chosen. We're the constellation of Mary, Queen of Hope."

And with that, she pulled herself out of the lounge chair she was ensconced in. "I'm feeling quite peckish after that homily. I wonder what's on the menu for tonight?"

And we laughed. "Indeed, the show must go on, and one of my favorite scenes is coming up."

Sr. Gertrude thought that was a riot. "You've got it, kid."

That night after "my favorite scene" and helping to wash and put away the props, I slipped into the chapel and just sat there quietly in the presence of the Lord in the Blessed Sacrament. I closed my eyes, and for an instant I was back at St. Vincent Ferrer's on East 65th. I had just wandered in to light a candle for my friend Gracie. And He was waiting for me. I was a Jewess, one of God's chosen people. Little did I realize that brisk autumn day that indeed I was chosen.

Thirty minutes passed by quickly, or so it seemed. The community bell was calling us to the community room for evening recreation. I paused on the way, standing in the cloister and looking out at the night sky opened up above the garth. It was a clear, cool September night, with an almost-full October moon. And the sky was full of stars.

thirteen

*T*he *Stars Were Out Last Night*, read the headline of the October 2 *Village Voice*.

The gala on opening night at the new Penguin Pub on Barrow Street had patrons lining the sidewalk to get in. Ruth Steinway opened the show with an uproariously funny parody of Broadway show tunes, written by newcomer Malcolm West. Steinway, dressed like the Tudor "Virgin Queen" of England, introduced each act in a modern vaudeville style, which brought the house down.

Gwendolyn Putterforth, owner and producer of Penguin Pub, welcomed invited guests and passed out tea and "biscuits." She also gave out free passes for tonight's performance to those unable to get in. Barrow Street was bouncing like it's never bounced before, with Pam Mertle and Jonathan Parker-Jones singing "Try to Remember," from The Fantasticks. *Indeed, the show recalled many showstoppers, to the delight of all the tea toddlers.*

Gwendolyn Putterforth and Ruth Steinway certainly have introduced something new and exciting to the New York scene, and without a drop to drink!—except the tea, of course. Bravo to Ruben the Penguin King, who promises more to come.

My heart leapt with joy at the news. Mama must have been pleased to see Ruben the Penguin. I hope she had a VIP seat, if they had such things. This was the morning edition of the *Voice* and had been hand-delivered by a Brooklyn Heights patron on behalf of Penguin Pub to Sr. Paula, who, in turn, came to the library in search of me. "I knew you wouldn't want to wait to find this in your mailbox. It was personally delivered by a distinguished gentleman who only said his name was Ralph."

My first impulse, of course, was to run over to the infirmary. But I knew midmorning was not a good time. I would go in the afternoon when jigsaw puzzling, cemetery gazing, and checkers would be in full swing. Sr. Gertrude would be thrilled and would probably want to begin a thanksgiving novena to St. Genesius.

As it turned out, she did more than that. Unbeknownst to me, she and Sr. Bernadette, the infirmarian, arranged to have chilled bottles of Martinelli's sparkling apple juice, complete with champagne glasses (albeit plastic ones!), fancy napkins, and paper plates left over from the previous year's New Year's Eve. They also got a lovely tray of almond cookies and walnut and prune rugelach from our Jewish deli down the street. *Of course,* I thought, *we're in the middle of Sukkot.* I remember staying overnight in a real *sukkah* with my cousins in Westchester County. The roof was made of wooden beams with wide gaps so we could look out at the stars. Inside were hung fruits and candies, and pictures of all our special *ushpizin*: Abraham, Isaac, Jacob, Moshe, Aaron, Joseph, and David. The monastery was like a permanent *sukkah* as I stood there the night before, gazing at the stars.

I was very touched that the whole infirmary had planned this celebration, all at the instigation of Sr. Gertrude, with the help of Sr. Bernadette, of course, and Srs. Gerard, Benedict, Amata, and Angela. Sr. Bernard was there in her wheelchair with a paper crown over her veil. And poor Sr. Mary Aquinas, who was in the beginning stages of Alzheimer's—she was all sparkles as she drank her fizzy apple juice.

Sr. Gertrude had everyone's glass filled, and then pronounced the toast: "Here's to Penguin Pub Productions and our Ruthie Steinway—mazel tov!" To my surprise, everyone shouted back, "Mazel tov!" Sr. Mary Aquinas shouted, "And Happy New Year!"

I brought out the review and read it aloud, and everyone cheered again. I began to wonder if ol' Sr. Gertrude hadn't slipped something into those Martinelli's bottles. But I realized then how much they had all been praying for a grand opening night, especially since they all knew Ruthie, both from me and from Sr. Gertrude, who followed her career more closely than I did.

Everyone settled down with more fake champagne and the rugelach. (The prune ones were a favorite in the infirmary.) Sr. Benedict wanted me to read the review again, which I did, and when I got to the part about Pam Mertle and Jonathan Parker-Jones singing "Try to Remember," Sr. Benedict broke into song:

"Try to remember the kind of September
When life was slow and oh, so mellow . . ."

160

And everyone joined in, as if on cue:

". . . Try to remember the kind of September
When grass was green and grain was yellow.
Try to remember the kind of September
When you were a tender and callow fellow.
Try to remember, and if you remember,
Then follow . . ."

Sr. Gerard added the "follow . . . follow . . . follow . . ." and everyone applauded themselves and laughed. The melody lingered in the air and, I'm sure, in everyone's mind. The infirmary was a place where they sat and remembered. It wasn't a sad nostalgia by any means. The old sisters seemed to have come to terms with the battle wounds and mostly remembered the happy times or the funny times. There was always more laughter in the infirmary than there were tears.

Poor Sr. Mary Aquinas was still wishing everyone a happy New Year, though she said she couldn't remember which year this was. She said she'd ask her mother, who was "coming to visit me tonight here in this lovely hotel." The sisters wished her a happy New Year back and promised to save some rugelach for Mom. They took care of each other.

That night, after Vespers, I stayed in the choir instead of running back to the infirmary or to the library or to our cell. I just sat and tried to remember how it all happened . . . Ezra, Gwendolyn, Fr. Meriwether, Greta. But most of all, I remembered the Lord. And I followed. *Dear Lord, I remember. I remember the first time I went into St. Vincent's. I remember riding the crosstown bus that evening after visiting Gracie in the hospital, reading the pamphlet about the cloistered Carmelite I would come to know as the Little Flower. I remember that first night in my room when I opened the New Testament and Matthew, Mark, Luke, and John introduced me to You. It's good to remember, isn't it, Lord? Because sometimes I forget. I can get so lost in my own head and in all the peaceful commotion around me that I forget why I am here and that it was You who brought me here. And, Lord, I remember giving You my heart forever and ever. I'm sorry if I have forgotten that and wanted to run away. I can't run away from You. I don't want to run away from You. I know I have never been Your "little flower," but please make me Your little blessing, Your little Baruch.*

The chapel had become dark, the only light coming from the sanctuary lamp flickering on the other side of the grille and the candles in the choir in front of St. Joseph, St. Dominic, and Our Lady, Queen of Hope.

I knew the best way to always remember was to live in the all-pure heart of Mary, our Mother—the Advent heart that pondered all these things. It didn't matter what I did, whether I established the biggest and best library in all the monasteries of the world, or washed dirty dishes in the infirmary kitchen; it didn't matter if I was prioress or house chantress or the scullery maid in the pantry. I belonged to the Lord Jesus in the heart of Mary our Mother, His and mine. I knew that here was where I belonged. I didn't need a sign to prove it.

I nearly missed supper, which would have been a first. I came into the refectory late and knelt for a moment; then Mother knocked, and I got up and went to my place. I was smiling to myself. Tomorrow was Simchat Torah in the Jewish world. The end of the reading of the Torah, and the immediate beginning again: "In the beginning . . ." Our life in this little monastery, tucked away in a corner of Brooklyn

162

Heights, New York, was like a Simchat Torah . . . a finishing and a beginning.

We had a delicious homemade vegetable soup for supper, with Sr. Simon's homemade bread. And afterwards, on the middle serving table, were trays of rugelach, a gift from down the street.

Sunday afternoon was clear and bright—a perfect day to walk outside around our small garden stretched out over a half acre of land. Over the years it had been subdivided by shrubs and flower gardens, and three trellises marked the winding path, each with different flowers. The rose trellis was my favorite, even in early October. There was a swing just past the trellis which could easily hold two, maybe three sisters. It looked onto the rose garden and what used to be a goldfish pond that had turned out to be too difficult to keep it up.

After None I thought I'd pop into the infirmary and thank everyone for the lovely post-show party, which I'm sure was more joyous than the one Ruthie went to. I also wanted to call Gwen and congratulate her, but I knew she must have been busier than ever, especially since they had a show that night. I sat down in the swing for a rest; my feet don't touch the ground, but I can get a swing going with one foot before sitting down. It hadn't been more than three minutes when Sr. Catherine Agnes came strolling under the rose trellis and smiled at me.

"May I join you?" That was a delightful invitation. I don't think Sr. Catherine Agnes had ever asked to join me in a walk, let alone a swing.

"Oh, of course, Sister, that would be neat." *How lame is that*, I thought to myself. *I should have said "awesome" . . . but she's probably no more up on the latest jargon than I am.* I stopped the swing and held it with one foot on the ground while she sat down. Both her feet touched the ground, so I sat back and let her give it a good two-footed push back.

"I heard about the little celebration in the infirmary yesterday—the sisters were still talking about it this morning." She was pleased about all this, not reprimanding.

"Sister Gertrude—well, you know Sister Gertrude, she had the whole infirmary praying a novena to Saint Genesius for the opening night. I think she's followed my sister's career closer than I have."

Sr. Catherine laughed. "It's very good, you know. It keeps the old sisters—like me, mind you—" she chuckled at her own insinuation "—it keeps the old sisters from thinking too much about themselves. I've always felt that once you move into the infirmary, your world becomes very small."

I just *hmmmed* and added, "I know what you mean. Sometimes that world is reduced to special diets and medication. They must feel terribly disjointed from the community."

"They do, although we do have speakers now in all the rooms so they can follow the Office and pray the rosary and *Angelus* along with the community. And they get to hear the reading at supper. But you're right: *my* doctor's appointment, *my* medication, *my* visitors—it can all be very focused on oneself."

"I'm afraid I can be very focused on myself, and I'm nowhere near the infirmary . . . yet." I hoped that didn't sound too self-deprecating. I wasn't good at expressing humility, but the self-focusing was true.

"Oh, I know, Sister. I know." Another push back with both feet. And she chuckled again, "I didn't mean regarding you—well, I do know that about you, but I meant regarding me . . . regarding all of us. We're all self-focused, even after many years of this life."

I didn't respond. This was Scar speaking to me like we were equals. And, of course, we were equals in regard to profession, but she had always been my nemesis looking over my shoulder, scolding me for something or other. I remember being so intimidated by her when I first entered that I didn't think I'd make it through the novitiate.

"I've never thought that about you." There, I said it, and it was meant as a compliment. "I was always afraid of you, but I never thought you were self-centered."

Sister laughed her little down-in-the-throat laugh again. "Yes, we're good at putting on appearances. I was always tough with the postulants and novices, as you know, but I did it to help them grow a thicker skin. You have to be tough to live this life, you know, because sometime along the way, you're gonna get the wind knocked out of you."

I just sat staring at her, mesmerized, because I understood what she meant. After a brief time of silence except for the swishing of the swing, Sister looked at me and said, "You've had the wind knocked out of you several times just these past few months, and look at you, you've pulled through."

"Thank you, Sister, thank you for that, and thank you for being so tough on me in the beginning. It's true, I've been out of breath for a few times, losing Mother John Dominic and my friend Greta. I don't know how strong I've been. I was close to throwing in the towel." I couldn't believe I was sharing all this with her.

"I've figured as much, my dear. I've been keeping an eye on you. It's just in my nature!" And we both laughed at that.

"I think Greta's death has hit you harder even than Mother's, and I know how close you were to Mother."

"I think it has, you know. I didn't see Greta that much this past year. I knew she was ailing from something. She wrote me a beautiful letter of good-bye and shared things about herself which I never knew, over all these years . . . I never knew . . ."

"Well, she must've loved you enough to want to share them with you before she died. And sometimes we do better writing than talking."

"Did you ever want to leave and start all over somewhere else?" I hoped that didn't sound like prying too much. I never thought I would ask her such a personal question.

Sister was silent for a moment, staring at the roses. She pulled her crocheted white shawl tighter around her shoulders, like a sudden chill had swept in under the rose trellis.

"I suppose I have, Sister. You know, I suppose we all do at one time or other. Mine was usually over an injustice, or what I thought was an injustice—this life isn't always fair. But I knew I would be leaving for all the wrong reasons. I'm an old nun, Sister. I've managed to stay out of the infirmary because I'm a tough old bird, and I'll be damned if I let the old devil get to me."

I couldn't help but laugh at her wonderful candor. Coming from her, it was . . . it was truly awesome! She kicked back for another swing and laughed along with me.

"You can't let him get you down. When we start feeling sorry for ourselves, or start comparing ourselves to others, or start getting down on ourselves because we don't have it all together, then the devil gets his nasty foot in the door. You believe there's a devil, don't you?" For a moment I heard the old voice of my postulant directress!

166

"Yes, Sister, of course I do."

"That's good, because I don't think most of the world does. We've psychologized him away as an aberration of our imagination, or the projection of our weaknesses. Even here. When's the last time we've heard a sermon on the devil? Not even before we renew our baptismal promises when we renounce him and all his pomps and works."

Another two-footed pushback. I had never been back that far in that swing in twenty-five years. It was neat. And Sr. Catherine Agnes was on a roll.

"There was a time after my solemn profession when I was thrown into utter darkness. I didn't know if I believed in anything or anyone. This life seemed like the epitome of repression and joyless robotism, if there is such a word. I had been named subprioress and the Chapter wouldn't confirm it, so the prioress named someone else. I didn't have any friends in the community—we weren't allowed to have friends then. I had a brother who had enlisted in the army and was sent to Vietnam. He had two tours of duty, as they called it. He came home on leave after his first and came to see me. I hadn't seen him since my solemn profession. Well, it was during Lent, and I wasn't allowed to see him, even for a half hour. I was so filled with rage at the prioress—I won't say who it was—I was so filled with rage that I could've spit bullets at her like she was the Viet Cong. That was the closest I ever came to leaving. Another sister who witnessed all this told me to take it all to the Lord in prayer. I think I laughed in her face. But she didn't flinch. She repeated herself: 'Take it all to the Lord in prayer, otherwise the devil will win.' I didn't laugh. I knew in that instant that she was right. The devil was winning in the crazy world—people hating each other, killing each other, using each other as objects of their own greed and lust. He was infiltrating the schools and the government and the family, and sports and entertainment too. I saw it all in an instant, even in my darkness and unemotional response to life. I didn't have any revelation of God's love and joy and peace—none of it. But I knew that the devil loathes us. He loathes this monastery of women who dare to love God and praise Him morning, noon, and night, who dare to adore Him all night long. He loathes every breath we take because we sing to God and promise Him our obedience and chastity until death. And you know why the devil hates us so much?"

I don't think she was asking this to be answered. I couldn't say anything anyway. I just shook my head. The swing was slowing down and the air seemed very still.

"He hates us because we belong to Jesus, because we are espoused to the Lord our Redeemer, the Crucified One whose death and resurrection destroyed the works of Satan. In that one instant I saw the truth of this. I saw that the death and resurrection of the Lord saves the world. And this sacrifice, this saving sacrifice, is made present in the Blessed Sacrament. And we adore Him there. And the devil loathes us for it. After that, I was determined not to let hatred, disappointment, rejection, or anything get in the way of mercy and love." The swing had come to a complete stop. Sister's face was not filled with anger; rather, it was a face of peace and acceptance.

"Did you see your brother after Easter?"

"No, he was killed on his second tour of duty. His body was sent home with others. I didn't go to the funeral—we didn't do that at all then."

"Oh, Sister!" I leaned on her shoulder. "I lost my brother in Vietnam also. I never knew you did too."

Sr. Catherine Agnes of Mercy put her arm around me and put her head down next to mine. We just held on to each other there in the rose garden. It was a time when silence spoke louder than words.

We sat up again. Sister kicked back for one last go at the swing. And I told her all about the night we took Mama and Papa to see *Fiddler on the Roof* for their anniversary. And about my brother Josh's gift he had sent weeks in advance to David, the eldest. There was a Timex watch for Papa, and for Mama a beautiful silver brooch with five tiny flowers, each set in a precious stone—one for each of her five children. A week later the telegraph came that Josh had been killed in action. His body never made it back to us. And Mama never wore her brooch again.

I told Sister how that changed me. I began to think about life and death differently. And I told her about Gracie and my going into St. Vincent Ferrer Church to light a candle.

Sister listened intently. She said, "You lit a candle. You see, you were not going to let the devil get to you. And you didn't even know it. You took it all to the Lord in prayer— and look where you wound up!" We laughed. She got up from the swing with great grace for an "old nun," while I had to kind of jump off and catch my balance. Not bad for a nun in her middle ages!

"I'm going to the infirmary to thank the sisters for their party yesterday and to make a huge pitcher of decaffeinated iced tea," I said. "Wanna come?"

"Don't mind if I do. I'm not too keen on the iced tea, but there may be a leftover bottle of champagne."

"It was Martinelli's apple cider, Sister, it wasn't real champagne."

"Ha! That's what you were told. Sister Gertrude and I go back a long time, you know. We theater people know how to disguise things. Props, you know."

"Well, I'll be!" I was shocked and delighted at the same time. "I knew Sister Gertrude was up to something!"

"Oh, she's taught me many a lesson . . . like there's more than one way to kick the devil in the pants."

"How's that?"

"Dance with the Lord and never let go!"

"Oh, I know. It's a *pas de deux*." And off we went, our own *pas de deux* to the infirmary.

fourteen

Autumn months always seem to go by too quickly. I wish they would linger a little longer when the leaves are in full array. This was a time when I especially missed Central Park, but our little array of trees gave us a little color show every year.

Six weeks had passed since Penguin Pub's grand opening, and it had caught on like wildfire. Gwendolyn never made it to Brooklyn Heights, but she called me twice on the phone. Mid-November was the last time.

"M.B., you wouldn't believe the crowds we're getting. And to think, they come to drink tea and watch a show! The show will be changing before Thanksgiving and will have a Christmas-Chanukah theme, as will our menu. Would you believe we made a decision not to serve coffee? It will be a tea-only venue, and only a couple people have complained."

"That's great—" I was trying to get a word in edgewise, but I was also enjoying the excitement in Gwen's voice. "How's Ruthie doing?" I got that in.

"Oh, she's doing great. She's already rehearsing the new show, and decided to advance from Tudor England to Victorian, which, of course, will mean I can pull out all my Victorian jewelry and decorate to the hilt."

"But how's Ruthie doing with . . . you know, her problem?"

"Well, I want to say she's doing fine . . . but I really don't know. She's becoming somewhat belligerent over the smallest things. I don't think she's going to her meetings, and she runs off after the last show with some friends. I'm not sure where she goes or what she does. She's missed a couple afternoons of rehearsals already, which is not like her. But she knocks herself out every show. Everybody loves her."

"Well, tell her I'm thinking of her and hope she'll come visit during the holidays. We only have two weeks left till Advent begins and visiting will be limited, but she knows that. Tell her Sister Gertrude would love to see her too, as would the whole infirmary!" I had told Gwen about our party the first time she called. She said she wished she had known, she would have sent a box of Penguin Pub Pups, her latest creation. They were really just sugar cookies with licorice icing, shaped like miniature penguins. They were almost too cute to eat—Gwen's words, not mine.

I was looking forward to Advent, as I did every year, but this year especially. It was our Simchat Torah—a time of rejoicing and beginning again. I had been dragging myself around trying to get back in the spirit of things. I love how the liturgy really changes the scenery, as Sr. Gertrude would say.

Mother and the Council had finally gotten around to implementing some of the liturgical changes. A change in the *horarium* requires a Chapter vote, and I was surprised that the change to eliminate the Midnight Office had passed by a wide majority! I guess it was good. We get a better sleep and can get seven or eight hours if we go to bed right after Compline. We now have Office of Readings at five thirty and Lauds at six thirty and Mass at eight o'clock. That's a little later than before too, but still early enough for people on the outside to attend and get to work on time.

We also began singing Lauds and Vespers in English; that was a big change. But the psalm tones we use are close to the Latin, and I like praying the psalms in English. We have kept the *Benedictus* and *Magnificat* in Latin though. And Compline is still in Latin.

Mother also said some changes in our charges would be happening come the First Sunday of Advent. I had a feeling my days as librarian were about to be over. A year before, I would have been anxious about that and would have hoped it wouldn't happen, but with Greta's passing, it almost seemed appropriate for me to move on to another charge. I just hoped I wouldn't be in the laundry or in charge of maintenance—especially maintenance, because it's too much of a responsibility, and you have to have your finger on all the workings going on, like boilers and heating systems, electrical networks, and the condition of the roof or the walls in the cloister. I never knew what any of them were, let alone how to fix one. That's what you have supers for. And the laundry was simply too hot and boring. I suppose I could have offered it up if I had been put there, but I suspected some of the younger sisters would take over.

Speaking of the laundry, Sr. Anna Maria had seemed so distant from me lately, even before Mother John Dominic and Greta died. *Something's going on*, I thought, *and she's not telling me.* She used to blab everything to me, but recently she had been acting more withdrawn and didn't seem to laugh as much. Of course, I hadn't been a barrel of laughs myself. But we used to share our gripes and comments about everyone with each other—I avoid saying "gossip," as I told Fr. Wilcox I would try not to indulge in it ("indulge" was his word). I once confessed that I gossiped with another sister about another sister, and he said, *"Tsk, tsk"*—he actually made the sound—"Sister, one should not indulge in gossip. *Tsk, tsk.*" He did it twice. None of my other sins ever merited a single *tsk*. Stealing raisin oatmeal cookies from the infirmary kitchenette cookie jar never got a *tsk, tsk*. Reading a letter that a sister accidentally left in a returned book didn't get a *tsk, tsk*. Not making up an Office I missed didn't merit a *tsk*. And when I told him I let more cats out of more bags, it hadn't fazed him one bit.

Now the one with whom I talked about everybody was one of the everybodies. I decided to suppress it all, however, rather than talk to someone about Sr. Anna Maria. If something was going on, she would tell me when she was ready. Of course, I first wondered if I had done something or said something. But I racked my brain for an entire Vespers, and I couldn't think of a thing I'd done to offend her.

I never talked to her about being with Mother John Dominic when she died. She hadn't come over to the infirmary, at least at the same times I was there. And she hadn't spent any time with me after Greta's death. Even Scar spent time with me and showed an interest in what was going on in my heart and soul.

I feared, of course, that she was going to leave. *But why wouldn't she share that with me? Nobody ever wants to share their heartaches with me*, I thought. I didn't understand it. The only ones who opened up to me were the strangers, or at least one stranger . . .

It was probably three years before all this. Sr. Paula had just begun sitting in the little extern room we call "reception" (reminds me of a five-star hotel in Manhattan!). We usually had lay volunteers there answering the phone and taking care of Mass requests. People would come through the main door of the monastery (not the church): the mailman, delivery-men, and anyone coming in to have a parlor with a sister. Sr. Paula wasn't quite up on what to do with people wandering in off the street, usually looking for a handout or specifically asking for money. This rather elderly woman came in want-ing to talk to a nun. She was obviously having a terrible time. Sometimes such people are content to know that we are praying for them, and Sr. Paula was good at assuring people of that. But it just so happened that I was at the turn collect-ing the mailbag, and the old lady shouted, "I want to talk to you, please, I need to talk to a nun!" I don't know how Sr. Paula took that; after all, she looks just like the rest of us. Maybe there was someone else there whom she was attend-ing to. Anyway I simply told the lady to go into the first parlor on her left.

I went in on our side, and the lady did not stop talking for a second. She told me every sordid detail from her past: how her children had all abandoned her, how her boyfriend stole everything she had in savings and she lost her apart-ment, how she thought she should check herself in somewhere because she was afraid to live in a shelter, how she had a devotion to St. Anthony but she hadn't lost any-thing (she tells me that after her litany of losses!).

I remember my head kind of spinning; it was a whirlwind of troubles. The funny thing was that she was very articulate—manic, but articulate. It was obvious she was well educated but had fallen on hard times. She said she had been married to a soldier who died in Vietnam—like that's what I needed to hear!

I had a lovely holy card of St. Anthony that someone had given to Sr. Paula, who had put it on our "giveaway table." I took it, thinking I'd make a card for Sr. Antonia, our novice who would be making her first profession on Christ the King. But I was inspired to give it instead to this poor woman. She told me her name was Willa. I remember telling her I thought that was a beautiful name. There I was, fibbing again. I couldn't imagine being named Willa. But it seemed to calm her down, just hearing my mellow, non-manic voice. "Willa . . . what a beautiful name."

She blinked a few tears away. *Please, Lord, don't let Willa weep.* Instantly the song popped into my head: "Willow, weep for me . . ." I think it was Billie Holiday. *I'll have to ask Sr. Gertrude*, I thought, *she probably has a recording of it.*

I told Willa I didn't have anything I could give her—no money, no clothes, no place to rest her head . . . but maybe I could give her a little hope. "I want you to take this holy card and go into the chapel and tell Saint Anthony that you are very lost. And then just sit there for as long as you'd like. He will help you find some peace and clarity so you won't have to panic and will know what you should do next. The Lord always opens a door."

It wasn't much, and it was probably very naïve on my part, but it seemed to work. Sr. Paula told me later that night that the old lady was in the chapel for an hour or more and when she left she smiled and said thank you. Sister also gave her two subway tokens.

I thought about Willa a lot that night too. She was just one of thousands wandering around New York, not knowing where to turn. I can't imagine how many are spiritually lost and wandering around, sometimes all their lives.

Well, back to Sr. Anna Maria. She had always appeared a little restless. . . . *But then again*, I thought, *I would be too if I was surrounded by washers and dryers all day.* So I took refuge in my stack of books that needed to be reshelved. It was quiet in the library. I sat down for a little while with the latest issue of *The Sign* magazine—they always had such great covers.

Even three years later, I hadn't forgotten about Willa. I put down the magazine and looked around at the library and felt very warm and safe and secure. I didn't have to worry about where my next meal was coming from or where would I sleep that night. I wasn't feeling guilty so much as safe and secure and grateful, and I made a place in my heart for all those Willas out there, and I prayed for them. I realized it was no accident that Willa had just happened to be there that day when I just happened to be picking up the mailbag.

Willa was still in my mind all during Vespers and afterwards when I stayed to pray. The light had changed in the choir by November. We were back on standard time, so it was already dark by Vespers. The overhead lights were turned off after Vespers, and flickering light from the few burning candles cast long shadows along the floor.

I felt a wave of sadness flood over me like the long shadows: *There are so many lost souls like Willa.* I understood then what is said of our Holy Father Dominic, that he would weep at night and cry, "What will become of sinners?"

It was one of those times when you realize your union with all the Mystical Body of Christ, that our prayers and sufferings, our sacrifices, and even our little triumphs and joys, have an effect on the whole Body. Ruthie thinks our life is sad, and my older sister Sally once told Ruthie (who told me) that she thinks our life is selfish, that it's all about us.

That can happen, of course. We once had a wonderful retreat conference by a Fr. Kitchens, O.P., who said that one of the dangers of the contemplative life is that we become self-absorbed, and so the remedy is to be keenly aware of our place in the Mystical Body, even if we never see the graces and conversions we have a part in for others. He was our Carmelite expert who loved St. Thérèse. "She wrote a beautiful autobiography out of obedience," he told us, "but she was never self-absorbed. She came to realize that her vocation was to 'be love, in the heart of the Church, my Mother.'" We all knew that and loved that quotation. But I didn't always remember it, especially when I became too self-absorbed.

Later that evening, a note in my mailbox from Mother reminded me that she had said she was changing charges in Advent. I knew she would never just surprise us with a charge but would discuss them with the individuals involved. Her note said that she wanted to see me at nine thirty the next morning. That gave me a whole night to obsess over what she might have in mind, and to practice acceptance. I didn't think she would ask what I would like to do; that wasn't her style. Mother Jane Mary, under whom I had become librarian, didn't even discuss; she informed.

I hadn't really thought about what charge I would really like, had it been left up to me. I thought more about which charges I hoped I wouldn't get, like the laundry, maintenance, and the kitchen. Sitting in the presence of the Lord in the Eucharist for my hour of guard, I realized that I would love to be the sacristan. It was a demanding charge, but there would be at least one assistant, and several for the "high holy days." It would be such a privilege to be so close to the sacred vessels of the altar, to dress the chalice every morning, to choose and lay out the vestments for the priest, to repose the Blessed Sacrament at night. I suddenly felt unworthy and decided that the Lord would not want me to be the one to do these things. I can be clumsy and forgetful. I remember once when Sr. Ambrose Marie, the sacristan at the time, forgot to put the priest's host on the paten, and how embarrassed she was when Father held up the empty paten for all to see. Poor Sr. Ambrose had to walk past all of us to go to the sacristy and bring out a host for Father. *But if Mother asks me if I'll be sacristan*, I thought, *I'll say yes, of course.* Maybe being sacristan would help me grow in holiness, and I really wanted that under all my fickle emotions and moods. It would help smooth them out, which living this life already does, but being sacristan would accelerate that, or so I thought. Then again, maybe she was going to ask me to continue as librarian or to train another sister to be that. I knew Sr. Anna Maria had always wanted to be in charge of the altar breads. But we were phasing out that job altogether. *I wonder if she's got an appointment with Mother too*, I thought.

The next morning I was anxious, but hopefully also abandoned, as I softly knocked on Mother's office door.

"Come in . . ."

"*Laudetur Jesus Christus.*"

"*In aeternum.* Sister Baruch, come in and sit down. I'm glad to see you're looking a little more rested these days."

"Thank you, Mother, I am. The autumn weather always invigorates me." I was still anxious, but I was much more at ease than with the last two prioresses.

"Well now, you know, I want to mix up the charges come Advent. I think it's good for us to have a variety of responsibilities and to serve the community in different ways. Maybe like the autumn weather does for you, it can invigorate us when we have a new charge."

"Oh dear . . ." I didn't mean for it to slip out like that. But Mother smiled.

"Don't worry, I'm not putting you in the kitchen!" How did she know I had an aversion to cooking for so many people? Of course, she would have known from the nights when I had the evening meal to prepare. S'mores might not be considered a healthy monastic supper!

"Thank you, Mother. I think the community would thank you too." Mother laughed at that.

"You have done marvelous work in the library, for many years now. I don't know who could ever fill your shoes, but I'd like to give Sister Antonia a try at it, if you would help to . . . what? Train her? As you know, computers are the up-and-coming thing, and I think it's time we made that transition. Sister Antonia has had a little experience with computers, and you can train her in how everything is catalogued."

"I'd be happy to do that, Mother. I'd like to learn about the computer myself."

"Well, that's good, Sister, because I have another charge in mind for you. It's something I've been wanting to do ever since I've been prioress. I was able to talk about it with a couple of the other prioresses too, and it's working remarkably well for them."

180

Oh my, I thought, though I didn't say it this time. *Whatever could she be thinking?*

"I'd like you to be my secretary, for lack of a better word. I am overwhelmed, as you can imagine, with correspondence. We are very unorganized in our mailing lists, our benefactors, and just daily responding to people who ask for our prayers, make donations, and even have theological questions that I guess they are afraid to ask a priest about. You would be wonderful for answering questions and organizing our lists and writing letters."

I didn't say anything yet. I just kind of gulped and wondered if Mother heard it.

"I would set you up in an office next to the bursar's office—she doesn't really need two rooms. You'll have a typewriter and perhaps a new word processor, and probably down the road a computer. You'll be doing a lot of the work of the subprioress without the title or any of the other responsibilities. You would actually be freeing up the subprioress to do her job. Of course, you would also be privy to private things that would remain just between us, but your many years in the library have shown me that you're most trustworthy in all I've just said." She stopped talking. She sat back in her chair and smiled.

"So what do you think?"

"I—I—I'd be very honored to have that job, I mean, charge. And being something brand-new, as you say, I could develop things as we go along, like I did with the library."

"Precisely." She said it like it was the gavel coming down in a court decision.

"Now, that's not all, Sister. I don't want this to be all-consuming, and it could easily become that when you see how much there is to do just in answering mail alone. As you would say, 'Oy, such a blessing this should be?'" And she threw back her head and laughed.

I laughed out loud too. She was really being funny. It was the first time she ever made a joke of my Jewishness, but she did it in a humorous and almost loving way.

"I'm also going to name you assistant infirmarian. This would not involve any of the nursing care, but more just being there and helping the sisters there feel a part of the community. You're already doing this, so I don't want you to stop. I'm just giving it an official title so no one will criticize you for being over there. And four nights in the kitchen fixing supper." She saw my jaw drop. "Only kidding, only kidding." She laughed.

"Such a blessing that would *not* be." And we laughed again.

"Don't mention this to anyone, of course, till I announce it at Chapter. For one, Sister Bertrand doesn't know she's losing a room for her work as bursar. I will send Sister Antonia to you now, however, for the morning work period. She can begin learning right away. She knows about it and is very happy to take over the library."

As elated as I was, Mother's last sentence struck a chord of sadness. I'd be leaving my library. *My* library—that alone was a good reason it should have been done years before! It passed quickly enough. I left Mother's office a couple inches off the ground, or so it seemed. I hadn't felt that joyful in a long time. To think, two months before, I had been in the doldrums, thinking that nobody appreciated me and that maybe I didn't belong here. And Mother made me feel important. Well, that might not be the right word—not so much important, as needed and capable and appreciated.

I was looking forward to Advent now with a different anticipation than ever before. Not saying anything to anybody was the hardest part. Since Sr. Anna Maria and I were no longer kibitzing in the laundry or infirmary kitchenette, it made that part easier. But I was anxious to share it with Sr. Gertrude, who would be sure to put a theatrical spin to it.

Around noon I checked my mail slot out of habit, and there was a letter from Matthew Goldman with a U.S. postmark. Not *Rev.* or *Fr.*, just *Matthew Goldman*. My stomach flipped over. I put the unopened letter on the table next to Squeak; I didn't want to open it. *Dear Lord . . .*

fifteen

The afternoon and evening jubilation was somehow dampened with fear of what was in that letter. At least the return address didn't say *Mr. and Mrs. Ezra Goldman.* That was my hidden fear, that he'd left the priesthood and married Barbara Parker and was teaching social studies in some high school in Boston. The postmark was from Boston, and I remembered Barbara was from there.

I was sitting in the infirmary kitchenette with Srs. Gertrude, Gerard, and Benedict. Summer iced tea had been replaced by hot apple cider. The pumpkin from Halloween still sat plopped in the middle of our round table on top of the oilcloth autumn leaves table cover. The old pumpkin was beginning to droop and look a little moldy. Its triangle eyes were getting shriveled up in the center. I made a mental note to get rid of it when everyone had retired for the night.

Like Ruthie, they all knew Fr. Matthew and the story of our meeting in Manhattan, and that Fr. Matthew was my godfather. They knew he was in Africa for the last ten years. So when they had blessed themselves and were staring at the pumpkin cookies from down the street and the sad-looking pumpkin on the table, all I said was, "I got a letter from Father Matthew but haven't opened it yet. It has a Boston postmark."

Sr. Benedict quipped, "It's not Advent yet, go ahead." And Sr. Gerard added, "Remember when all our mail was already opened for us?" That, of course, sent them on a sentimental journey down memory lane. Only Sr. Gertrude picked up on my anxiety.

"It's probably good news, Sister. He's back in the good ol' U.S.A. and is stationed in Boston, and has been elected provincial." That got a laugh. All eyes were on me.

These sisters may have been in the infirmary, but they were not dumb. They had been through the last fifty years or more of religious life; they probably all knew at least one priest or sister who had left and gotten married.

Sr. Gerard said, "If it's not good news, you're going to find out sooner or later, and if it's good news, you're depriving yourself and all of us of another party, not to mention heartburn from these cookies."

"You're right. I'll open it tonight after Compline."

"After Compline? What are we supposed to do, wait till tomorrow to find out?" Sr. Gerard was leading the pack. All of them stared at me again.

"Okay, I'll go get it and open it here." I headed out the door.

"Pick up a bottle of Maalox while you're there," came the final word from Sr. Gerard.

Every imaginable scenario went through my head as I walked discreetly, as always, to our cell. If he had left, he probably would go back to being Ezra, and the return address said *Matthew*. That was a good sign. Maybe he was just home on leave as he had been several times before . . . although he had always come back to New York then.

I retrieved the letter and, passing the common closet, grabbed a bottle of Maalox, although I'm sure the infirmary had a whole case of the stuff.

When I arrived back at the kitchenette, Mr. Pumpkin Head had disappeared and Our Lady of Fatima was on the table, and the sisters were in the middle of the Third Joyful Mystery. Finishing the rosary, they sat without saying a word, looking at me.

Sr. Gertrude broke the silence. "We decided to pray a rosary for Father Matthew regardless of what that letter says. You once said he used to call Mary his other Jewish mother, so what's there to be afraid of? You're schvitzing, by the way."

She knew she would get me with her Yiddish. "I know I'm schvitzing, I walked too fast. . . . So, here it is." I handed the Maalox bottle to Sr. Gerard and laid the letter on the table.

"Would you like me to read it to you?" Sr. Gertrude was joking . . . I think.

"No, I'll do it." Sr. Benedict slid over a butter knife. I opened the letter and two photos fell out. There was Fr. Matthew in his habit, surrounded by about twenty African boys in shorts and tee shirts. The other one was of him standing by himself under what we presumed was a banana tree, and perched on his shoulder was a black-and-white monkey with a really long tail and beady eyes.

Dear Sr. Mary Baruch,

Greetings from Holy Redeemer Mission in Zimbabwe. Enclosed is a photo of me with all the boys from our new orphanage, a project that has been near and dear to my heart, as you know, for the past three years. We're finally established and financially on good footing. I wish you could see it. The boys come to us through social workers and family care agencies, and the youngest directly from another orphanage run by the Missionaries of Charity.

I thought you would like to see one of the banana trees in our backyard, and my faithful companion, Baruch.

"The monkey," Sr. Gertrude said in case we didn't get it. "The monkey's named after you. How sweet is that!"

"Sweet?" I said. "He names a monkey after me? Not one of his little orphan boys, not a sleek and beautiful pet gazelle, but a monkey!"

"He's kind of a cute monkey," added Sr. Benedict. "I think it's sweet too. He's reminded of you every time he talks to him."

"Thanks a lot!" Everyone thought that was a riot and laughed, including me. "He probably named him Baruch because he eats all the bananas." And they laughed even more. The letter went on:

Thank you for your letter, which just arrived yesterday. I am so sorry to hear of Greta's passing and offered Mass for her this morning. She was such a good friend and influence on you. I think of her whenever I write in my journal. She was the first one to get me to do that.

Wonderful news too about Gwendolyn and Ruthie. I'm looking forward to seeing the new Tea on Thames, but I must confess I'm going to miss the original.

These were exactly my sentiments too, as if I'd ever get to go there again!

I especially enjoyed the "infirmary sisters" praying for a smash hit on opening night. I thought, only in New York! Or rather, only in a New York monastery! I think the cast should come and do a couple numbers for the community in the large parlor!

"Yes to that!" said Sr. Gertrude—of course. The others all nodded their approval and laughed. "We could make it like a Tony Award, and present a . . . a 'Ruben' to Ruth Steinway for Leading Host in a Variety Show." Sr. Gertrude was off and running. The "Ruben," of course, would be a penguin.

"Go on with his letter," said Sr. Gerard, bringing us back to reality.

Please ask your infirmary sisters to pray for me. I haven't been in the best of health. I had a second bout with malaria, and the mission director wants to send me home to the States. I told him I was fully recuperated, but he's not convinced. Nothing has been definitively decided, and won't be until after the Christmas holidays. I'm grateful for that, as I would hate to leave my boys before the big day. We've got some wonderful benefactors preparing Christmas boxes for each of them, which will include baseball uniforms, or at least hats, bats, and gloves. They are more into soccer, but I've introduced American baseball, and they're excited about it.

Between you and me, I've been struggling with other things too. I'm thinking of leaving the Passionists, but after all these years, is it possible, and is it even prudent? Be at ease, dear Sister,

I'm not thinking of leaving the priesthood. That may be another reason the provincial wants me back in the States.

I would love to have a couple hours with you in your parlor and talk about all this. I depend so much on your prayers.

You remember Barbara Parker. She has been here with a team of visiting doctors and dentists. She's leaving tomorrow, and they will fly into Boston, so I've given her a few letters to mail for me. I'm not in Boston.

Know I remember you every day at Holy Mass, and I pray for you and your family and all the sisters at Queen of Hope, especially the infirmary sisters.

Blessings and prayers,
Ezra Matthew

The sisters sat speechless for a change. They were touched by his letter, I know, and deep in their immediate thoughts, already planting him in their prayer; it didn't have to be said.

I too resolved there and then to pray more earnestly for Ezra, that it would all go according to God's holy will. *It will be wonderful to see him after the New Year*, I thought. *That's a Christmas star to look forward to.* Funny how we get kind of nostalgic in the middle ages. Ol' Fr. Ezra Matthew and I would have a lot to reminisce about.

So there were lots of things to look forward to that Advent. Blessed be God in His gifts.

The Chapter was scheduled for Saturday evening after supper. It was also now Christ the King, as Vespers was First Vespers of the Solemnity. Mother had some news about different monasteries and then said she would like to announce the changes in our charges, which would officially begin a week from that night, meaning after First Vespers of the First Sunday of Advent.

"Sister Mary George, you will begin to serve as assistant bursar." This was a good choice, as I think Sr. Mary George had worked in the business world, maybe even ran a business. She was with a teaching congregation for ten years before transferring to us. Her canonical transfer was over, and we had voted at the previous month's Chapter to accept her. Poor thing, she probably hoped to have a life free of accounting and figures, and now she was assistant bursar, which also meant she was in training to be bursar.

"Sister Ruth Mary, you will be in charge of the laundry. We thank Sister Anna Maria for her many years keeping our habits, clothes, napkins, towels, and sheets all washed and cleaned and smelling brand-new." And neatly folded, Mother forgot to mention, neatly folded.

"Sister Anna Maria, you will assist in the altar breads department, and help to make the transition easy. You will also be assistant cook three days a week." *I wonder how she feels about that?* I thought. *She wanted to be head of altar breads years ago, and now that we're phasing it out, she's only helping to end it. Poor thing. She's looking rather piqued.*

"Sister Bernadette Mary, you will move from the infirmary to the kitchen as first assistant." *Oh my, that's a big change. I think the infirmary sisters will miss her gentle way with them. First assistant is a big job, especially with ordering food. She is nutrition-conscious, though—maybe that will help keep us out of the infirmary longer!*

"Sister Joanne, being solemnly professed since the Solemnity of Our Holy Father Dominic, you will serve as infirmarian." We all knew that was coming eventually. Sr. Joanne was a registered nurse before entering. *That's good,* I thought. *She has a lovely way with the elderly sisters. I'll be under her guidance, I suppose, which is fine. I like her.* She had introduced me—well, the whole community—to granola bars.

"Sister Mary Baruch"—*Okay, here we go*—"you have worked many years in the library and have certainly done a marvelous job in bringing it up to date and up to monastic snuff." *Monastic snuff? Oy.* "You will now initiate a new charge as the prioress's secretary. I suppose in the world they call it 'administrative assistant.' You will be in charge of all my correspondence, especially to our benefactors and businessmen. This will also relieve the subprioress of a lot of secretarial work and free her to direct the other charges in my absence. You will also serve as assistant infirmarian three evenings a week.

"And now, to fill in the empty space in the library, Sister Antonia, you will take over as librarian. Sister Mary Baruch, you will assist her if needed." I liked Sr. Antonia. She had been solemnly professed for about a year, and was one who kept an almost perfect silence. *She and the books will get along very well*, I thought. *She may struggle with the German, Greek, and Latin volumes, but don't we all?*

"The other charges all remain as they have been. Our help is in the name of the Lord."

"Who made Heaven and earth," we all replied in unison.

We filed out in silence, with a few whisperings. Sr. Anna Maria came up beside me.

"Mazel tov, Madame Secretary." I didn't know how to take that. Was she teasing or being cynical? So I ignored it and asked instead, "Aren't you happy to finally get out of the laundry?" But she didn't answer me. Strict silence in the cloister . . . although *that* had never fazed her in the past.

* * *

Sr. Myriam, our only novice that year, lit the first Advent candle of our Advent wreath in the middle aisle of the refectory. There was snow predicted for tomorrow, according to Sr. Mary Aquinas, who listened to the radio in the infirmary.

I had remembered to call Gwendolyn before Advent began. Ruthie was not available to talk, Gwendolyn said; she was panicking over her new show. It had opened after Thanksgiving and hadn't gotten very good reviews. I told her about Ezra's letter, and she said to tell him he had a reserved orchestra center seat, for him and his friend the Earl of Grey. Ruben was now sporting a Santa hat (she called it a Father Christmas hat) and the wise-penguins were making their way to the crib. I laughed. The world doesn't really keep Advent and had been into Christmas since before Thanksgiving.

But I was keeping Advent with a happy and renewed Advent heart that year. I fixed up my little office and loved the word processor, which was incredible. Mother didn't mention that my job would begin with Christmas cards and acknowledging gifts and donations. But with this word processor thing, I could save several styles of thank-yous and simply change the name and the amount. It was "awesome."

I had even had to go to the parlor several times already on behalf of Mother and arrange for special Christmas gifts for special people, like our workmen and volunteers. It was the first time I had met with Max, the owner of the Jewish deli down the street. He loved my ideas about a gift basket with delicacies from the store. He said he'd make up a few samples and bring them to show me. He was pleased and surprised that I was so acquainted with their products. I just smiled.

The Third Sunday of Advent I was going to the infirmary and caught myself wanting to whistle down the cloister, I was so happy. Little did I realize what the morrow would bring.

Monday of the Third Week of Advent will be forever emblazoned in my memory. I was walking down the front cloister towards the mailboxes when Sr. Paula met me. It was just after Terce.

"There's an old lady in the parlor who asked for you."

"An old lady? My goodness, do you think old Willa is back?" I was just at the parlor door when Sister said, "No, she asked for Rebecca Feinstein."

My hand began to tremble as I opened the door.

sixteen

I opened the door slowly, my hand still trembling. A woman was standing with her back to the grille, but she turned when she heard the door close.

"MAMA!" My whole body began to tremble. I wobbled over to the grille. There she was, her silver hair falling softly from beneath a black felt cap.

"My Becky! Oh, Becky . . ." She put her hands on the grille, and I put mine through the open grate and enclosed her fingers in mine.

"Mama" was all I could get out, and for the next three minutes we held on to each other's fingers and sobbed our tears of welcome.

Mama looked up at me through the lattice work of the grille. "Look at you, my baby . . . a real nun. You . . ."

I knew Mama was having a hard time speaking, but I was tuned in to every syllable and every sigh and wouldn't let go of her fingers.

"You look so beautiful." That just brought a flood of tears rolling down my cheeks. My nose was running and my lips were still trembling. I had to let go to retrieve my handkerchief (a mere Kleenex couldn't handle this one). Mama followed suit and dug in her handbag for a handkerchief.

I then noticed her shoulders were slumped and her head down.

"Mama, what is it? Are you okay?"

She looked up at me, the tears still falling. "It's Ruthie." She took a deep breath. "Ruthie was found dead this morning around four o'clock."

"Oh, Mama!" I pulled over the wooden chair next to me and sank into it. "Oh, dear God. I don't believe it . . . oh my, oh my." I was finding it hard to breathe. *Ruthie dead—it can't be.*

"The police came to the apartment and woke me up. Gwendolyn was with them—the dear girl, she looked like she had been dragged through I don't know what. Oy, the poor schlimazel. She insisted the police come to me in person and not phone me. And she came with them. She's with me now, in the chapel."

"What was it, Mama?"

"It was those damn drugs, God forgive me in such a place." She looked around like an alarm might go off, but then she just stared at the grille. "God forgive me for not seeing that Ruthie was in such trouble. I should have seen it coming. Ruthie was not herself, but I thought it was just the showbiz stuff. Gwendolyn said it was crack cocaine. She died of crack cocaine." She sank into a chair, still inches from me through the grille.

We both sat in silence.

"Becky," Mama was looking through the grille, her eyes puffy from crying, her mascara making black rivulets down her cheeks, her upper lip trembling. "Becky, my darling

Becky. I'm sorry I have never come to see you. Your father, may he rest in peace, spoke of how beautiful you looked as a nun." She gave a little sob. "I just couldn't bring myself to come here. But I can see it now. You haven't aged a bit, and your face is so peaceful."

"Peaceful?" I said. "Such a blessing to see you, dear Mama. I can't believe it."

"I couldn't let you find out about Ruthie with a phone call either. Ruthie and you were so close. She used to say you were praying for her all the time." The frog got caught in Mama's throat. She blew her nose again and wiped her tears, which made the mascara smudge even worse. Good thing we didn't have mirrors in the parlor. But I looked beneath all that—Mama was still so beautiful.

"Dear Hannah of a Thousand Silver Hairs." I managed to get it out. Mama remembered.

"I know you're not allowed to ever come out from behind these bars, but—"

"I can, Mama. I can." Before I could say anything more, both our parlor doors opened. On my side, Mother Agnes Mary came in swiftly and came right over to embrace me with her own sigh and a few tears. I was very moved. Mama saw this too, and her eyes sprang new tears watching this.

On her side of the parlor, Gwendolyn came through the door, a silk scarf around her neck flying in the breeze. She was already sobbing when she saw me. She made her way to the grille, her fingers already through its square bars.

There we were. Four weeping women.

Gwendolyn had not been in the chapel. She had asked to see Mother in the parlor right away. That's how Mother knew, and she came in as soon as she learned.

Mother was the first to speak. "Mrs. Feinstein, I cannot tell you how sorry we are for your loss. And how grateful we are that you have come here to tell Sister in person. And thank you, too, Gwendolyn, for bringing her here. I have sent Sister Paula to get some coffee and something to eat. Tell us, if you can, what is happening now and if there is anything we can do to help."

Mama was genuinely touched by Mother's quiet voice and her concern. Gwendolyn had pulled over another chair and was sitting next to Mama, and she took her hand. I looked at Gwendolyn and didn't—couldn't—say a thing. We both blinked away our tears.

Sr. Paula knocked quietly and entered with a tray with a Pyrex coffeepot full to the brim, four cups and saucers, and a lovely cut glass plate with miniature cheese Danishes. Mama looked at it all with wide eyes as her face streaked with smudged mascara. "Such a blessing—cheese Danishes?" And we all laughed. It was so incongruous after a flood of tears.

"Oh, Mama, you haven't changed."

"And let me tell you, Mrs. Feinstein," Mother Agnes said, "this daughter of yours has us all thanking God for 'such blessings' He sends us every day."

Mama smiled and looked at me again with unbelieving eyes, "Such a beautiful nun I should have?" Poor Gwendolyn scrunched up her face, searching in her huge bag for a hankie. Sr. Paula, meanwhile, had our two cups filled and put on the turn, along with a Danish each, which we probably wouldn't eat. Mama watched it all. The turn always fascinates people.

Mama took a few sips of her coffee, without comment, and then said, "We will not have a viewing, of course, but

Ruthie's body has been taken to our funeral home. Our synagogue has a *chevra kadisha*, so she will be washed and dressed in a plain dress and wrapped in a *sovev*."

"A *chevra kadisha* is a group of people from the synagogue who prepare the body and take care of the arrangements," I said. "It means a 'holy society,' or I guess a 'burial society.' The *sovev* is like a shroud that will go all around her. Is that right, Mama?" I was doing my best.

"Yes, that's right. You remember. Such a blessing we have, to live so close to the synagogue, practically across the street. That's where the service will be tomorrow late afternoon or evening. Sally is flying in from Chicago tomorrow, and my son David is at a conference in Brussels. He's been called and hopefully will fly in tomorrow morning. Then we go to the cemetery. She'll be laid to rest next to my Ruben." Mama's voice cracked again. She paused and took another sip of coffee. "This coffee's good, but it could take a little milk." Gwendolyn was out the door in a flash, I think to get some milk, and to get a hold of herself!

Mama went on. "I'm not sure what will happen, whether we will say *Kaddish* at the cemetery or at the synagogue. Probably the synagogue, because we can be sure of a *minyan*."

"That's ten people," I said quietly. "You have to have ten people to say *Kaddish*."

"We are not the most observant Jews, but we keep Shabbat, and we'll go to my apartment afterwards and sit *shiva* for the night."

Mother looked at me as I explained, "Sitting *shiva* is when everything is over, and you go home and people come to pay their respects and bring you food. *Shiva* means 'seven,' and in a really orthodox home one keeps this mourning for seven days."

Mama listened intently, amazed, I think, at my explanations. "It is our way of mourning," Mama added.

At that point Gwen had returned with a little pitcher of milk. She refilled Mama's cup with the requested addition.

Mother Agnes Mary had remained silent, taking all this in. She spoke very softly to Mama.

"We have the custom now of going to our family's funerals. Years ago we did not do this, as the rules governing our cloister were, shall we say, stricter. Today the rule of charity has loosened some of our old ways. Sister Mary Baruch would be able to go home with you today and be with you tonight, so you won't be alone. Since you are just across the river, she may stay overnight in your home if you have a room for her and are comfortable with that, or she may return each evening here and go back in the morning. It's entirely up to you."

"You mean she could come home with me today? To West 79th Street? Oh my." And Mama began to cry a little. "That would be such a blessing. Ruthie would be so happy to know that. My Ruben would be so happy."

"What about David and Sally, Mama?"

"Sally has her old room, and you still have Ruthie's room. David's just across the park. If they don't like it that Ruthie's sister, the nun, should be there, they can go fly a kite."

In another context that would have been hilarious, but none of us laughed. I think I was more stunned by Mama's attitude than anything else.

"Such a blessing it would be."

That's all Mother Agnes Mary needed to hear.

"If it's agreeable with you, we will prepare a little lunch for you in our guest dining room, and Sister will go and put a few things together. She is free and has my blessing to go with you. We don't want to do anything to upset you or your family, but I know it would mean the world to Sister to be able to be a part of this, at least a part of the parts she can be. Does that make any sense?"

I think Mama was speechless, which says a lot. I certainly was myself. But I'm sure Mother could tell from my expression how grateful I was. Gwendolyn took Mama with her to the dining room, and Mother waited for me in the cloister.

"I am so sorry, Sister, about your sister. It must be a great shock to you and to your mother. Isn't it something, though, that it took your sister's dying to bring your mother here? God's mysterious providence. Now, listening to your mother, I know you would not really have to go until sometime tomorrow, but that would mean your mother will be all alone tonight. I think God has worked it out for you to be with her. You can discern when you are together what you should do by way of the services, and do what you think is the best thing."

"Yes, Mother. All of this hasn't really sunk in yet! I'm terribly grateful to you for . . ." I started to choke up again.

"I know, my dear, but we are your family too, and we want what is best for you. Mother John Dominic used to talk to me about your mother, and it was always her great desire that there would be a reconciliation before—well, before your mother passed away. I'm awfully sorry it took your dear sister's death, but perhaps this is Mother John Dominic's first miracle."

By that point I couldn't speak at all. How would I ever get through this?

"Now, you go and pack a night bag for yourself. And stop by my office. I will give you . . . what? A hundred dollars to cover cab fares. When you know the details, you call me, so I can put up a notice for the community."

"Thank you, Mother. The sisters in the infirmary? They will be very upset to hear this."

"I will go there myself and tell them. You know they will immediately begin to pray, for both your sister and certainly for you. That your mother came here today, I think, may also very well be an answer to their prayers."

I don't even remember what I put in the overnight bag: my night habit and veil certainly, and my cappa, a toothbrush, my slippers, and my breviary. Mother handed me a little black purse, like a pouch with a zipper, and inside were ten ten-dollar bills and four quarters and a key to the front door of the monastery. There was also a slip of paper with Mother's private phone number, which I've never called in all my life; I didn't even know she had one!

"Do you have room in your bag for this?" She handed me a neatly folded black shawl—not heavy, like a woolen or yarn shawl, but a light cotton.

"Well, I am taking my cappa. I thought that would be appropriate."

"Oh, of course, that's most appropriate. Sometimes a little extra wrap helps if it's chilly out. This used to belong to Mother John Dominic. I think she would be happy to know you have it with you."

I was very moved by this. I tucked it in my bag. I asked Mother to pray for me, which she promised to do. Then she gave me a hug. "You call me at any time. We'll be praying for you. Now, Gwendolyn and your mother are waiting for you in the guest dining room."

I let myself out of the enclosure door and down the short hallway to the dining room. Mama was standing there waiting for me, and as soon as I walked in she began to tremble again. There was no grille here separating us. We fell into each other's arms and had a good cry all over again.

Gwendolyn, trying to keep her stiff upper lip (and not doing a very good job of it), headed for the door. "I'll be out front, getting a cab. Don't be too long."

A couple minutes had passed when Sr. Paula popped in and told us the cab was here. Mama and I headed out arm in arm. Gwendolyn insisted on sitting up front with the driver so Mama and I could have the back seat. And off we went.

"I have lots of money, Gwen." I fidgeted in my habit pocket to get the pouch.

"You put that away. This is on me."

There I was, in a cab with my mother, crossing the Brooklyn Bridge. It was surreal. It had been more than twenty-five years since I'd been in Manhattan. Mama had taken off her felt cap and let her hair fall naturally. She was in her mid-seventies, but looked like her fifties, or maybe early sixties. She had been able to wash her face and didn't put on any more mascara or lipstick. She looked even younger without all that. Her eyes were a bit puffy, but clear and alert. She kept looking at me and stroking my arm. It was like she was trying to make up for these twenty-five years of not seeing me. Whatever fear was behind that decision had been washed away with our flood of tears.

We were driving around the tip of Manhattan past the World Trade Towers and heading uptown on the West Side Highway. Gwendolyn leaned over towards the driver and whispered something I couldn't catch. There was a plexiglass barricade between the front seat and the back seat. It was like a taxi grille. It was missing a "turn" but had a movable slot where one would put the money. The driver was wearing a kind of men's turban and had a strange name on the license displayed next to the meter, which was already up to over ten dollars. I couldn't believe it!

When we got to Greenwich Village the cab turned right onto Christopher Street heading east. It was then that I realized what Gwendolyn was up to. I rapped on the plastic enclosure. There were holes in it as well, so one could talk to the driver.

Gwendolyn swung around and talked to me through the plexiglass grate. "I know what you're thinking, M.B. We're just going to go by the place so you can see it. That's not breaking any rules."

So I laughed and sat back and enjoyed the ride. The Village looked as seedy and interesting as ever, from all the little shops lining Christopher Street to the subway intersection where Seventh Avenue crosses over. We made our way to Barrow Street, and there, in black and white neon lights, was a huge penguin, tipping his hat. Penguin Pub.

Gwen told the driver to pull over in front. The show was advertised on the front window, but now a wide banner stretched across:

All shows cancelled till after Christmas as we mourn the passing of our dear Ruth Steinway.

We sat there in silence reading it. Gwen finally said, "I wanted to make sure they got it up. Drive on—West 79th Street between Columbus and Amsterdam."

Mama was again speechless and didn't say anything till 23rd Street. "You will lose a lot of good holiday money . . . Ruthie would want the show to go on."

"We lost a thousand times more than money, Mrs. Feinstein, when we lost Ruthie. The show will go on again, but the Penguin needs to mourn too." And she couldn't say any more.

I took Mama's hand as we drove up Eighth Avenue. I was amazed at all the people on the street. Of course, it was right before Christmas. Everything was decorated to the hilt. We didn't go by way of Sixth Avenue, or I would have caught the back of the public library and Bryant Park. I would have liked to have seen the wreaths on the lions out front. I was looking at the city like a tourist coming to New York for the first time, mesmerized by it all.

Gwen leaned into the driver again, telling him to stop. "Pull over at the corner, right now." And once the cab stopped she leapt out the door. I had to scrunch down to see where she was going. And when I saw it, I didn't know whether to laugh or cry. She was buying two soft pretzels on the corner. She returned in a flash, opened the back door, and handed them to me.

"Welcome home, M.B.!"

Mama and I shared the pretzels, of course. It was like the best treat I'd ever had.

Mama said, "The salt. They put too much salt on these things. And it's too dry. This one is—" and she stopped and looked at me "—this one is too dry, but delicious. Eat your pretzel before it gets cold."

The cab swung around Columbus Circle. I couldn't believe how much it had changed, but the old movie theater was still there. Lincoln Center was a sight to behold even in midafternoon: *The Nutcracker* was advertised everywhere, and a beautiful Christmas tree filled the center of the plaza. The Metropolitan Opera House glistened in the afternoon sun. And before our pretzels were completely gone, we were turning onto West 79th Street. Gwendolyn got out and opened the door for us like she was a doorman. She hugged both of us and said she couldn't stay but would be in touch. She got back into the cab, in the back seat now, and off she went.

Mama and I watched the cab zip down the street, and we turned, and there was my old home. It looked older. Large potted shrubs on either side of the door were new, and the door itself was not what I remembered, but it was the same entrance. The doorman, of course, didn't know who I was. He bowed to my mother, who didn't say a word to him and took my arm as we walked to the elevators. The lobby still smelled the same.

How can I describe what it was like, walking into the apartment where I grew up? I reverently kissed my hand and touched the *mezuzah* on the door lintel. I remembered when Papa put it on the door brand-new. I must have been five years old then, but I remembered.

We stepped inside. "Oh, Mama, it is so sad to be here because of why I am here. I still can't believe Ruthie is gone. I expect her to run down the hallway here, yelling out something outrageous that she just read in the theater section of the *Times*." I looked down the hallway towards the front parlor and could almost see Papa sitting there in his chair reading the paper.

I followed Mama into the kitchen, which looked totally different to me. It had been done over a couple times.

"I have a microwave—it's such a blessing when you live alone. Sit down in my new kitchen chairs. They should be more comfortable for what they cost, but your brother bought them for me, I can't complain."

I sat down, not saying anything, and just took it all in, not believing I was there.

"That pretzel was so dry—we should have something to drink." Mama headed for the fridge, and pulled out a large bottle of Mogen David elderberry wine. "It's a little early in the afternoon, but it's not every day my Becky comes . . ." The words stuck in her throat. She took two wine glasses out of the cupboard and sat down. She shakily poured two full glasses of wine. "Welcome home, my Jewish nun. Tell me all about yourself."

seventeen

Mama and I sat at the kitchen table till the sun went down. I was feeling a bit woozy, and I knew Mama was too when she started to repeat herself. I had not eaten anything since the pretzel! So I convinced her to go in and wash her face and change into something more comfortable, and I would fix us something to eat.

"My Becky is going to cook? This I have got to see." And she toddled off to her bedroom. I had left my overnight bag in the entranceway, and Mama picked it up and put it in my room. I scrounged around the kitchen looking for stuff to cook, but there were only some frozen soups in the freezer and a few plastic containers of leftovers. There was an unopened container from Zabar's: chicken livers. Perfect. I also found a box of whole wheat crackers, some saltines, and some stuffed green olives.

"Mama, I lied. I'm not going to cook tonight. There isn't anything here to cook, and tomorrow night we'll have more than we can eat. I'm gonna call out for Chinese. Is there some place you like that delivers?"

Mama came out in a housecoat and slippers. "I'm not getting ready for bed, just getting comfortable, like you said. The Cherry Restaurant on Columbus has the best Chinese, and they deliver. The menu is by the phone, with their number. I'll call. What do you want?"

"I haven't ordered Chinese in over twenty-five years, and you're asking me what I want?" I knew I shouldn't order pork or shrimp, Greta and my favorites. "Order me whatever you're getting."

"White rice or brown?"

"I get white, but Ruthie always gets brown . . . so I'll have the brown. And Mama, I'm paying for it. Mother Agnes Mary gave me a wad of money, and Gwen paid for that cab ride."

"I should argue with a nun?" We hugged each other again. It would be hugs all night long, which was just fine. We had many years to get caught up on. "Now you go and get in something comfortable," she said.

I laughed. "I am in something comfortable, Mama, this is it! I have another habit that I sleep in, but it's not much different from this. But I'll go and wash my face."

Walking into my old room which I had shared with Ruthie flooded me with such memories and emotion. There over her bed were the Comedy-Tragedy masks. There was just one bed in the room now, but the night table was still there, and on the bottom shelf, our old Maxwell House coffee tin where we'd save our allowance money for movie tickets. She had a vanity table and bench, with a big round mirror, and a dozen pictures of herself, mostly taped to the mirror. But on the bottom right side was a small round photo of a Dominican nun standing behind a grille, grinning from ear to ear. Ruthie had taken that at my first profession. I'm glad I was grinning and not looking sad.

I had brought my penguin slippers with me, which I slipped on, and I made my appearance back in the kitchen. Mama was on the phone, which I hadn't thought about before. I thought we'd be undisturbed for the entire evening, but of course the phone would be ringing off the hook once the evening papers had come out.

The doorman buzzed the apartment, so I opened the door for the delivery boy, who didn't know what to make of me. I'm not sure if he'd ever seen a nun before. I paid for the Chinese food and gave him a good tip—some things I remember! He did a profound bow and walked backwards.

I touched the *mezuzah* again, thinking, *It's still here after all these years.* The Word of the Lord: "Hear, O Israel, the Lord your God is God alone." In my mind I added, *And the Word became flesh and dwelled among us.* How close Mama and I both are to the Word of God.

That was my little meditation as I was unwrapping the Chinese food (which smelled as wonderful as it did twenty-five years before). God has revealed Himself and made known to us His Name and His will. The Law, this Torah, is at the heart of Judaism and so beautifully revered in the *Sefer Torah*, the handwritten parchment scroll which contains the five books of Moses. The world doesn't believe that God has spoken. "I am the Lord your God. Have no other gods besides Me." *Maybe idolatry is still the biggest sin in the world*, I thought. *And when did they begin to serve Chinese food in these Styrofoam containers?* Only the rice came in the old-fashioned cartons with thin metal handles.

Mama joined me in the dining room. "That was Sally on the phone. She'll be in around noon tomorrow. She couldn't believe you were here and wondered what you were wearing."

"And what did you tell her?"

"I said, 'She's wearing nuns' clothes, what do you think? The dress goes all the way to the ground and is all white, except for the veil—that's black.' I told her it's quite beautiful, and you still look like you're twenty-five years old."

I laughed. "I wouldn't go that far. I don't quite look twenty-five without the veil."

"You have to wear that all the time, huh?" Mama wasn't sounding impudent, just curious. And before I could answer, she mused, "I guess it's like Orthodox Jewish women who never show their hair except to their husband. They always have the beauty of their hair covered, with a scarf or even a wig." Looking at my veil again, she said, "It must be pretty hot in the summer . . ."

"It is, and you know me, how I hate to schvitz. But we offer it up. I love your comparing it to the Orthodox women—I'm gonna use that myself."

Mama smiled. "Sally said she can't wait to see you. Wait till you see her! I think she found all the weight you've lost. And she quit her job with the paper, after all those years, and now she's a dog barber or something like that, along with her partner."

"Ruthie told me that some time ago now. I didn't know what she meant by 'partner': a business partner, right?"

"Have another glass of wine." Mama brought another bottle of Mogen David into the dining room. "You're gonna need it. Such a family I have! Her partner is her lesbian girlfriend."

"A thespian, like Ruthie, that's nice."

Mama started laughing. "Lesbian, Becky, not thespian."

"Oh my . . ." Mama couldn't stop laughing. I don't know if it was my mistake, the Mogen David, or just the release of the day's stress. But we couldn't stop laughing.

"The lesbian, she's a nice girl, but she kind of bosses Sally around, if you can believe that. And you know what her name is? Mitzie!"

"Mitzie?" I repeated. "Her name is Mitzie? That sounds like one of the dogs' names." And we both got laughing our heads off. We finally settled down with our chicken moo shu and chicken with broccoli and bean curd with mushrooms. "Mama, you ordered enough food for an army."

"You should eat up, I've never seen you looking so thin. Don't they feed you in that place?"

"They feed us fine—too good, sometimes. We even have a great Jewish deli down the street that keeps us in pastry, bagels, and even challah once in a while. We have our own baker though, Sister Simon, who makes great homemade bread at least three times a week. But no one can match your challah." Mama just smiled.

We dug into the moo shu before we dug into the Sally-and-Mitzie story.

"I always kind of wondered about Sally and her roommates," I said. "You told me all about the one she brought home for Thanksgiving—the Chicago cop, Bobbie. She had hair like . . . well, she had hair like I have under this veil." And I laughed at myself.

"Oy, don't I know," said Mama, taking a big sip of wine. "What's a mother to do? I don't understand it. I don't think your father would be happy to know this. I don't ask any questions. Years ago, I thought it was just a phase she was going through, you know? Your generation was experimenting with everything. I thought, 'My Sally, she just needs to meet the right man who will sweep her off her feet.' But it never happened—instead she brings Bobbie and Charley and Mitzie home for Thanksgiving. It was our Ruthie who told me what's up. So what's a mother to do? It's her life, and I know I can't do anything to change that."

I didn't comment on that. I knew she was talking about Sally, but maybe she had to wrestle with all her children's so-called lifestyles: Sally's, Ruthie's, probably David's too . . . and, of course, me. I had always thought I was the biggest black sheep in the family, but maybe Mama had come to see that I was a white sheep with a black hat. Papa once told me that Mama thought my becoming a Catholic was just a phase too, that I just needed to meet the right Jewish boy to sweep me off my feet. Of course, I did—but Mama didn't quite get that either!

The phone rang, and Mama left me in my thoughts with moo shu chicken and brown rice. The brown rice was really good. I made a mental note: *We should have "Chinese night" once in a while in the infirmary. I don't think they could handle the moo shu or the bean curd, but you never know.*

Mama returned, and before she could take a bite the phone rang again. She didn't even sit down. She came back five minutes later with a glass plate, on which she piled her supper.

"See, I can microwave this and it will be hotter than when it arrived. That was Rabbi Stein. He's the new rabbi at the reform synagogue on 76th Street. We will have the service there at three o'clock tomorrow, the burial right afterwards, and then come back here. I'll call the funeral director in the morning. He'll know all that, but if you want, we can go to see the body before they close the lid. I think it would just be the two of us, Becky, and maybe that's what God wants." Mama hustled off into the kitchen before I could say anything. *It's nice*, I thought, *Mama is thinking about God's work in all this.*

I heard the microwave ding, and Mama came back, her chicken with broccoli steaming on the plate. "I haven't heard back from David. He might not make it." She didn't sound sad or terribly disappointed, just kind of resigned to the fact. "I still can't believe you are here."

"Oh, that reminds me, I should call Mother Agnes Mary around seven o'clock and let her know everything's okay, and probably Gwendolyn too. She'll want to know what's up."

"Of course, and how about the lovely lady who you lived with? Is she still working at the library? And tell me, whatever became of your old boyfriend that became a priest? I can't think of his name . . . Ezra!"

So I filled Mama in on Greta's passing, and assured her—again—that Ezra was never my boyfriend and that he was a missionary priest in Zimbabwe. I'm sure Mama had no idea where that was, but she pretended to know. The phone rang again, and while Mama gabbed to whomever, I washed up the dishes and put away the leftovers. Then I wandered into the front parlor and sat down in Papa's chair. Under the television was a collection of VHS tapes. I knew that because people gave some to us as gifts, and on a rare occasion we'd actually watch a movie. I glanced over Mama's collection: *Oliver, Fiddler on the Roof, Showboat, 42nd Street, Anything Goes* . . . and there it was, *The Sound of Music*! It had been *The Sound of Music* which had changed Papa's image of Catholic nuns. Maybe Julie Andrews and Peggy Wood were still pulling off their magic on Mama!

I heard Mama holler from the kitchen, "Coffee?" I thought that was a good idea. After all, we did have the night ahead of us, and Mogen David and I hadn't been palsy-walsy for a long time!

I called Mother at seven o'clock, and she was grateful for the call and happy that everything was going along well. I told her about the times for everything, and that I wasn't sure if I would stay over tomorrow night, but I would let her know. She asked about sending flowers and I told her not to—it wasn't really a Jewish thing, and we would be sitting *shiva* all evening. About my staying over a second night, she told me to do what I felt was best, and especially to make the most of the reunion with my mother. She also told me she went to the infirmary and told the sisters there. They insisted they pray an extra rosary immediately for Ruthie's soul, and that we should have a memorial service for her at the monastery—not a Mass, but a "para-liturgical service."

"I must say," Mother said, "the sisters in the infirmary are up on all the latest. Sister Benedict said something like the Office of Readings would be good, from the Hebrew scriptures and psalms. And Sister Gertrude chimed in, 'And maybe something from a show she was in.' I could see her already dreaming up something! Something from a show? That must be the 'para' part of para-liturgical!"

"I hope she's not planning on any liturgical dancing." And Mother laughed along with me.

I thanked Mother again and asked her to remember me at Compline, which I knew they would be praying in less than an hour. I couldn't reach Gwen—apparently she was not even at Penguin Pub.

Mama and I settled down at the kitchen table again, close to the phone and the coffee. Almost like it was on cue, there was a knock on the door. Mama went, and it was Mrs. Hutner, her neighbor, who wanted to express her condolences and handed Mama a plate of double chocolate fudge brownies. Mama invited her in, but she made excuses and said she would come in again tomorrow evening, and would get things ready for us while we were at the cemetery.

"Such a blessing to have such neighbors. When I am in Boca, she takes care of all my mail, comes in and waters my plants, and airs out the place before I come home. She always has a microwave dinner waiting for me. My friend, Esther Bellsey—you remember her—she died last summer. That's why I'm not in Florida right now. It was Esther's condo, and her son, the lawyer, took it over and sold it, the schmuck."

Mama hadn't changed a bit. She could praise you and insult you in the same sentence. I wondered how Fr. Wilcox would handle the likes of Hannah Feinstein.

The phone and door both sounded at the same time. Mama took the phone and waved at me to get the door.

I opened the door and two neighbors, I presumed, nearly dropped their covered dishes when they saw me.

"I'm Mrs. Levinson in 9-H, and this is my granddaughter, Leah. Are we at the right place?"

"Yes, Mrs. Levinson, come in. Mama's on the phone. I'm her daughter, Rebecca, but my friends call me Sister Mary Baruch. How kind of you to come over."

They came in, casserole lids clinking. "Let me help you with these." And I took the larger one from Mrs. Levinson, who had momentarily lost her voice. The granddaughter, maybe fifteen years old, followed me into the kitchen. Mama waved at her from the phone and said, "I'll be right out."

Regaining her voice, Mrs. Levinson said, "We're so sorry to hear about Ruth's sudden death. We didn't know she had a sister."

"How kind of you to think of Mama. It's been a very trying day for all of us. Ruth has two sisters, me and an older sister who lives in Chicago."

"And where do you live?"

"I live just across the river in Brooklyn Heights."

And with that, Mama came bounding into the room. "Imogene and little Leah, thank you for those lovely casseroles—you remembered how much I love your tuna and noodles. I see you've met my daughter, Sister Baruch. My deep dark secret is out of the bag, and I'm glad she is."

So I've been Mama's deep dark secret, I thought. *This should be an interesting couple of days.*

"May the nun in the family offer you a glass of wine?" I looked at both of them and instantly won Leah's full approval. No one had ever offered her a glass of wine.

"Thank you so much, but we can't stay. Leah's dad will be by shortly to pick her up. But it's been very nice to meet you. I'm sorry it has been under these circumstances, but perhaps another time we could have that glass of wine. I'd love to hear all about your life. I didn't know there were still nuns around."

"Oh yes." It was Mama this time. "The monastery is on a lovely street in Brooklyn Heights, and the Mother Superior is . . . well, she's such a blessing to know her." I couldn't believe my ears, and my smile certainly betrayed the tears I felt gathering behind my eyes. Mama sounded like she and Mother had been friends for years. "The service for Ruthie is at Temple Beth Sholom tomorrow afternoon at three o'clock." And with that the Levinsons did a quick about-face and departed as quickly as they had come in.

Mama shut the door and moved me into the kitchen by the arm. "The old biddy—the news that I have a daughter a nun will be known in the Hadassah and half the building by nine o'clock tonight." And she giggled.

I think Mama was taking quite a delight in all this, and I was thrilled to go along with it all. I glanced down the hallway again at Papa's empty chair and thought, *Mother Agnes Mary thinks Mama's coming to the monastery may have been Mother John Dominic's first miracle—but she's with Papa now, and look what they can do together!*

"Dump the tuna casserole in the garbage, but save the creamed string beans and almonds. I think those double chocolate fudge brownies could stand a little Mogen David." And with that, the doorbell rang again.

"What'd I tell you? Half the building knows you're here. . . . You go and open it."

Laughing, I went to the door and opened it. And there stood Lady Gwendolyn Putterforth, who trilled, "Chardonnay, anyone?"

eighteen

Names: *only we human beings among all creatures give names to things, and to places, and to ourselves. Our names identify us—someone once said they capture our very essence. When we know people's names we "have them," and until then we don't know who they are. It's no wonder that usually the first thing we do is give someone our name or ask someone, "What's your name?"*

Such thoughts were going through my head as I sat silently in the limo with Mama and Sally and Aunt Ruth. Everything had gone quite smoothly. Mama and I had gone to Hirschfeld's Funeral Home at one o'clock in the afternoon. This would be the most difficult part of the whole day, and I was so grateful to be there with Mama. Lydia Hirschfeld met us at the door and didn't blink an eye when she saw me. We looked like quite a pair. Mama was in her best black dress and a lovely black jacket over that, plus black shoes and handbag, and a black hat—not quite out-of-date, but perfect for the occasion. I had my cappa on and wrapped around to cover all my white tunic. The smell of the place just about knocked me over when I walked in. There must have been a

Gentile wake going on—the scent of hyacinths reminded me of Easter. We were brought into a small viewing room, with very low lighting and no scent of flowers. Mama and I made our way arm in arm to the casket. Without thinking really, I blessed myself.

"Oh dear Ruthie." We held on to each other. It was Mama who broke the silence. "She looks better than I was expecting—a little drawn in the cheeks, but it's our Ruthie."

"She's at peace, Mama, you can see that. No more struggling with it all."

"Say a prayer for her, Becky. The rabbi will do a good job, I'm sure, but you pray a prayer for her now."

I was moved at Mama's request. And so I did. "*Baruch atah, Adonai Eloheinu.* Blessed are You, Lord God of the universe, for You are the giver of life and the peace of all who call on You. Look with mercy on Your child, Ruth, our daughter, our sister, whom You have called from this life, and bestow on her the rest of Your eternal Sabbath. May her earthly father welcome her to the eternal life You have prepared for her from all eternity. Blessed are You. Blessed are You. Amen."

Lydia came in shortly afterwards. Mama and I arranged the *sovev* neatly around Ruthie and over her face, and Lydia closed the coffin quietly. She pointed out a small pitcher of water and a basin, where we wet and dried our hands, and then we went back out into the larger room with the air heavy with hyacinths.

"It was a beautiful prayer, and you remembered your father. How proud he must be of you, and your sister too. He followed her star right to the end. She was a real comedian, our Ruthie. She had the audience in hysterics." Mama paused for a few seconds. "I wonder if she knows we put her in such an awful dress!" And the two of us got the giggles as we found our way out the front door.

The synagogue service was short and sweet, as Sr. Joanne says about certain homilies. The psalms were recited in both English and Hebrew; the translation was different from ours, but it made the words stand out more. I think Mama was surprised at the number of people who came: many young people, no doubt fans of Ruth Steinway.

It was even more dramatic at the cemetery when a line of young women, like the *corps de ballet*, but moving more like Martha Graham, flowed up to the casket and placed a red rose on it. A few placed a stone instead, and one could hear each one say her name: Ruth. Ruthie had taught a modern dance class at Barnard as a guest lecturer for three semesters.

We were at least thirty people at the graveside. The rabbi led us in praying *Kaddish*, first in Hebrew and then in English.

Names: of all the names, how awesome, how holy, how intimate it is to say the Name above all other names. "At the name of Jesus all knees should bend under the earth and every tongue proclaim that Jesus Christ is Lord." That, of course, was not prayed, but the great reverence for the Holy Name of God is what wraps our loved one up in the *tallis*, or prayer shawl, of death.

Glorified and sanctified be God's great name throughout the world which He has created according to His will. . . .

The opening line of *Kaddish*. David should have been here to begin it, but he wasn't. Rabbi Stein began in Hebrew, and Mama joined in for the English. *Glorified and sanctified be God's great name throughout the world which He has created. . . .*

How close that is to our Divine Praises, I thought. *Blessed be God, blessed be His Holy Name.*

> *. . . May He establish His kingdom in your lifetime and during your days, and within the life of the entire House of Israel, speedily and soon. Amen. . . .*

I don't know the state of Ruthie's soul, of course. She wasn't a very religious person, but she was deeply in touch with her soul. I think God touched her deeply in beauty and the arts, especially the art of make-believe, which is very spiritual too. Only human beings pretend and create new worlds from their imaginations. How like unto God is that! Some of our greatest saints certainly knew the hole in the soul of human beings, and how we try to fill it with everything but the One alone who made us for Himself.

> *. . . Blessed and praised, glorified and exalted, extolled and honored, adored and lauded be the name of the Holy One, blessed be He, beyond all the blessings and hymns, praises and consolations that are ever spoken in the world. Amen. . . .*

Kaddish captures it so beautifully. Ruthie always searched for a happiness that would lift her out of herself. Maybe everyone who gets high, as they say, wants to touch the Highest. (That "Higher Power" thing again.) And this is precisely where the evil one sticks his ugly foot. Our surrender and obedience to God's Word open the door, and self-will and disobedience slam the door on Him. I have come to see that the whole drugged world is not of God; it is the false god of another getting-high kingdom that takes away one's human dignity, one's free will and reasoning. Addiction enslaves one to . . . to one's self. How much of the so-called civilized world is under the influence of drugs? Is it not the nectar of the Prince of Darkness? It may very well be an illness, as Ruthie once proclaimed, but does the devil not take advantage of even our weaknesses and illnesses? Oh, for the need for divine help, for grace. "God, come to my assistance. Lord make haste to help me." Thus we begin our Divine Office at every hour.

> . . . *May there be abundant peace from Heaven, and life, for us and for all Israel. Amen.* . . .

Standing there at the graveside, I held on to Mama's arm and helped to hold her up, and she let me. She leaned into me without any self-consciousness. Our souls were on the mend after many years. Moments like these put everything else in a different perspective. I glanced at Sally standing alone. Her face seemed puffy and blotched to me, with a perpetual frown. I wondered, *Is she really happy?* I wrapped Mother John Dominic's black shawl tight around my shoulders. I had my black winter cappa on too. it was my poor hands that felt the cold, and my eyes were tearing and my nose running. There we were, the Feinstein girls, saying good-bye to our Ruthie. And deep down inside of me I knew a deep peace, because I knew that somehow, by a silent and strange presence, the Lord was there, with His Comedy-Tragedy mask, His Sacred Heart, loving us.

There was the threat of snow in the air. "Threat" is used by people who don't like snow. I hoped it would snow. This was my first time standing by Papa's grave as well. Papa and I loved to walk in the snow. I put a smooth stone on his tombstone and secretly blessed him. I would have stayed longer, but the limousine awaited us and the ride back to West 79th Street.

The crowd at the synagogue hadn't followed us to the cemetery, but we were expecting a goodly number back at the apartment.

Sitting in the black limousine, after watching my sister's coffin lowered into the cold ground, I hated crack cocaine, I hated heroin, I hated every drug that stole my Ruthie's soul away from her. She was meant to be a star, a bird soaring above the treetops of life, bringing others to laugh and cry and stand in awe and wonder at the spectacular drama we call life. And it was snatched away from her.

When we got back to the apartment, Mrs. Hutner from next door was already there and had the coffee going. I told Mama that if she was uncomfortable with me sitting with her and Sally and Aunt Ruth, I could busy myself in the kitchen and keep things moving along. Maybe I would be too much of a distraction or simply *too much* for some of them to handle! But Mama insisted that I stay; she would have her two daughters on either side of her. Aunt Ruth could help out in the kitchen, carrying plates and casseroles and bowls of cherries.

Sitting *shiva* is more involved for a truly Conservative or Orthodox household, but we did take off our shoes, because we were "poor" at the death of a daughter, a sister. I thought to myself, *I'm a Discalced Dominican.* People coming in usually had a plate of something, and would wait to speak till Mama or Sally spoke first.

I'm glad I was at the end, as it were, because some people, interestingly, wanted to linger a bit, and many expressed their joy or appreciation at seeing me after all these years. Some didn't know what to say.

We were surprised at the number of young people again who came in, probably from the theater. One noted actress, presently starring on Broadway, came in, and leaned down to Mama and told her how much she loved Ruth, and that the whole theater community would miss her tremendously. I think Mama was quite startled and moved by this.

Gwen arrived, draped in her finest black pantsuit and floppy hat. She handed Mama a basket with black-and-white decorated hard-boiled eggs. "And if you dig deep enough. Mrs. F., you'll find a little Mogen at the bottom, for later on."

Mama hugged her and thanked her and whispered, "Take it into the kitchen and don't let Becky's Aunt Ruth see it." Aunt Ruth, from Cherry Hill, New Jersey, was Papa's youngest sister. She was widowed now, but had been married to a saxophone player, and sometimes she would sing at wedding receptions and bar mitzvahs. Enough Mogen David and she might be tempted to render us a tune, Heaven help us!

After about a half hour, a little old lady in a gray parka and a black knit cap and a homemade knit scarf that seemed to weigh her down came in and came immediately to me, saying, "Becky . . . Becky." She kind of resembled Mother Teresa with her wrinkles, but I recognized her right away. "Aunt Sarah!" Ezra's aunt from Uptown.

"Aren't you something for coming down in this weather. Mama, you remember Aunt Sarah, Ezra's aunt. She spent Thanksgiving with us, remember?"

Mama took her hands. "Remember? Of course I remember! I thought you were the yenta getting those two together! Little did we know! Oy." And we all laughed, which was a bit incongruous in the somberness of the front hallway. It would have been better down the hall in the front parlor.

224

"Becky, dahling, you look like a holy card. I got a letter from himself the other day. We'll have to talk." Aunt Sarah headed to the kitchen with her foil-covered nondairy apple cake. (I kept my eye on it for later!)

"We shall, we shall." I think Sally had been feeling out of it, till a few of her old friends made their way through the door, and Sally got up and led them into the kitchen.

I was just getting ready to get up myself to go fix a little something for Mama, when everyone gathered around the entranceway hushed themselves and stood back. Standing at the door and making their way in were four nuns, one in a wheelchair, being pushed by none other than Fr. Wilcox. Mama stood up and embraced Mother Agnes Mary, who kindly got her settled back in her chair and introduced Sr. Catherine Agnes, Sr. Anna Maria, and Sr. Gertrude of the Sacred Heart, who was weeping in her wheelchair. I was on my feet, of course, and hugging them all and thanking them for coming. I kissed Sr. Gertrude on the cheek, and even hugged Fr. Wilcox! I had no idea they would come.

"Thank you, Father, for coming all this way, and for bringing Sister Gertrude."

"She insisted!" Lowering his voice to a half whisper, he said, "Actually, she *enlisted* me. . . . It was the only way Mother would let her come." And we had a little laugh together. Fr. Wilcox and me!

I thought, *This will be on the front page of the Hadassah Newsletter, if there is such a thing: "The ladies came to pay a* shiva *call for their friend, and Catholic nuns were popping up all over!"*

For being a cloistered nun, Mother Agnes Mary knew how to work a room. She very discreetly made her way around, introducing herself and the others as "Sister Mary Baruch's sisters—that is, Rebecca Feinstein, of course, dear

Ruthie's older sister." Making her way back to Mama, she continued, "We always enjoyed Ruthie's visits to the monastery, and Sister Gertrude here followed her career with uncanny devotion." I don't think anyone caught the irony in Mother's remarks, but they were all rather impressed that Ruth Steinway had such a following. Sr. Gertrude, in full control now, pulled out an eight-by-ten scrapbook, filled with clippings about Ruthie's performances beginning twenty years ago. Even I didn't have such devotion. She presented it to Mama like it was a folded flag.

Gwendolyn came in from the kitchen to welcome them and escort them to the food table. Others quickly gathered around to ask questions and some just to gawk. Five nuns in an Upper West Side apartment is not something you see every day.

One impervious blue-haired lady, however, not so impressed, spoke so all would hear: "Hannah Feinstein, we had no idea you were so . . . so ecumenical."

Mama stood up. "Well, Bloom, darling, I'm not sure what ecumenical means, but I've had a sudden awakening since two policemen woke me up yesterday morning to tell me my youngest daughter was dead of an overdose. And you know what, Bloom? My heart was crushed. What mother should hear such news? And my heart ached, because I realized that for thirty years another daughter of mine, who did not sing or dance or entertain people, who did not do drugs, who did nothing in her life but what was good—I cut her off like she was dead. But she is alive and happy and, if I may say so, very beautiful, and always, always, loving towards me, towards my Ruben, and towards Ruthie, whom she never let pass away from her life. Come here, Beck. Sister Baruch, forgive me for losing you, and pray that God will forgive me too." And she broke down right there in front of all of us.

I rushed over and held Mama in my arms. And the somber silence was frozen and then melted in an instant of applause. The Hadassah ladies scurried around Mama to comfort her and to embrace me in a way that I never experienced in all my life. My own "Hadassah sisters" in black and white, plus Gwendolyn and Fr. Wilcox, were there to comfort me too.

Sr. Gertrude was showing Father the way to the Mogen David table, and Sr. Catherine Agnes followed right behind. As she passed me, she whispered in my ear, "I think the old devil got kicked in the pants royally tonight! It's the best 'para-liturgical ecumenical service' I've ever been to." This from Scar!

Sr. Anna Maria stuck close by me. "I can't believe I'm here, in the apartment where you grew up. Can you show me your room? I've got something to tell you."

I grabbed her arm. "Come with me." Actually, we went by way of the beverage corner and grabbed a plastic glass of Mogen David. Sr. Anna Maria had never had Mogen David, but it was an instant friendship. I led her down the hall and into Ruthie and my bedroom.

"So here it is. It's smaller than I imagined it."

"Funny, I was thinking the same thing. I guess things seem bigger when we're little, and back then there were two twin beds in here."

"There's your infamous theater masks. I always thought they were one piece, but they're not. I like them."

"When we were kids, we would have one mask over each of our beds, for a month at a time. We were not superstitious, mind you, but if you had the Tragedy mask over you, you would be sad about something, like getting an F on a test. And if you had the Comedy mask, you would be really happy about something that month. We always wanted the happy mask, of course. . . . So what do you want to tell me? Is it a happy mask or a sad mask? You're okay, aren't you?"

"I'm fine. I've been dying to tell you, but Mother put me under obedience until she broke the news to the community, which she did last night. I kind of purposely avoided you because, well, you know, I'm not very good at keeping secrets."

"What is it? What is it? You aren't leaving, are you?"

"No, of course not. I love our life—every towel and bed sheet and pillowcase." We giggled. I was so happy to hear that giggle again; especially today, I needed it.

"Well, Sister Dominica has not been in the best of health and asked Mother if she could resign from being subprioress. Mother, of course, understood and said yes right away. And to my big surprise, she called me into her office and told me she would like me to be subprioress. Can you imagine! I've been the laundry mistress for years, and she wants me to be subprioress."

We both took a big gulp of our wine. And then, of all times, I got the hiccups. "That's wonder—*hic*—ful news. You'll be a—*hic*—great subprioress—*hic*. Dear me." And our giggles turned into irrepressible laughter.

"Is that a picture of you on the mirror?" Sister pointed, and I walked over to get it, not knowing she was right behind me. I turned, and—

"*Boo!*"

I jumped a foot off the ground. "Don't do that!" And we waited. The hiccups were gone. Sr. Anna Maria had done that to me more than a few times in our twenty-five years in the monastery. It always worked.

"I want to meet your mother and sister, but I wanted you to know my news. I've missed our little chats. And . . ." She suddenly got something caught in her throat. "And I want you to know how awful I feel about Ruthie. You know . . . you've got all of us, especially me."

I thought I was all cried out by that time, but the waterworks began again, and the sisters hugged in the sisters' room. We blotted our faces with tissue from Ruthie's vanity table and made our way back to the dining room. Sr. Anna Maria scooted off to help Sr. Gertrude, who didn't need any help. She was rather holding court from her wheelchair. The little circle of theater people who witnessed her handing over the album were now gathered around her every word.

I couldn't tell how Sally reacted to it all. She got her journalist's inquisitive look back, and wanted to be a part of it. We hadn't really had any time to talk, and I knew she was not at ease with my being there. It was also her first time seeing me in the habit. She edged her way over to me.

"I'll say one thing, Mama was right. You do look beautiful." She had never ever said that to me; I was always her fat little sister who ate too much. All barriers were down. We hugged each other without more words.

"I love your hair, by the way. You'd never know you're the older sister." There I was fibbing again, and in the same room as Fr. Wilcox.

"Do you have hair under . . . under that?" Sally was genuinely interested.

"Enough gray for the both of us! Come, I want you to meet Sister Anna Maria. She's been my best friend for all these years. We knew each other before we even entered. You'd never believe she's over fifty, would you?" And off we went, to introduce my sister to my sister. I think Sally was quite amazed by it all.

Mrs. Levinson and Leah appeared again, not as nervous as the previous night. "My father said I could come," Leah told me, like it was a secret. "I'm a huge fan of Ruth Steinway. I can't believe she's . . ." and she couldn't get it out.

"I know, Leah, none of us can. I'm glad your father let you come. Ruthie would be very happy." Leah was all wide-eyed, taking it all in.

One strange man came in whom none of us recognized. We thought perhaps he was an actor or another of Ruthie's fans. He was a bit inebriated and a bit too loud. Mama didn't know what to do.

"I loved her, I did. And we had a roller coaster of a ride together." He laughed. Gwendolyn recognized the voice and came to the rescue. She thanked him for coming and said there was a pot of coffee in the kitchen.

"Gwenovin! I loved her. How could she leave me?" To my happy surprise, Fr. Wilcox was right behind Gwen and knew just how to coax him away from Mama and into the kitchen. And he went with him without protest. The power of the collar!

Gwen came around to my side and informed me that that was Alex, Ruthie's ex-husband, "the one she married on the beach at Coney Island." *Ah,* I thought, *hence the roller coaster reference.* Ruthie never spoke to me about him, other than saying that he was a bit brutish, but a lot of fun too.

Eventually Fr. Wilcox got him down to the street and headed towards the subway. I overheard him telling Sr. Gertrude, "The poor soul. I think his grief over Ruth's passing was most genuine. It would be hard for us to understand, but he mourns too."

What an emotional evening it was. It was close to eleven when the last of them left. Mother and the sisters left with Fr. Wilcox around seven thirty. Poor Sr. Gertrude, who didn't want to leave so early, seemed to have more energy than any of us. She waved good-bye to me, saying, "Holy obedience." Aunt Ruth also took off for a late train to Philly: "Christmas office parties call." At the end there remained "four old ladies" around the kitchen table: Mama, Sally, Gwendolyn, and me.

Gwen said, "It's something how we always end up at the kitchen table, wherever we are." I had a comment on that, which I kept to myself. But took I comfort in the thought that Our Lord wanted us to wind up around the table too, to remember Him. Sally said she was sorry Mitzie wasn't here for this. Mama and I just glanced at each other. Mama made the only comment: "Such a job you two have, haircuts for dogs."

"Speaking of dogs," Gwendolyn said, "my little one is probably sitting cross-legged by the door. I'm off. Sister M.B., are you sure you can get home tomorrow on your own? I can come up and go with you."

"You are too kind, as always. But you forget I *am* a New Yorker and a big nun now. I can handle it."

Thus did Lady Gwendolyn make her exit. As she grabbed her coat from the front parlor, she cried, "Oh look! It's snowing out!"

Sally said that she was quite done in by the whole thing, by "the mystery of it all." "I'm the oldest girl in the family, I should go first. And where was our older brother?"

"He called this morning from Brussels," said Mama. "He said he's delivering a paper on something technical that psychiatrists get together all over the world to talk about. He said he would miss seeing the two of you." I wondered if Mama was fibbing.

"Well, I hope the paper wasn't on the nature of addiction or the effect of psychedelic drugs on the brain." Sally hadn't lost her edge. And before we could make any comments, she announced she was making herself a cup of valerian-and-catnip tea, and would either of us want one of her Ambiens? She kissed us both on the top of the head, grabbed the evening paper, and took off to her room. "Good night, you two. It's been some night. I still can't get over how warm and friendly all the nuns were."

I didn't say a word, but just let her dwell on that thought. Mama looked very tired. I wondered what she was thinking.

"We've got enough lox and bagels here for a scrumptious breakfast tomorrow morning." Feinstein thoughts indeed.

Midnight struck, and Mama and I sat alone in the kitchen. I told her this was when we used to get up to start a new day of prayer, and how often I would think of her sitting here doing the crossword puzzle and having some elderberry wine.

"Aha! Elderberry wine—we need a little nightcap before we go to bed?" Mama was up before I could answer.

"Why not? And I think your friend Ester Goldberg brought a large container of chopped chicken livers from Zabar's."

232

"That Zabar's—such a store. I wish you could stay for a few days and see it. It's completely done over. But I think it was your friend Aunt Sarah who brought it."

"No, Mama, it was Ester Goldberg. She even said, 'Into your hands, Rebecca Feinstein, I'm putting the best chopped liver in New York.' Aunt Sarah brought a nondairy apple cake."

"Oh my, that's better than New York's best chicken liver. I haven't had nondairy apple cake since I can't remember, and it sounds like it would go very well with my elderberry. . . . Oh look, it's really coming down hard out there. Maybe you'll have to stay." Mama pushed back the café curtains and we stared silently at the falling snow, dancing peacefully around the streetlight. Snow makes the city quiet. It was nice.

So we settled down with Mogen David and a large slice each of Aunt Sarah's apple cake. Mama raised her glass: "Merry Christmas, Becky."

"Happy Chanukah, Mama." We clinked our glasses, and then we both jumped with a start as we heard something fall in Ruthie's room. We looked at each other, and together made our way down the hall into Ruthie's room. There, on the floor, lay the Tragedy mask. Only the big smiling mask still hung over Ruthie's bed.

It was too eerie for words. We kind of tiptoed back into the kitchen and refilled our glasses.

Mama spoke first. "Such a thing to happen? What does it mean?"

"I don't know, Mama. Life and death are full of mysteries. Like . . . Ruthie's death was such a tragedy, but now, I believe, she's free. . . . She's happy."

"My daughter, the nun."

nineteen

I woke up early the next morning. The apartment was very silent; I could hear the faint muffle of someone snoring. I got up and was as quiet as I could be in the bathroom. Like the previous morning, it was startling to get dressed in front of a huge mirror. It was like getting dressed in slow motion. I love our habit. The only change over all these years was going from a chain-link rosary to wooden beads and rope cords. These are much quieter, and there are no more accidents in choir when one's rosary gets stuck in the seat and even sometimes breaks. (It never happened to me.)

I quietly made my way down the hall, through the dining room, and into the kitchen. Mama had a nice coffee maker; she called it "Mr. Coffee." I made a pot with Zabar's ground French roast. This was a little touch of Heaven. I realized I hadn't prayed my Office—I let a whole day slip by me! I had prayed Vespers and Compline around one in the morning, if that counts. The Lord would understand, I thought. I wasn't so sure Fr. Wilcox would . . . but today was a new day. I took my coffee to my room, settled in Ruthie's lounge chair, and

234

prayed the Office of Readings and Lauds. I looked at the time . . . six thirty. I knew Mama and Sally wouldn't be up for at least another ninety minutes.

I wasn't thinking of this before at all, but I had such a yearning for Our Lord in the Blessed Sacrament. I had missed one day, and it felt like a month. And then it crossed my mind. I entertained the thought for two minutes and decided just to do it. I got up, put on a black sweater from Ruthie's closet, and wrapped myself in my cappa and Mother John Dominic's shawl. I wrote a hurried note for Mama:

Mama and Sally, I'll be back for breakfast before 9:00.

I took the apartment keys Mama still kept hidden in the soup tureen in the dining room and quietly closed the apartment door.

Stepping out onto 79th Street a little after seven o'clock was wonderful. It was cold, and the sidewalks were shoveled from the snowfall. The morning doorman tipped his hat to me, and I told him I needed a cab. He quickly hailed one for me, even opening the door for me.

"Sixty-fifth and Lexington." And the cab headed for 81st Street to go across the park. The Hayden Planetarium was still there, but it looked completely done over. I remembered Ruthie and me walking around with our heads back like we were watching a show at the planetarium. I bet the shows today were spectacular, with all the new technological stuff they had. We came out on East 79th Street and turned down Lexington instead of going over one more block where Greta and I had lived. The cab pulled up in front of St. Vincent's.

I just stood there at the bottom of the steps leading into the church. It had been over thirty years since I walked up these same stairs for the first time. It was a little too cold for my sentimental journey, so I made my way into the church, through those same heavy doors.

It was like walking into another world, a familiar world that has always been a part of my soul and opened up again to embrace me in its warmth: the smell, the subdued light coming through the magnificent stained glass, and the silence that prevailed despite the noise of traffic outside.

I turned right and started to make my way down the side aisle, passing the baptistery where I was joined to Christ and His Church when all my sin was washed away: my real passing through the Red Sea. The Sacred Heart chapel with St. Dominic's statue, just like thirty years ago, was ablaze with vigil candles. Then I stopped at the shrine of St. Vincent. The fire was still coming out of his head—or alighting on it? He was still preaching. I knew who he was this time and had celebrated his feast every year. He was my Dominican brother and my friend.

I caught my breath as I approached the statue of Christ the Priest, gesturing to His Sacred Heart. It had been painted, and the face wasn't exactly what I remembered, but it was still the same Sacred Heart that moved my heart all those years ago. The vigil candles were no longer there, but they were close by.

A candle was three dollars. They had gone up three hundred percent! But here I was. . . . It all began with my lighting a candle, so I had to do it. I certainly had the money, and I couldn't call Mother to ask permission, so I made an administrative assistant decision and lit five candles! The first was for Ruthie and the repose of her soul; one was for Greta, who loved this church as I do; one for Papa who, like me, made his Passover to Christ's life right here and, like me, received the Lord in the Eucharist for the first time; one for Mama, in thanksgiving; and the last one for Mother Agnes Mary and all my sisters, living and deceased.

The bell rang, signaling the priest entering the sanctuary. I made my way into the third pew on the right side, what we used to call the epistle side. The Dominican Father was young; he almost looked like a boy—a sign that I was getting old! I thought of my dear Fr. Meriwether and all the Dominican Fathers I had come to know and love here in the five years Greta and I came to Mass almost every day.

The young priest read the Gospel and gave a lovely reflection on it. He looked over at me once and smiled. I think I must have blushed, but I smiled back and put my head down. I was so happy to be there. All the emotion, grief, and exultation of those days were lifted as we entered into the Eucharistic Prayer.

The immense love of Christ was made present on this altar. His very sacrifice on the cross and glorious resurrection are re-presented through the ministry of the priest, conformed to Christ so intimately that he acts in His very person.

I gave everything to Him and offered my poor life again, and all my loved ones, to our beloved Lord, in union with His holy sacrifice.

Returning to my pew after Holy Communion, I buried my face in my hands and adored Him. *Stay with me, Lord . . . stay with me.*

I left by the side door on 66th Street with a small wave to the modern statue of St. Thérèse, who was flanked with her own blaze of white vigil candles. I walked the short block up to Third Avenue so the cab would be going uptown. I think three cabs veered over to answer my call. I sat in back, smiling to myself; the old Italian New York cabbie had beat the others to the punch. "Where to, Sista?"

I entered the apartment quietly, but Mama and Sally were both up and futzing around in the kitchen.

"We waited for you," Sally announced. "Coffee?"

"Such a blessing to have all this lox," Mama said, "and look at this: three kinds of cream cheese. The bagels could be a little fresher, but twenty seconds in the microwave, they're like new. Were you out walking in the old neighborhood?"

"No, actually, I took a cab across town and went to Mass at Saint Vincent's, for old times' sake, and to pray for Ruthie and Greta . . . and Papa."

Mama and Sally didn't say anything. Sally poured the coffee, and Mama talked to the microwave, and we sat, the three of us, at the kitchen table.

Sally broke the silence in between bites of her cinnamon raisin bagel with cinnamon walnut cream cheese. "You know, I was very moved by all the people who came to pay a *shiva* call, so many young people I didn't even know, but they knew Ruthie."

"Ruth Steinway," Mama interjected. "Such a name, like a piano."

Sally went on, ignoring Mama's comment. "But I was amazed that your nuns came . . . to pay a *shiva* call, yes, but I couldn't get over how peaceful and happy they seemed, how caring they were towards you and Mama. I think I've had the wrong idea about nuns for a long time. Are all of you that happy?"

I took a good swallow of coffee and smiled at Sally. "I never thought of it that way, but yes, we are all that happy.

It's not a superficial or sentimental kind of happiness, but we certainly love each other and care for each other. It's something, when you think about it, because we never get away from each other, you know. We don't have vacations or all the little escapes and escapades regular people have, like going out to eat, or going to the movies or the theater. We don't even watch television."

"Such a life you should have. What do you do for fun?" Mama's old sparkle was back in her eyes.

I laughed. "We don't have radios or television, but we get together almost every night and talk to each other. We learn about everybody's family. And we pray a lot, of course—that takes up a big part of our day. We sing our prayers together, like at temple, we sing the psalms of David. And on big feasts we have special everything: special words to sing, special meals to eat, and sometimes we have little shows and perform for each other."

Mama and Sally just stared at me wide-eyed.

"Sister Gertrude, the one in the wheelchair last night, she used to be a tap dancer and always dreamed of being on Broadway. She still loves the theater and the dance. She's put away her tap shoes, but she'll still do a soft-shoe across the infirmary floor." I chuckled. "We all hold our breath, of course. I love the old sisters in the infirmary. That's one of my jobs, to help look after them."

Sally said, "I wish Mitzie were here. We're not always so happy and caring, I don't know why. Most of our friends are women, but . . ." and she didn't say anything more.

I waited a minute and poured us all more coffee. "I think we're happy because . . . well, because we all love the Lord. That's what makes us sisters. He's why we leave everything and live locked up behind bars, as Ruthie used to say. She thought my life was sad, but it really isn't sad. It's serious, and it's sacrificial, but it's peaceful and full of a quiet joy, if you stay long enough." I stopped, hoping I wasn't sounding too pious or homiletic. I took refuge in my lox and bagel.

"Your father used to say things like that. He was certainly keen to pick all that up the few times he went there."

"Papa was a wise man." That's all I said.

Sally was moving her coffee mug back and forth from one hand to the other.

"So you think we should pray or something? I don't know if I could do that," Sally said pensively.

I took a deep breath and interiorly called on the Holy Spirit. "Praying is a good place to begin. Our life, my life in the monastery, doesn't make any sense, really, apart from its ultimate end. Everything has an end, you know. The end for Mr. Coffee here is to brew coffee. That's a silly example, I know, but everything and everybody has an end. We know it's ultimately not marriage or relationships, because they end, they change, they may fall apart. They may be finite ends in themselves, but certainly not the ultimate. Our ultimate end—for all of us, for all human beings, for you and me—is union with the God who made us for Himself. It's that simple, and that mysterious. Even our poor bodies age and begin to break down, but our souls—the spiritual part of us—don't have physical parts to break down: they're eternal. So our in-between job is to keep our souls aimed at eternal life. Lots of things can get in the way, you know."

They sat motionless and silent, just staring at me. "I'm sorry, I should climb out of the pulpit now and . . . and have another bagel."

Mama laughed. "Such words coming from my Becky. If the rabbi spoke like that I would go to temple more often."

"You should go to temple, Mama, not for the rabbi, but for God."

Sally was lost in her coffee mug, like she was reading tea leaves, thinking. She's always been a thinker.

"Sometimes Mitzie goes to this kind of temple where they chant and dance for Gaia, woman spirit. I never went—all that stuff gives me the heebie-jeebies."

"It would give me the heebie-jeebies too. I'll stick to good old revelation, beginning with Abraham and Moses, and the Torah, like a good Jew."

"But what about—you know—what about Jesus?" Mama was picking up the ball.

"Jesus was a Jew too, and, we believe, fulfilled all the sacrifices and prophecies of the covenant, and gave us a new covenant, a new Passover, a new Pentecost, in Himself. We pray at Mass to 'Abraham, our father in faith.' I always think of you every time."

I knew they had reached a saturation point. Mama was up microwaving three more bagels, and Sally was scrounging around the refrigerator for Aunt Sarah's nondairy apple cake. I opened another wrapper of Zabar's Alaskan lox, and we delved into our second breakfast like we were Jewish hobbits.

The conversation came back to earth with talking about different people who came to pay a *shiva* call, and the famous actress who paid her respects.

"But none was quite as touching as that sister in the wheelchair." Mama couldn't remember her name.

"Sister Gertrude, the tap dancer."

"That's right. Do you know she had clippings about Ruthie which I've never seen? It was so kind of her to give me that album. Please thank her for me."

241

"You can thank her too, when you come to visit me. The infirmary sisters love to be pushed into the parlor."

Mama smiled. "I'll do that. I'll bake them something special. And you, look at all the food we have. You should take some back with you. There's enough potato salad to feed an army."

"Or a nunnery," added Sally. And we laughed.

Clearing the dishes and putting things away, I knew it was time for me to be on my way too. Sally was staying on with Mama for a few days. Even though there was a pre-Christmas rush for groomed dogs, there were others who could do it.

The doorman buzzed us to tell us a visitor was on her way. To our surprise, Gwendolyn came streaming into the apartment in a black-and-white overcoat that could be mistaken for—well, you know what: a penguin. She had a Father Christmas brooch on, which lit up at a touch.

"M.B., I know you're a big nun now and can negotiate with New York cabbies, but I want to go with you. I haven't been alone with you face to face in years. And remember, I am your godmother."

Mama and Sally fed her while I packed my bag and took one last look at my old room. Mama had agreed the night before that I should take the Comedy mask with me to remember Ruthie and to pray for her. I didn't need the mask to do that, but it gave Mama some comfort. I also took one of her self-photos from her vanity mirror and put it in my breviary.

I kissed Mama and Sally good-bye. Sally promised she would write. I kissed my hand and touched the *mezuzah*, and out we went on West 79th Street. To home.

epilogue

December 31, 1996

Dear Lord,

 Here I am on this snowy New Year's Eve, writing on the first page of the new journal Greta left me. We have sung the glorious First Vespers of the Solemnity of the Mother of God, and a great silence and peace have settled over the monastery. The snow is so lovely and will wrap us in an even greater silence when the new year comes in. Millions, no doubt, are gathered at this very moment in Times Square waiting for the ball to fall. I am content to be right where I am, which is a nice feeling to have on New Year's Eve.

 This has been some year, Lord, and I wonder what the next year, the next three years, will bring, before the change of the millennium. Our Holy Father John Paul II will hopefully carry us through the Holy Door at that time. He calls it the "threshold of hope."

I am filled with much hope this new year. Ezra will be here next week with all his news. Sr. Anna Maria will begin as the new subprioress after the January Chapter. I think she's sad to leave the laundry, if you can believe that. My being Mother's secretary will mean Sr. Anna Maria and I will get to work together. She'll be keen on thinking up jobs for the infirmary sisters, hopefully without spiders. We bought Sr. Gerard a rubber spider on top of a cupcake as her infirmary Advent Pal gift. She glued the feet together and told us we were safe.

Weather permitting, Gwendolyn and Mama are coming here for a visit tomorrow afternoon, and Mama plans to come for Ruthie's memorial, which is still being worked out by Sr. Gertrude.

An interesting encounter: before she left Mama's apartment, little Leah Levinson asked me on the sly if she and her best friend from high school could come visit me someday. "She would love to meet you and see your monastery," she said. "She's my best Catholic friend—her name is Gracie."

. . . squeak . . . squeak . . . squeak . . .

Made in the USA
Middletown, DE
27 July 2017